TIME WALKER

IN THE PRESIDENT'S SERVICE—BOOK 19

ACE COLLINS

A Christian Company
ElkLakePublishingInc.com

COPYRIGHT NOTICE

Time Walker
First edition. Copyright © 2024 by Ace Collins. The information contained in this book is the intellectual property of Ace Collins and is governed by United States and International copyright laws. All rights reserved. No part of this publication, either text or image, may be used for any purpose other than personal use. Therefore, reproduction, modification, storage in a retrieval system, or retransmission, in any form or by any means, electronic, mechanical, or otherwise, for reasons other than personal use, except for brief quotations for reviews or articles and promotions, is strictly prohibited without prior written permission by the publisher.

This is a work of fiction. Names, characters, businesses, places, events, locales, and incidents are either the products of the author's imagination or used in a fictitious manner. Any resemblance to actual persons, living or dead, or actual events is purely coincidental.

Cover Design: Derinda Babcock
Interior Design: Deb Haggerty
Editor(s): Cristel Phelps, Deb Haggerty
Author Represented By: WordServe Literary Group, Ltd.

PUBLISHED BY: Elk Lake Publishing, Inc., 35 Dogwood Drive, Plymouth, MA 02360, 2024

Library Cataloging Data
Names: Collins, Ace (Ace Collins)
Time Walker / Ace Collins
342 p. 23cm × 15cm (9in × 6 in.)
ISBN-13: 9798891341098 (paperback) | 9798891341104 (trade paperback) | 9798891341111 (e-book)
Key Words: Strong female protagonist; World War II; mystery/suspense; multi-cultural detective team; presidential service; assumed identities; Indian reservations
Library of Congress Control Number: 2024931417 Fiction

DEDICATION

To Joni, who defines the spirit of acceptance
and unconditional love.

PROLOGUE

Wednesday, August 5, 1942
1:12 a.m.
Five Miles from Paris, France

The covert mission had been a disaster since the twelve American soldiers parachuted behind German lines. From their first day in France, they had run into one issue after another. Initially, their underground escorts were late, forcing a harrowing twenty-four hours hunkered down in a filthy chicken coop just a hundred yards from a Nazi camp. An hour after the Americans were finally picked up by the French Underground, two of the soldiers were killed in an automobile accident just a mile out of Paris. A day later, another was shot while talking to a lost child. The only good part was the German who killed Private Todd Malvern never spotted the other nine, but even then the bad luck just kept coming. The plans they'd been sent to recover were delivered a day late, which gave them very little time to get back to the rendezvous point. Five miles from the spot the C-47 was to pick them up, they'd been surrounded by unwitting German soldiers on a training mission. Even though the Nazis were unaware the Americans were within a stone's throw of where they were camping, the Yanks were still bogged down.

"All this way for nothing," Private Steve Grimes whispered as he stared at a busy bridge used to ferry troops and equipment from Germany to the French coast. "If we didn't have bad luck, we wouldn't have any luck at all."

Grimes had always been a pessimist—a person who found the dark side of every situation. Yet this time, the tall man from Fargo had every reason to be in a bleak mood.

"It's not for nothing," the team's leader, Captain Jim Watson, argued. "We have the two women we were assigned to pick up, and they have the plans for Hitler's new fighter plane."

"But there's no way to get to the pick-up point," Grimes grumbled. "We're surrounded by Germans, and we have three hours to get five miles. If we miss the plane, we never get home. We'll either be killed, or if we escape that fate, captured and sent to a POW camp."

Grimes was right. The odds were slim to none. Dejectedly, an exhausted Watson took off his helmet, ran a hand through his thinning blonde hair, and frowned. Each man on the mission was a volunteer, but that didn't make their situation any easier for the officer. He was the man in charge. He was supposed to bring the men back. Three were already dead, and the rest were as good as dead or captured now. He had failed. After somberly studying the bridge and praying for inspiration, he looked back at the others hidden behind trees.

"What do you think, Cap?" Private Ruffin Redman whispered.

Redman was the one member of the group Watson knew the least. He was from out west, but he'd never said where. Throughout their four weeks of training and during the mission, he'd never mentioned his family. He hadn't shared any photos or stories of a girl he'd left behind or discussed how much he missed his hometown. He talked so little about his personal life that if he were interested in music or movies, they wouldn't have known. He was just six feet and one-hundred sixty pounds of man stuffed into an Army uniform. A guy who followed orders without question, whose expression never changed, and whose voice never revealed emotion. He seemed more machine that human.

Pushing off the ground, Watson creeped back to Redman. "What do you think?"

"We have to get those plans back to London. That's the most important thing. That's why we're here. So, sitting and watching a bunch of Germans camp out in a valley is a colossal waste of time."

"Tell me something I don't know. Son, the fact is, we can't move. If we take one step out of this stand of trees, we'd have a hundred eyes locked onto us and each set of eyes would be aligning a gun at our heads."

"Right now, that's true," Redman agreed. "But what happens if we stay here?"

The captain shrugged, "In time, we'll be spotted and caught. There's no way to remain here for very long. There will come a time when one of those Germans will get close enough to spot us."

"So, sir, we are damned if we do something and damned if we do nothing." Redman pronounced as he glanced over his shoulder. "Captain, those two women risked so much getting those plans to us. Sure, the Nazis might capture us and put us in a POW camp, but those two women would be tortured and executed. It'd be a shame to have them die for nothing. They gave up everything, including their pride and innocence, to help our side. So, for their sake, we can't sit here and do nothing." The darked-eyed, black-haired Redman frowned and announced, "Do you know what one of them asked me?"

Watson shook his head.

"Sir, they want me to shoot them in the head rather than let them be captured. They begged me to execute them if the Germans headed this way. Sir, I have a problem with that."

The captain shook his head and spat. "War's not pretty, son. And those women have been dodging death for a few years now. They knew the odds when they signed up."

"But I'm not going to shoot them," Redman whispered.

"If you can't," Watson offered, "then I will."

"Captain," Redman asked as he shifted his eyes toward the road, "how much stuff do the Germans move across that bridge every day?"

Watson shrugged, "Why does that matter?"

"It's a lot, right?"

"They're supplying their operations in several sections of France with that road. The bridge is a key to keeping that line open. Since we've been here, there have been thousands of vehicles crossing it. Listen, you can hear the parade now. But why is that important?"

"We've got a bag full of dynamite," Redman explained, "and I think it's time we use it."

"What do you mean?"

"That bridge up there ... there's a deep gorge below it. If that bridge goes down, it'll take months for the Germans to rebuild it. That'll interrupt a lot of transportation."

"That's not our job, that wasn't in the plans."

"Plans change, sir, I know that as well as anyone. And if the bridge blows up, it'll give us the cover we need to get to the rendezvous point. Let me take it down, and you can sneak off while those Nazis are racing to see what happened."

Watson glanced toward the bridge. It was a mile away and there was nothing but open ground between where they were and where they had to be to blow it up. The officer shook his head. "Private, we'd get mowed down the minute we stepped out of the woods."

"If all of us tried it, we would," Redman agreed, "but I can do it."

"It would be suicide. Even if you got there, they'd take you out before you could get away."

Redman signaled for Watson to follow and then crept to the edge of the trees. "Cap, do you see that truck?"

"Yeah, it's been there all night. It's likely hauling supplies for the training operation."

"There are two men assigned to that truck," Redman explained. "They're lookouts, but I've been watching them, and they've not been looking out much. They've been paying attention to the radio, some kind of music show. If you listen close, you can hear it."

Redman was right. Though the radio was turned down, when he concentrated, Watson could make it out.

"One of them," Redman continued, "is asleep, has been for more than an hour."

"How do you know that?"

"My eyes are as good as my ears." Redman let the observation sink in before suggesting, "Sir, I can crawl down there and take out both of them. One is about my size. I'll put on his uniform and drive down to the base of the bridge. Before anyone can question me, I'll set off the charge and take the bridge down."

"Odds are against you getting to the truck," Watson argued. "Even if you made it that far, it's still a suicide mission. You couldn't get back alive."

"Yeah, I know that, but I also wouldn't have to shoot

those two women. That would be on your hands."

"I don't send my men on suicide missions."

"Cap, you look at us like we're more than fodder for the war effort, and those who serve with you admire and respect you for it. I really appreciate the importance you put on my life. But beyond just the plans, those other men on this team are good people. They all have reasons to live."

"Don't you?"

"I've got nothing waiting for me back home but trouble. Dying here for a purpose would be better than going home."

Redman took one last look at the truck before creeping back to get the duffle bag filled with the explosives. He retrieved it and moved quickly to the edge of the clearing.

"I don't know you," Watson announced as he starred directly into Redman's face. "I know everyone else, but you never let me in."

"No one gets in, no one has for years."

"What are you running from, son?"

"Nothing, Cap. I assure you I've done nothing wrong. But sometimes fate deals us a hand we can't play. For the last six years, I've been holding all the wrong cards. I was bitter about that until tonight. Now I realize that my not having a past or a future gives the rest of you a chance to complete your jobs."

"I don't want you to do this," Watson argued. "Let me figure something else out."

"You'd have to shoot me to stop me," Redman said, "and a gunshot would expose the women and the rest of the men. Good luck. Please get everyone home. That'll mean my life was worth something."

Silently, Redman crawled out from behind the tree and into the meadow. The clear skies and the bright moon made him an easy target, but as the hundreds of Germans had no idea there was a group of Americans so close, so no one seemed to notice.

"What's Redman doing?" Grimes demanded.

"Trying to save us," Watson grimly explained.

With the eight soldiers and the two French women intently following Redman's trek, time seemed to stand still. As he eased across the ground, Redman made no sound, his form somehow blended in with the terrain. Each of his moves was almost catlike—he'd become a stalking predator that was one with nature. It took him almost twenty minutes to get to the truck and work his way to the back side. Pulling himself upright, he hid in the shadows as he passed the German sleeping on the ground. The soldier then eased toward the lookout leaning against the vehicle's hood. The moonlight caught a flash of the knife's blade before it entered the Nazi's chest. There was no celebration. Redman just held onto the dead soldier and eased him to the ground.

After glancing up the hill, Redman silently stole to the other man. A second later, with one single thrust of the blade, this German would never awaken from his slumber.

"Wow," Grimes whispered. "Where did he learn that?"

"Not in boot camp," Watson assured him.

Redman stripped the second German of his shirt and helmet, dragged him back to the truck's bed, then lifted him in. A minute later, the first victim joined the second. Redman glanced back at the woods a final time before entering the cab, starting the engine, and slipping the truck into gear.

"What's he doing?" Grimes asked.

"He's going to try to take out the bridge," Watson explained. The captain then turned to the others and in a low voice announced, "If Redman's successful, every

German within miles is going to be headed towards that explosion. We'll wait five minutes or until they're all at the bridge, then we'll sneak out the back of these trees and head to the rendezvous point. We'll have to move quickly and be on guard for patrols. If we see one, we hide and let them pass. We can't afford to have to fight our way to the plane."

Satisfied his team was ready to move, Watson turned his attention back to the valley. What happened next would determine the future of this mission and everyone on it.

Redman was smart. He'd driven at a leisurely pace to the base of the bridge. Once there, he parked, and with backpack in hand made his way to one of the supports. He lit a match before moving quickly back to the truck. Still acting as if nothing was amiss, the private pulled forward and slowly headed the vehicle between two supports. A few seconds later, an explosion lit up the night sky. The entire region shook as if it was at the epicenter of an earthquake. The night was filled with flames and chaos. Men screamed as trucks crossing the bridge were tossed like toys into the valley. Initially, only one small section of the bridge fell but, with the rapidly spreading fire, more of the structure began to weaken and collapse. Within a minute the whole thing was nothing but ruins.

Its noise and destruction brought Germans from every direction pouring onto the scene. For the moment, the Nazi army's entire focus was on that bridge. Redman's plan had worked.

"Okay, men, "Watson announced, "let's get moving. We have a plane to catch."

"Redman didn't make it?" Grimes asked.

"No, but he made sure you did."

Chapter 1

Thursday, September 23, 1943
9:17 p.m.
Waco, Texas

It had been a long day. The flight from Chicago had been bumpy. Once on the ground in central Texas, the information Helen Meeker and Teresa Bryant received from the military was scant. A man supposedly dead had been smuggled back to London a few weeks before. By all reports, he was one of the most courageous and selfless soldiers in the army, yet he didn't want any part of being honored for his valor. Private Ruffin Redman was an enigma.

Redman had been deposited at Meeker's hotel door five minutes before by a military escort. He was five-ten, one-sixty, eyes dark, hair black, skin tone olive. His gaze was piercing, but his expression stoic. He didn't want to be there, and it showed. She quickly discovered that rocks were more talkative than this man.

"Private Redman," Meeker began, "I want to thank you for meeting with us."

"I wasn't given a choice, ma'am. Just following orders."

"And so are we. Miss Bryant and I are here at the request of the President. He wants to award you the Medal of Honor, and we've been told you want no part of it."

"That's correct."

As Meeker considered the soldier's abrupt response, she took a moment to evaluate her accommodations. For a small city, the Regis was an upscale hotel. The room she'd been given was a suite with a living area and connecting bedroom. It was decorated in the Art Deco style that had been the rage a decade before. The room's windows overlooked the city's sprawling downtown, which at the moment, was almost as quiet as a tomb. One car was on the street traveling north toward the Brazos River—otherwise, Waco appeared to be a ghost town.

"Private Redman," Meeker announced as she continued staring at the downtown lights, "to my knowledge, from the Civil War when it was first given, until now, no one has ever refused this honor." She turned back to face her guest. "I've seen your record. I read what you did. I know how you were wounded and left for dead by the Nazis. I know all about the underground unit that rescued you, saved your life, and smuggled you back to England. I know the bridge you destroyed upset the German supply chain and the diversion you created allowed your group to complete their mission and return to London with important plans for a German plane. I know the two women who escaped with your unit shared detailed information about Nazi operations in France. In my years working with the President, I've never known anyone who deserved this honor more than you do."

"Maybe that's true," Redman agreed, "but there's no rule that says I have to accept it."

"You're a good soldier," Meeker shot back. "Why don't you want it?"

"I don't want to deal with the press. I don't want to pose for pictures or meet the brass. I don't want to be used as a publicity pawn. I did what I did thinking I was going to die.

I got lucky and somehow lived. If you want to send me to Europe or the Pacific, I'll follow those orders, but you can't order me to accept an award. That's my choice."

Redman's response made no sense. No one refused the Medal of Honor and all that went with it.

"You do know," Meeker suggested as she smoothed her gray suit and eased into a chair, "accepting this award would assure you would never have to go back to combat. This is not just something you deserve, it's your ticket to surviving this war. You've already given enough to your country and the war effort."

"I want to go back into combat, so what you just told me gives me an even greater reason to say no."

"From what I've been told," Meeker continued, "and boy, it took some digging to find out about Ruffin Redman. You're from Chicago, grew up on the east side, and you didn't list anything about your family when you enlisted. By the way, you're the only Ruffin Redman in this whole country. If there had been others, we likely still wouldn't know anything about you. I've done my homework. I know your father was a butcher, your mother a nurse. You have a sister. She's a schoolteacher in Indiana. And, as I understand it, you have refused the request from the military to inform your sister about your honor. In fact, you have refused to let the Army tell her you are no longer missing in action. In her mind, you are likely dead."

"I like it this way. I want her to think of me as a ghost."

Meeker wagged her finger. "Do you know how many people you could inspire? Do you realize if you let us make this announcement your hometown would hold a celebration? Chicago's mayor would likely give you the key to the city."

"That key wouldn't open anything. Besides, I don't want any of that, I just want to get back to the base."

As a confounded Meeker studied Redman, Bryant, dressed in blue slacks and a gray blouse, moved into the bedroom and made a call. She spoke in low enough tones that neither Meeker nor Redman could understand what she was saying. Only when Bryant finished, almost fifteen minutes later, did Meeker pick up the questioning.

"This is a huge deal for you, the army, and your country," Meeker argued.

"The war will go on without it," Redman assured the women. "Now can I leave? If I'm going to catch a bus back to the base, I must be downstairs by ten. And I don't want to waste the money for a taxi."

Meeker glanced at Bryant. "You have anything to add?"

"Tell me about your family," Bryant demanded as she stepped closer to their guest.

"I haven't seen them for a long time. We had a falling out."

"So, no special memories of your mother?"

"I keep my memories to myself."

"What about riding the interurban and seeing the Cubs play in Comiskey Park?"

"Ma'am, that was when I was a kid. I've been to war—that was a lifetime ago."

"But surely those times mean something to you," Bryant argued.

"Back then they might have," Redman agreed, "but not now."

Bryant raised her eyebrows. "Didn't you enjoy eating at the counter at the Marshall Grant store or walking along Lake Huron?"

"Every kid likes those things, but I'll never be a kid again. Can I go now?"

"Sure, but we're not finished with you. We'll talk again soon."

Redman stood and moved across the room. He was reaching for the knob when Bryant said, "*Cehecares.*"

"Cehecares," he politely replied as he opened the door and stepped out of the room.

"What was that about?" Meeker asked.

"Cehecares is Seminole and Creek and means 'I will see you later,'" Bryant explained.

"And the stuff you said about Chicago was all wrong," Meeker noted. "It's the L not the interurban. The Cubs play at Wrigley Field. It's Lake Michigan not Huron."

"Yeah. That guy's never been to Chicago. There's no doubt he's a hero, but he's not Ruffin Redman. I called Napoleon to see what he'd dug up. Our partner had a wealth of information on the real Redman. And there is no way he is this guy."

"Spill."

"Helen, Redman had a few run-ins with the law when he was in high school. Therefore, the Chicago cops had a mug shot. That photo was of a pale-skinned man with red hair and green eyes. According to what Nap found out, Ruffin is stocky and about five-six. He's also at least a decade older than our visitor. And I figured this out even before I checked with what Nap had uncovered."

"How did you know?"

Bryant, her dark eyes aflame, explained, "When he entered the room, I saw a tattoo on the inside of his wrist. As you know, I have one as well. You got that when they sent you to an Indian school. As his record said he enlisted in Tulsa, I took a leap of faith and thought he might be Seminole."

"Why didn't I pick up on him being a native American?"

"Americans come from all over the world, Redman could have been the product of several different ethnic groups that produced his dark hair and eyes. So, there was no reason to think he couldn't have been from Chicago. But the story just starts there."

Meeker moved to a couch and took a seat. As she did, Bryant retrieved a pad and reviewed her notes.

"Redman left Chicago sometime in the early thirties. He had a few more run-ins with the law in Los Angeles, Utah, and then New Mexico. And then nothing. He simply disappeared."

"So, Teresa, our Redman is not Redman, he's a Seminole from Oklahoma."

"And if he accepted the Medal of Honor," Bryant added, "the ruse would be exposed. Then he would have to let the world know who he really was."

Meeker leafed through the army file of the man who was pretending to be Redman. "It seems that our hero became Redman in 1936. He joined the military in Tulsa. Now, listen to this. He has turned down advancement in rank a half dozen times."

Bryant nodded. "Any man who voluntarily remains a private is doing it for a reason. So, he's been trying to stay out of the spotlight for a long time."

"It's ironic too that he would choose the alias 'Redman,'" Meeker noted.

"No native would choose that name unless some conviction led them to," Bryant scoffed.

"Teresa, you told him goodbye in Seminole, and he answered without thinking. Now he must have figured out that you're onto him. So, how do you suggest we handle this? Would you be better off visiting with him one-on-one? Would he trust you more than me? This is now more than just a man refusing an honor, this is a missing person case. Maybe even more."

"I'll see if I can talk to him tomorrow," Bryant suggested, "but I don't think he'll open up to me or anyone else."

"Then how do we solve the mystery?" Meeker asked.

"We start by finding out what happened to the real Ruffin Redman. Our hero surely didn't choose that name by chance. I'm betting the two of them crossed paths."

"Whoever this guy is," Meeker pointed out, "he earned that medal. He deserves it."

"The medal, yes," Bryant agreed, "but what does this soldier deserve if we discover he killed Ruffin Redman before assuming his identity? This might just be the first time in history the United States executes a Medal of Honor winner."

A cold chill ran down Meeker's spine. She rubbed her arms before asking, "Teresa, would it be better for the war effort to just forget this? Let this guy get his wish, go back to combat, and pretend we don't know what we know?"

"Probably," Bryant agreed, "but we're not going to do that. If we did, it would haunt us for the rest of our lives. I'm going to my room, going to get some sleep, then tomorrow I'll take another crack at discovering who this guy is. In the meantime, I think Napoleon needs to find out more about Redman and his brushes with the law."

After her partner exited the room, Meeker walked back to the window. If the soldier had been killed when he blew up the bridge, he'd have taken his secret to the grave. Living was probably the worst thing that could have happened to him.

Sitting by the lamp, Meeker once more opened the military file. There was no next of kin listed. When he joined, he gave his address as an apartment in Tulsa. In the last seven years, that information had never been updated. But there was one small, interesting nugget. In case of his death, his effects and military insurance were to be sent to a Nancy Blue Sky on the Seminole Reservation in Oklahoma.

CHAPTER 2

Friday, September 24, 1943
8:22 a.m.
Waco, Texas

At eight o'clock the next morning, Teresa Bryant ordered a light breakfast while keeping her eye on the door. The small restaurant located off the Regis Hotel lobby was mainly filled with men in uniform. As the Army Air Corps trained in Waco, that was to be expected. These young men, so relaxed and unassuming now, would soon be half a world away taking on the best pilots the Axis powers threw at them. Sadly, many of those now laughing and sharing stories would not live to see their next birthdays. She was sure most, if not all, wanted to be heroes, they wanted to make their families proud, they wanted to be remembered and lionized in their hometowns, and they wanted most of all to live. And yet, the soldier she was meeting this morning didn't seem to want any of those things.

The man claiming to be Ruffin Redman entered through the street door. Dressed in his uniform, he appeared little different than the scores of enlisted men who surrounded him. Still, there was something that set him apart—his expression was one rarely seen outside a funeral. While everyone else seemed happy and upbeat, he was obviously displeased.

Bryant watched Redman search the tables before spotting her. When their eyes met, he began the trip through the crowded restaurant to her table.

"Istonko," she announced when he arrived.

"You caught me last night," he admitted as he eased into the seat opposite his host, "but not today."

After the light scolding. Bryant held her tongue until a plump, middle-aged waitress waltzed over. "You need anything, son?"

"Coffee, black."

"I'll have it in a jiffy."

Once the waitress left, Bryant made an observation, "There's no reason trying to spin a story about you being Ruffin Redman. Though, I do appreciate the irony of one of my people using the name Redman as an alias."

"And why do we know that?" he asked.

"Here's a wire photo of a mug shot of Redman. That's not you."

He glanced at the photo and shrugged. "A lot of people have the name Redman."

"You've never been to Chicago," Bryant jabbed. "That was easy to expose. I'd guess you're from Oklahoma and you're likely, at least, part Seminole. There's a long list of things I can hit you with that will continue to expose you're not who you claim to be, but I really don't want to waste your time or mine."

"What are you?" he asked.

"Caddo." She held up her tattoo. "Now let's both admit we spent time in the Indian schools with people trying to make us White. With me, it didn't take, but I'm not sure about you."

The talk paused as the waitress returned with the coffee. Once she'd left, Bryant pushed deeper.

"What do I call you?"

"Let's try Lucky. I'll come up with something better tomorrow."

She nodded. "I doubt that's your name, but it has to be closer than Ruffin. All I'm asking you to do is level with me."

"Okay, my name's not Redman."

"Why do you use it?"

"I needed a new name and picked this one. Believe me, the irony you noted was a part of why I chose Redman."

"So, you're running from something?"

He took a sip of coffee. "That should be obvious."

"What did you do?" Bryant demanded.

"In truth, nothing. I was just in the wrong place at the wrong time. But if I'd stuck around, I'd be dead now. That's the way the White man's justice works."

Bryant shrugged. "Maybe I can help you."

"The frame was perfect," he suggested.

"Tell me about it."

"No, I'm not going to give you more than you've got. Haul me in, charge me with anything, but I'll never tell you who I am, and you won't ever be able to find out. And that shouldn't surprise you, Seminoles were taught to cover their tracks as children. I'll bet you were too."

She shook her head. "I don't want to charge you with anything, but I'd like to see you get rewarded for what you did. You're a hero."

"And somehow, I'm alive. If I get the medal Roosevelt wants to pin on my chest, I won't live long. There's a very deadly man who'd make sure of that. Just so you know, I'm not the only one he'd kill. And you or your friend can't touch him." He took another draw from his cup before making a request. "As someone who shares my heritage, just allow me to continue to be Redman. And keep any publicity as far away from me as you can."

"Here's the deal," Bryant offered, "I'll keep this thing buried for a while, but I'd like to help you. If I could clear your name, would you accept the award? I mean, winning the Medal of Honor would be a huge thing for your tribe."

"I quit being Seminole in 1936. I'm not ashamed of my heritage, it's just something I had to do. I can't go back to who I was. What I did in France was to make sure a mission succeeded. That's all. I don't want to be rewarded for that. I'm asking you to make sure I remain an unknown private so my personal mission can succeed as well."

Bryant leaned closer to her guest. "Can you promise me on the honor of your ancestors that you did nothing wrong?"

"The only thing I did wrong was leave the reservation. I returned when I got out of school and should have stayed. Because I didn't, I will never again ride a horse across the land where I was born on or visit the graves of my parents. I'll always wander the world as a lost soul, having no past and no future. That's the way it must be. But I didn't do anything to deserve this fate except being at the wrong place at the wrong time. I hope you believe me."

"I do."

"What is your real name?"

"Morning Song."

He got up and smiled. "Morning Song, never turn your back on who you are."

"I never have," she quietly announced as she watched him leave.

Bryant was in a quandary. How do you help a person who doesn't want to be helped? She was still considering that problem five minutes later when Helen Meeker walked up to the table and sat down.

"What did you find out?" Meeker asked.

"Very little. He wouldn't tell me his name is or where he's from. And we aren't going to get him to accept the medal. He assured me he's done nothing wrong, but he's just as sure that the White man's law wouldn't see it that way. Maybe you can't understand that, but I can."

"So, we just drop it?"

Bryant shook her head. "No, but we must be careful. He claims there's someone powerful who could bury him. What did you find out about the woman who gets his insurance and personal effects?"

"Nancy Blue Sky is dead," Meeker explained. "She died in 1940 on the Seminole reservation in Oklahoma."

"I need to go there and talk to those who knew her."

"I'll go with you," Meeker suggested.

"No, I need to go alone. A White face would stand out in that world. Perhaps whoever could bury our hero knows who you are. If I go in just as an Indian, it likely won't bring any unwanted attention. Why don't you go back to Chicago and see if you can figure where Ruffin Redman went when he left town. This guy and Redman must have met. Knowing what happened to the real Redman might reveal more than anything I can find out on the reservation. I want to know who this guy was and why he became who he is now."

CHAPTER 3

Friday, September 24, 1943
3:35 p.m.
Elmwood, Indiana

There was no way to not stand out. Napoleon Lancelot was a large, muscular black man, and all the faces at Elmwood Grade School were White. Dressed in a blue suit, white shirt, and red tie, he'd checked in at the main office before being directed to room 417. The kids were all gone and one teacher, likely about forty, sat behind her desk grading papers. She was so consumed by her task, she only looked up when he knocked.

"Mrs. Rachel Lewis?" Lancelot asked.

The plain brunette in a green flowery dress nodded. Anyone could have seen she was confused. Though she said nothing, her blue eyes screamed, "Why is a black man visiting me?" Maybe that's why she remained mute.

"Mrs. Lewis," Lancelot repeated her name, "I work for Helen Meeker, who works with President Roosevelt."

A suddenly relaxed Lewis nodded. "You must be the one the newspapers call the Black Knight. I've read about you. The latest case you and Meeker cracked involved a Missouri congressman."

"That was a difficult one," Lancelot admitted. "It hit very close to home."

He glanced around the classroom. It looked no different than a thousand others all over the country. There were twenty-four desks arranged in four rows. Children's drawings of birds were taped on the far wall. The chalkboard displayed simple math lessons. The floor was scuffed, four-inch-wide wood strips.

"Why would you want to visit with me?" Lewis asked.

"May I sit down?"

She got up, pulled a chair beside her desk, and nodded. "This is the only adult chair I have in the room. I usually use it for parents."

After he was seated, Lancelot announced, "I'm not a parent. I wish I were here to talk about school, but I'm here to talk about your brother."

"You've found Ruffin?"

"No, that's the problem, we need to find him. When was the last time you heard from him?"

As she considered the question, she drummed her fingers on the desk and glanced out a far window. Lancelot couldn't tell if she was unsure of a timeline or unsure if she even wanted to talk about a man who was likely the family black sheep. When she finally turned her head and answered, Lewis's tone was almost void of emotion. "Our parents were still alive, so that makes it more than eight years ago. We got a letter from Arizona." She again looked toward the windows and shook her head. "No, it was New Mexico. Give me a second, and I'll remember the town. It'll come to me because I'd looked it up on a map after I read the letter." She snapped her fingers before continuing, "It was Alamogordo, a place down by Mexico."

Lancelot lifted his eyebrows. That was not the answer he expected. Maybe Santa Fe, but Alamogordo? "What was he doing there, do you know?"

"He told us he had a good job with a business located in the town, but he didn't say what it was. He did tell us we'd see him soon, and when he came back to Chicago, he'd be driving a big, fancy Cadillac and handing out dollar cigars."

"Eight years ago, that would be 1935," Lancelot suggested.

"I think it was thirty-six. Mom died late that year and Dad in the following summer."

"You never heard from him again?"

"No. As far as I know, Ruffin never came back to Chicago."

"And that didn't set off any alarms?"

"No, he'd been gone for a while, and my folks' lives were far better without him. He was constantly in trouble. He couldn't hold a job, drank a lot, and was hanging out with the wrong kind of people. Somehow, he always had some money, nice clothes, and a good car." She paused and smiled, "Do you know anything about gardening?"

"Not much," Lancelot admitted.

"When you buy packages of seed, in almost every one of them there's a bad seed or two. It could be a weed that got mixed in. My brother was that bad seed. He was that way when he was four years old. Even as a kid, Ruffin wasn't honest. He started out bad and got worse. So, while Mom wanted to see him again, Dad and I didn't. When he didn't make good on his promise to return a wealthy, rich man, we counted it our good fortune. If he had come to town in that car, you can bet the cops wouldn't have been too far behind."

Lewis paused before admitting something she seemed to regret. "Mr. Lancelot, don't get me wrong, I love my brother, we share the same blood, but I have three kids, the oldest sixteen, and I don't want him around them. Now, can I ask you a question?"

"Sure."

"What's Ruffin done this time?"

"Maybe nothing," Lancelot explained, "so we're not investigating any crime. We'd just like to know where he is."

"I'd like to tell you. I'm sorry I can't help you, but in truth, I'd rather not know where he is."

"Thanks to you, we've got a starting point. Other than getting into trouble, can you tell me anything else about him? Maybe some kind of habit he has that might give us a clue?"

"He's always been drawn to trouble, he likes finding shortcuts to making cash, and if he makes a score, he spends the money quickly. Beyond booze, he finds many other vices, such as women and gambling, to fill the void. He's smart, and over the years, most people initially underestimate him. He can hide his rough edges when needed."

"That coupled with some photos we have of him might help."

"There's something else Dad and I suspected that Mom never knew about."

"What's that?" Lancelot asked.

"We thought he made some of his money by killing people for certain members of the underworld."

Lancelot took a deep breath. This turned up the heat a few notches. He leaned closer to the teacher's desk. "You mean a hit man?"

"We had no proof, but there were times when bodies turned up in the river, and when the stories made the newspapers, Ruffin was awash in cash. You don't sleep very well when your brother might be using his talents to snuff people out."

Lancelot had been expecting to hear Rachel Lewis talk about petty crime but not this. If Ruffin Redman was connected to certain crime bosses, then why had he been in a small New Mexico town eight years ago? Was he cooling off from a hit?

"Mrs. Lewis, where was Ruffin between the time he left Chicago and when he wrote that letter from New Mexico?"

"He left Chicago around 1933. I know he first went to Los Angeles. He was there for a year or so and moved to Salt Lake. The next time we heard from him in 1936, he was in Denver. Then came that last letter. There was nothing after that. I'm confused, if you aren't after him for any crime, then what difference does any of that make?"

"Sometimes to know where someone is going," Lancelot explained, "you have to know where they have been. I thank you for your time."

"Can I ask a favor?" Lewis's tone indicated a touch of self-loathing.

As he rose, Lancelot nodded.

"He has no idea I live here. He doesn't even know I've remarried, and my name is Lewis. My life would be much better if I never see Ruffin again. So, if you find him, don't tell him where I am."

"Okay, I can do that, but if I find him, would you like me to tell you where he is?"

"I've been pretending he's dead for a long time," she explained, "I'd like to keep on pretending."

Normally, her thoughts would have been chilling, but if Redman was a hit man, Rachel Lewis's wishes were understandable. Put in that position, he would probably feel the same way.

Lancelot nodded and said, "Thank you again."

"It was nice meeting you. My kids will be jealous I got to meet the Black Knight. Could you give me your autograph?"

After scribbling his name, exiting the building, and sliding into his 1941 Ford sedan, Lancelot considered what he'd learned. Why would a man use Ruffin Redman's name when he entered the service? Why choose the name of a person who might be wrapped up with the underworld? Perhaps their hero didn't want the Medal of Honor, not because of who he had been, but rather because he found out his alias was pure poison.

CHAPTER 4

Saturday, September 25, 1943
9:19 a.m.
Seminole Reservation, Oklahoma

Walking onto to an Indian reservation was never a pleasant experience for Teresa Bryant. Each visit presented a stark reminder of the hopeless plight of her own people. Essentially, in her view, this was the US government's version of a human zoo. Rather than lions and tigers being confined, it was the people who once called the whole continent home. And of all the reservations in Oklahoma, this was the smallest, and it seemed completely ill-suited for this proud tribe.

This region had little in common with the Seminole's original Florida home. The soil was too poor for farming, and the wild game was in short supply. Though there were areas that reflected a certain raw beauty, the reservation still represented a home that was as depressing for those who lived here as the Bronx Zoo was for a caged gorilla. There was no freedom—something the American natives had embraced and treasured for centuries. Then, everything changed. The best of this continent was taken away and given to immigrants, and those who claimed North America as their ancestral homes were pushed onto the parts no one wanted.

Bryant was standing on a hill overlooking the building that housed the Office of Indian Affairs. As it was run by a White man, it served as another stark reminder of who was in charge. She was choking on her own bitterness when an old man approached. His face was deeply wrinkled, his lean form slightly bent, but his shoulders were still broad and his arms strong. He was wearing a colorful, homemade, pullover cloth shirt and dungarees. As he walked, it was obvious he was sizing up the stranger.

"You look like one of us," he announced, "but you don't dress like us."

The welcome was unconventional but not surprising. Her gray suit, complete with jacket and slacks, blue blouse, black leather flats, and stylish hat would have been something Katherine Hepburn or Marlene Dietrich would have worn in a movie. After years spent in the White man's world, Bryant was comfortable in the ensemble, but she sensed the old man viewed her outfit with some disdain.

"Does the way I dress bother you?" she asked.

As he stepped up to the visitor, he announced, "I have no ill feelings for those who escape our exile, as long as they have not betrayed who they are to gain what they have."

"Have I done things I regret? Sure! But when the lion is on your trail, the choices are not always easy. The fruits of my labor have come from walking an honest path. On my clothes, I dress like this because of what I do. There are times I need to blend in for me to accomplish my job."

He nodded. "Even in those clothes, you still look like one of us. What is your tribe?"

"Caddo."

"There are very few of your people left," the old man observed.

"The Caddo are not alone. There are many proud names that were once spoken often who no longer walk the ground in this world."

"Where did you grow up?"

She pulled her blouse's sleeve back to reveal the numbers tattooed on her wrist. Being a product of an Indian school was not something she was proud of, but it was a part of who she was.

He solemnly nodded. "So, you were raised in hell?"

"In the Indian school, I was raised to forget who I was. I was beaten to remove the native from my fiber. I was starved of the wisdom of my ancestors. When I could escape, I did. I made it through my life doing whatever it took to survive. Yet, I never forgot when we were free to roam and borrowed our lands from the Great Spirit. When we weren't assigned property of a government we had no voice in. When we lived much more like Jesus than the White man ever has."

He carefully studied Bryant. His eyes looking deeply into hers before stepping back and observing her in full. When he finished his inspection, he announced, "You are strong in many ways. What is your name?"

"The White man calls me Teresa Bryant."

"And your people, what did they call you."

"Morning Song. And you are?"

"The Whites call me Bill. I was once Grey Wolf. In my mind and heart, I still am. Why have you come?"

Now was the moment of truth. By admitting who she served, she might well close the door to all future conversation. So, rather than immediately respond, she studied the draw that ran between two hills. A few goats were grazing there, completely oblivious to a world that was chaotic and cruel. Many of the western reservations were on land that constantly reminded people that in the White man's eyes, the Indian had no value. This place could, at least, feed those who lived here, but even that wasn't enough. It was still a zoo. And the person who ran the country and placed these people in this zoo was her boss.

She turned her gaze from the goats to the man. "I work for the President of the United States."

"Has oil been discovered on our land?" Grey Wolf asked. There was no humor in his tone. He was deadly serious. "Have they sent one of our own to inform us we will be packed up and moved as our ancestors were?"

"No. I'm looking for something far different. I need your help."

"As a member of the government or a sister?"

"A little of both, but mainly as your sister."

"Then speak."

Bryant nodded. "I need to know the story of a woman who died three years ago on this reservation. She is a part of mystery concerning a man from your tribe who is a hero but refuses to accept the award that recognizes his valor."

"Humility is a part of being a Seminole. Refusing to be rewarded for doing what is right is a part of our nature. We are taught to sacrifice and expect nothing in return. I therefore understand this man."

"It's more than that," Bryant explained. "This man is not using his real name. He is hiding behind a White name he has stolen. When I speak to him and mention the past, I see unrest and concern in his eyes. I need to relieve him of a burden he is carrying so he can once again be who he was intended to be."

"What does the woman have to do with this?"

"This brother listed that if he died she was to get his personal effects. If I knew who she was then perhaps I could learn who he is."

"Is that important?" Grey Wolf asked.

"Do you think we should bury someone before they are dead?" Bryant returned.

Her response appeared to catch him off guard. He considered her words and then pointed toward a creek. "Walk with me, share your story, and I will see if I, an old man of eighty, can or should help."

Bryant sensed she needed to remain mute as she followed the man across the rolling hill and into a valley. When it was time, he would invite her to voice her inquiries. After a half mile and fifteen minutes of silence, he finally spoke.

"Tell me what you know about this man."

"I'm guessing he's about thirty. He speaks the Seminole language. He tells me he can't reveal who he is, but he won't tell me why. He's going by the name of Ruffin Redman. I found out late last night that Redman once worked within the White man's crime world. But the member of your tribe is not that man, he is only using his name."

"Does the member of our tribe know the story of the man whose name he now carries?"

"He won't say."

"What happened to the White man?"

"We don't know."

When they arrived at the creek, Grey Wolf studied the clear water as it moved over ancient rocks and down toward a pond. He remained lost in his own thoughts for several minutes, and Bryant respected each of those.

"Morning Song," he finally said. "Let us sit on that fallen log. We will look at the clouds as we search for answers."

After they were at rest, their eyes fixed on the sky, Grey Wolf made an observation. "The clouds often take on the forms of the things that shape our lives. Some remind us of those who went before us. When I sit like this, I remember the stories told to me by my father and his father before him. In these moments, their voices are still alive in the wind."

"I often hear my grandfather's voice," Bryant admitted, "he told me about the times before the White man was here. His last lesson was on the day an eagle came and took his spirit."

"You were with him when he died?" Grey Wolf asked, his gaze still fixed on the sky.

"I was."

"And after that, the White man took you away to their schools?"

"Within a year."

He again studied Bryant as if trying to look into her soul. After several seconds of silence, he posed a question. "Who is the woman whose story you want to know?"

"Nancy Blue Sky."

The old man shook his head and looked back toward the clouds. This time Bryant didn't have to wait for answers.

"She was just another woman. During her younger days she had been a teacher ... one who kept the ancient stories alive. She taught my son and daughter. She walked with sadness because her only son was taken to the Indian School when he was just six. He would not return until he was sixteen. He stayed on the reservation for two years and then left."

"What can you tell me about him?"

"He was quiet. He loved horses. In fact, he trained ponies for others. Once, he broke his arm when a paint tossed him into a pile of rocks. Another time, he busted his leg when a stubborn raven horse spun him against a tree. But both times he recovered and got back, and those ponies became his. When he left us, he gave the horses to me."

"What was his name?"

"He chose Red Cloud as a way of saluting his mother. He wanted to be a cloud in her blue sky. The White school gave him the name William, but they didn't call him that for long. He was given another name by a teacher, but it had no meaning to me, and I've forgotten what it was. On this land, he always remained Red Cloud."

The man's eyes were still fixed on the sky when Bryant posed her next question. "When did Red Cloud leave the reservation?"

"1933."

"Where did he go?"

"His mother told me he was headed west, but we never heard from him again, so that may not be true."

"He never wrote letters?"

Grey Wolf sadly shook his head, "Why should he? He had one relative, and that was his mother. And she couldn't read." He once again studied Bryant before asking, "This man who is using a White man's name, do you think he is Red Cloud?"

"I don't know," Bryant admitted, "but he might be."

"Do you read books?" he asked.

"Yes."

"Three years ago, I read a book by a dead White man named Thomas Wolfe. He wrote something that spoke to me in a way much like my grandfather's wisdom. He said you can't go home again. For my entire life, I dreamed of going back to our ancestorial lands in Florida. It seemed to me that if I could move there, I would find peace and happiness. But after reading Wolfe's book, I came to realize that I am not the same kind of person my grandfather was when he lived there, and Florida, as the White man calls it, is a much different place now than it was then. Does that make sense to you?"

"Yes, I have found the same thing to be true. We cannot reshape the past to make the present what it once was."

"So, Morning Song, if that is true, then perhaps you should allow the Seminole who is now known by the White man's name to remain as he is. Because even if you were to find out that he is Red Cloud, he still couldn't come home again. He and this place have changed too much."

"But," Bryant argued, "if this man is captured and held hostage by a lie, wouldn't it also be correct that truth would set him free?"

Grey Wolf stood and began to walk the trail that had led them to the log. Bryant joined him, matching his steps. Neither spoke until they returned to where she had parked her rented car.

Grey Wolf once more studied the visitor intently. Finally, he said, "My grandfather once told me about time walkers. Did your grandfather ever mention them to you?"

"Yes, they are legendary figures."

"Is that all they are?" Grey Wolf demanded. When she didn't answer, he continued, "They are not bound by the passage of time. The Great Spirit has given them longer on this earth than he has given others. Their wisdom is as deep as the ocean, their vision is like that of a hawk, but they are restless like a mountain lion. Their curiosity drives them to explore, to see more, to experience more, and to learn more. They are bound by one thing ... they must know the truth."

Bryant shrugged and walked toward her car. After getting in, she looked back at the old man, "I know the legend of time walkers well, but that has nothing to do with this."

Grey Wolf leaned close to stare deeply into Bryant's eyes, "They are more than fables. My grandfather knew one. He described her to me. And she looked exactly like you."

"Lots of people look alike," Bryant argued.

"That's true, but you also have the other qualities. Can I give you a word from my own wisdom."

She nodded.

"The truth is this land the White man calls the United States should still be ours, but knowing that truth does not free me from this reservation. Perhaps the Seminole who carries the White man's name will find the truth binds him even more than the lie he lives. May your path be easy, Morning Song."

Before she could respond, he turned and walked away.

In her brief time with him, Grey Wolf had given her many things to contemplate and a few nuggets to run with. But his last observation made her question if she shouldn't call this case off. Yet, even if she walked away now, she knew the military wouldn't. So, perhaps the best way to protect the hero was to control where the case was heading.

CHAPTER 5

Saturday, September 25, 1943
3:30 p.m.
Alamogordo, New Mexico

Helen Meeker knew Sunday would be a wasted day. With no businesses open, she likely would spend more time in her hotel room than finding anything in the small city she could tie to Ruffin Redman. So on Saturday afternoon, when she landed at Holloman Army Airbase, she hit the ground running. Her first stop was at the *Alamogordo Daily News*.

The smalltown paper's office was on the main drag. On one side of the building was a Western Auto and on the other a small café. The structure was two stories, but apparently the business was all at street level. She guessed the second floor was either a residence or reserved for storage. As she entered through the front door, a bell announced her arrival, and a man sitting behind a Royal typewriter looked up.

"Can I help you?" he asked. He was crowding, if not beyond, seventy. Thin, balding, clean-shaven, and his choice of dress was white shirt, loose tie, dark slacks, and black cowboy boots.

"My name is Helen Meeker."

The man froze, his eyes suddenly fixed on the guest, and in time, a smile slowly emerged. After tightening his tie, he stood and announced, "Of course, I've seen enough photos to know you, and I've read a lot about you over the past few years. It's an honor to have you in my office."

"My life would be better if you'd read nothing," she shot back. "What fame I have I didn't ask for or want. It hinders my work rather than helps it."

He stuck out his hand, and after the two shook, he pointed to a chair. "I'm Hamilton Hodges. I own this little paper—have for fifty years. I do everything from write the stories to set the type and run the press. Even in a town this small, it kept me so busy I never had time to get married. Though I might have sold this old rag and walked down the altar if there'd been anybody like you here."

She smiled. "I'll assume that was a compliment."

"You assume right. Good-looking, smart, and brave, that's a rare combination in either sex. The only thing that could beat the honor of your visit was if your Indian sidekick had come with you."

Meeker raised an eyebrow. "I talked to her when my plane landed. She'll be here tomorrow, but a word of warning, she is an equal. If you ever refer to her as Tonto, we will not respond well."

"Advice noted. As few folks come to Alamogordo for pleasure, especially one of your status, what can I do for you?"

Meeker paused. How much of the information Lancelot had gathered should she reveal? Perhaps it was best to unwrap it slowly.

"I'm looking for a man who might have arrived here in 1936. His name was Ruffin Redman. He was about my height, stocky, red hair, and originally from Chicago." She reached into her purse and pulled out a photo. "Here's a mug shot I got via a wire transfer. He was a lot younger when this was taken."

"The name doesn't mean anything," Hodges admitted. "Let me look at the photo." He studied the picture for a few seconds before shrugging, "He kind of looks familiar, but it's not anyone I know. And if they'd been here for any length of time over the past five decades, I would know them. Maybe I saw him but never met him, but I just can't say for sure. That shot isn't setting off any bells."

Meeker figured having the first person she showed Redman's picture recognize him would be a long shot. So, she was hardly surprised. But rather than give up, she opted to share a bit more information anyway.

"He wrote his family a letter from Alamogordo about seven or eight years ago. That was the last they ever heard of him. In that letter, he was hinting at cashing in on some kind of big deal. And we're talking lots of money. Does that set off any alarms?"

Hodges shook his head. "We didn't cover anything that sounds like that. There were no gold strikes No one discovered oil."

"Do you have a newspaper morgue?"

"We sure do," Hodges assured her. He then smiled and tapped his balding head, "but the information's all here and much easier to locate. Now, let me be a reporter and grill you."

"That's fair."

"Why are you interested in this missing person?"

"He worked for organized crime in Chicago. We think he might have been a hit man."

"As you are usually dealing with the government or the war effort, I thought it might have been something in that line."

"Not directly," Meeker answered, "though it might tie in down the road. Here's something you'll find interesting. There's another man who is kind of missing we need to find information on too."

"Kind of missing?" the editor asked. His raised eyebrows spelled out the irony he saw in Meeker's description.

"I'm sorry, I can't give you any more information than that. And that's because of the war effort."

"So, you just tied everything together. You are here on government business."

"In at least one way, but we're trying to figure where these two men met. Teresa spent today in Oklahoma on one lead, and on a last-minute hunch, I came here rather than go back to Chicago."

"Do you have a photo of the other guy?"

"Teresa has it. When she gets here tomorrow, I can share it with you. Now, let's get back to the time that Redman's letter was written. Was there any big news in town back then? Any unsolved murders?"

"Do you have a specific date?"

"It's like I said a while ago, I'm guessing 1936. Redman's sister didn't remember the time of the year. She only recalled the location because she looked it up on a map."

Hodges leaned back in his chair, put his feet on the desk, and closed his eyes. Unlike many, when he thought, he did it out loud. His words clearly spelled out his thoughts.

"We were still battling the Depression. Times were lean and more people were leaving town than moving in. The White Sands National Monument helped create a little tourism, but those who came didn't leave much of their money behind. The WPA did some nice work, which created a few jobs. There was a bank robbery in July of that year. First State had been holding a shipment of bills headed west. They claim the amount stolen was about $100,000."

"That's a lot of money for a small town," Meeker suggested.

"Most of it wasn't local money," Redman offered. "A train derailed and shut down the tracks for about a week. A large shipment of cash was headed west. So, the hundred grand was railroad money. Anyway, a day or so before the rail line was fixed, the vault was blown open, and someone got away with the loot."

Meeker leaned closer. This news tied into something Redman had hinted at in his letter. That amount of cash could buy a Cadillac and a whole lot more.

"About twenty-five grand was found two days later," Hodges announced. "The bag of cash was next to a burned-out car about twenty miles east of here. There was a body in that car too."

"Who was it?"

"The WPA had been using some men for work. These guys came from all over. A billfold found about twenty feet from the wrecked car indicated it was a guy named Alan Jenkins. He was from somewhere in Alabama."

"You say you identified him by his billfold?" Meeker asked. "Couldn't one of his coworkers verify the body was his?"

Hodges chuckled. "I guess I forgot to mention the car was burned, and so was the body. No one could have identified that guy. The bank manager, who had only been on the job for a few weeks, was just thrilled to get at least one bag of cash back. That banker was a young man named Taylor Owen. First State was owned by a group from Santa Fe. They'd bought the building for a song back in thirty-five."

"The amount you mentioned was only a quarter of what you said was taken."

"The total amount was never actually verified," Hodges explained. "One of the women who worked at First State swore she put four bags of railroad cash into the vault. So, that's where the hundred thousand comes from."

Meeker nodded, "Can we visit with her?"

"No, you can't," Hodges explained. "Judy Walloch was her name, and she died in a car wreck about six months later. She was driving by herself and just ran off the road and into a bridge."

"Was this guy who pulled the job ..."

"Jenkins?"

"Yeah, was his body shipped back to his hometown for burial?"

"No, his family didn't have the money, so he was buried here."

"Did you see the body?"

"I did, and I saw the accident scene too. I took photos on both occasions. I was also there when the medical examiner, who's our local doc, did the postmortem. I took pictures for him. But I can tell you this. The guy was the same size and build as Jenkins. So, it passed the smell test. Best we could figure, it was late at night, he was driving too fast on a dirt road he didn't know, and just lost control. As it was a roadster, there wasn't much protection. Doc said there was no evidence he was alive when the fire consumed the body. So, he likely died instantly."

"How did he find out about the money?" Meeker asked. "I'm assuming the railroad didn't release that information. So, it had to be secret."

"Now, that's something none of us know. I didn't write about the money, the bank and railroad said nothing, neither did the sheriff, so maybe the guy heard Judy spilling the beans. She was known as a gossip. But more than likely, the news came from a young guy who worked in the bank. He might have found out and shared the information with Jenkins. Then the two of them worked together to blow the safe."

"Was the young guy arrested?"

"No, he disappeared the same night the money was taken. No one has seen him since."

A now captivated Meeker smiled. "What was the other man's name?"

"Folks called him Horse, but don't ask me why. Not long after he arrived, he got a job cleaning up the bank. He'd also run errands for the bank manager both at the business and at the house Owen rented. No one ever found out what Horse's real name was. He looked like an Indian, but some claimed he was Mexican."

"Mr. Hodges, you're a newspaper man, do you think Horse was in on the job?"

"I liked the boy. He must have been about twenty, but I guess he might have done it. After all, times were hard. But he wasn't very bright. I mean, he could barely string together a sentence. He had an impediment of some kind. He didn't take charity, either. He worked hard. I just don't see him as the type who would have been tempted by money ... even a hundred grand."

"Is that a hunch?"

"No, a bit more than that. There were footprints leading away from the car and out into the desert. I think there's a body out there waiting to be found. When it's found, that will spell out who was working with Jenkins. And, as Horse appeared to be the only one missing, I guess I might be wrong about him not being involved."

"Did they search for Horse?" Meeker asked.

"Yeah," Hodges solemnly added, "a big search party. It went on for several days. After all, if the rumor was right, there was more money out there, and he might have had it with him."

"Why don't you think the accomplice got away?"

"Because Miss Meeker, that desert in the summer is unforgiving. If he had shown up in any of the other towns around here, folks would turn him in for the reward. So, I'm pretty sure he died out there."

"So, the desert got him?"

"I didn't say that." Hodges replied. "My gut tells me someone found him. My guess is they shot the person working with Jenkins, buried the body, and kept the money for themselves. Could that have been Horse? Maybe, but I still believe the boy just left town at the same time as the robbery. Maybe the other guy was working for the WPA too."

"That bit about murder is a pretty bold statement. You have any proof?"

"Only that a couple of the locals suddenly left town for a few days and came back with new cars. They claimed they got lucky gambling in Santa Fe, but I never knew those guys to do anything but lose at cards."

"Who were they?" Meeker asked.

"Just a couple of rowdies. They were both drafted in 1942. One died in Italy. The other is serving in the Pacific."

"Is the bank manager still around?"

Hodges frowned, "No. After the robbery, folks pulled their money out of the bank, and it folded. He was gone almost as soon as he got here."

"Any other big news during that time?"

"No, just the normal stuff that happens in a town of four thousand. A few fights, babies being born, people dying, and life going on. When the military moved here after the war started—that's when things really began to hop."

Meeker looked at her watch before asking, "Any good places to eat that you could recommend?"

"If you want Mexican, try the joint on the right about a block. Otherwise, the café next door is your best bet."

"Mr. Hodges, I know it will be Sunday, but may I meet with you tomorrow after Teresa gets here? I want you to look at the other photo."

"Sure. I live upstairs. Just knock on the office door and I'll answer."

"Thanks for your time."

"Did I help you?"

Meeker smiled as she got up and walked toward the door. After she opened it and the bell rang, she looked back. "I found your story interesting. I wish it had been the guy I was looking for behind the wheel, but if he'd been pretending to be Jenkins, you would have recognized him. You know, if I had the time, I'd liked to have found out what happened to the rest of the money. But I have my own mystery to solve. Maybe tomorrow you'll recognize another photo and that will give me a lead."

Hodges smiled. "Nice meeting you, and it was an honor to have you in my office."

Meeker walked back out into the sunshine. If she and Teresa struck out tomorrow, and it sure looked like they would, this had been a wasted trip.

CHAPTER 6

SUNDAY, SEPTEMBER 26, 1943
10:47 A.M.
ALAMOGORDO, NEW MEXICO

After a quick breakfast, when Helen Meeker and Teresa Bryant exchanged information, they moved from the café to the newspaper and knocked on the door. A few seconds later, a smiling Hodges, dressed in his Sunday best, greeted them.

"So, this is Miss Bryant," he quipped as the women entered.

"I am."

"I've heard so much about you, but there is so much more I'd like to know. You're an amazing woman. Both of you are. Your exploits read like fiction. And I'm betting there are a lot of things you've done no one knows about."

Bryant, dressed in light blue dress tied at the waist and dark pumps, shrugged and then returned the compliment. "Helen has told me about your encyclopedic knowledge of all things Alamogordo. I've long believed a man who learns is well read, but a man who retains what he has observed is most often wise. I sense you are both of those."

"If not wise," Hodges added, "perhaps boring. I spend a lot of time talking about things no one wants to know."

He glanced over at Meeker. "Miss Meeker, I'd like to look at that photo again. The one you showed me yesterday. Why don't we climb the steps and have our visit in my small living quarters. It's more comfortable than this dusty rat trap."

The steps were at the back of the office. They were wooden, steep, and ended in a twelve-by-twenty-foot combination living room/kitchen. Like the office, it was cluttered. None of the furniture matched, and neither did the dishes stacked in the sink. Books, magazines, and newspapers were stacked everywhere.

"It lacks a woman's touch," Hodges suggested as he pointed to a green leather divan. Once the women were seated, he eased into a red velvet wingback chair and cut to the chase. "Two days before the bank was robbed, we had a community carnival. It was an annual event called Frontier Days. There were folks from as far away as Santa Fe and Roswell. People were selling food and ice cream on the streets, our city band had a concert, and there was even a hillbilly group that performed. Rather than enjoying the activities or the food, I did my job and spent most of the day shooting photos. Later than night, I printed a contact sheet and chose the ones I was going to use in the weekend edition of the paper."

Bryant glanced at Meeker who shrugged. It was evidently one of those times when they would just wait for the man to make his point, but she wondered how long that would take.

"Miss Meeker," Hodges asked while running his hand over his bald head, "can I see the photo you showed me?"

"Sure."

After taking it from Meeker, the publisher studied the print for a few seconds, then got up, walked across the room, and pulled an eight-by-ten from a file folder. He held the two side by side before giving both to Meeker.

"I didn't really see Ruffin Redman back then," Hodges explained, "but I got his picture. At least I think I did. He's fifteen years or so older than the one you have with you, but it looks like the same guy to me."

Meeker examined the shots before sharing them with Bryant. There was no doubt.

"I wish I could tell you more," Hodges continued, "but you can see he has a visitor's ribbon pinned to his coat. By the way, the man on his right is the bank manager, Taylor Owen. The photo has them in the same frame, but it doesn't seem like they are friends."

"What about this photo?" Bryant asked as she pulled a snapshot from her purse and handed it to their host.

"I don't know this guy at all," Hodges quickly answered.

"So," Meeker asked, "that's not Horse?"

"Definitely not. Horse was thinner, his face had a couple of scars."

The door alarm from downstairs momentarily stopped the conversation until Hodges offered an explanation. "That must be Doc Edwards. I asked him to come over so he could talk to you about Jenkins's body. I took photos of it at the accident and then later grabbed some pictures of the postmortem." Hodges stood and yelled, "Come on up."

The women listened as Edwards's footsteps strolled across the office and up the stairs. Bryant noted that, unlike the publisher, the doctor moved slower, as if each step was contemplated. When he finally appeared, Bryant sized him up. Edwards was likely in his fifties, a portly man with graying hair, a quick smile, and clear green eyes. When he spoke, his voice crackled like a winter fire.

"Nice to meet you, ladies. This old codger to my right is mighty pleased to have you in his office and this mess he calls an apartment. You're the biggest celebrities he's ever met. I guess that goes for me too."

Rather than waiting for Meeker, Bryant stood and took the lead. "I'm Teresa Bryant, and this is Helen Meeker."

"And I'm Roy Edwards, but most folks just call me Doc. I brought some pictures with me on the Jenkins's matter. Hodges thought you'd want to see them. Don't complain about the quality—he took them, I didn't."

Meeker grabbed the file, set it on the coffee table, and as Bryant looked on, she leafed through about two dozen eight-by-tens. When they finished, Hodges handed the women another eight-by-ten that had been taken at the crime scene.

"This guy was bigger than Redman," Bryant immediately noted. "He looks to be over six feet tall."

"Mr. Hodges," Meeker chimed in as she studied the new photo, "you said it was determined that Jenkins drove the car off the road and hit that boulder."

Hodges glanced at the shot and nodded. "It's pretty obvious."

"He couldn't have been driving very fast," Meeker suggested. "There wasn't much damage done to the front end of the Caddy. And the dirt doesn't show he attempted to brake. As soft as the sand was, I would've expected some ruts if that had been case."

Hodges took a second look. As he did, the doctor moved closer and studied the shot as well.

"Where was the billfold found?" Meeker asked.

"About twenty feet to the left," the publisher explained. "The bag of money was in that same area."

"So," Meeker opined. "Jenkins rolled down the road, gently bumped into a rock. His gas tank, which is in the back, caught on fire. He allowed the flames to slowly crawl to the front seat, where just before he voluntarily burned to death, he tossed his billfold and money bag far enough from the wreck to keep it from burning. Gentlemen, this was staged."

The doctor and publisher quickly shuffled through the photos of the crime scene. Their expression fully displayed their shock. When they'd finally grasped what had been missed so many years before, Bryant dropped a second bombshell.

"This photo shows a close up of the upper half of the body on the examining table." She passed it over to the two men. "Though it's badly burned, you should note the large hole at the back of the skull." As Edwards and Hodges's jaws dropped, Bryant handed them a second photo. "Note in this shot, the fabric on the man's wrist. He had been bound when he was shot."

"My Lord," Edwards whispered, "this was a murder."

"It was more than that," Bryant declared. "It was an execution. It was either someone framing Jenkins or Jenkins using someone else to buy him the time to get away and start a new life with the loot."

"I suggest," Meeker chimed in, "you alert your sheriff and tell him he has an unsolved murder to investigate."

"Aren't you going to stay and help?" Hodges asked.

"No. We wanted to confirm two things," Meeker explained. "The first was Horse was not the soldier in that photo. The second was that Ruffin Redman was here. If we find anything else that ties to his case, we'll let you know."

Meeker and Bryant stood and walked toward the stairs. The two men were so caught up in their own mystery, they failed to offer their thanks or goodbyes. Only when the women were outside did Bryant speak.

"Was Redman in on the heist?"

"Could be," Meeker suggested, "but as Horse is not our hero, then Alamogordo is not likely where the two crossed paths. We need to figure out where Redman went next."

"How do we do that?"

"I have no idea." Meeker glanced around the all-but-deserted main street before adding, "I don't think we'll find any answers here."

CHAPTER 7

Monday, September 27, 1943
2:42 p.m.
Chicago, Illinois

Napoleon Lancelot frowned. The call from Helen Meeker produced nothing new. Yes. Redman had been in Alamogordo in summer of 1936, but that didn't tie him to a man who deserved the nation's highest honor. That meant Lancelot had to get back to work. He'd spent most of Sunday afternoon at the Chicago Tribune going through newspapers from the twenties and thirties. His goal was to prove that Redman's money was earned by conducting mob executions. He'd found a host of unsolved hits, but they couldn't be tied to Redman. He was taking a break, drinking a Coke, and eating a Payday when a small man came into the newspaper morgue.

"You must be Lancelot?"

The man, slightly built with wavy blond hair, was dressed in a wrinkled gray suit, white shirt, and a black tie that was loose at the collar. Thick glasses framed hazel eyes. He was likely about forty.

"I'm Lancelot."

"I'm Goodwin, I've been covering the crime beat for this paper for almost twenty years. Charlie tells me you've been looking for information on a guy named Ruffin Redman."

"I might be."

"Don't be alarmed, I just came here to help you cut some corners." Goodwin perched on the corner of a long table, pulled a handkerchief from his pocket, and began to clean his glasses. As he worked, he made an observation and posed a question. "I know you work with Helen Meeker. That makes what you do important, so why do you want information on Redman?"

There was no reason to couch his story, so Lancelot shot straight. "I'm trying to determine if he's a hitman. And if so, who he worked for. But all I'm finding is there have been more bodies discovered floating in the Chicago River than fish."

"And there's a lot more on the bottom," Goodwin added with a wry smile, "bodies not fish. But the handiwork of the boy you're looking for won't be found in the river. That wasn't his style. Though the cops here have never been able to pin anything on him, my sources tell me Redman's taken out, at least, a dozen men and likely many more. I've got a lot of dope on him I will gladly share."

Lancelot leaned back in the chair and placed his empty Coke bottle on the table. "Who did he work for?"

"He started back in the early twenties as a free agent. But in time, Capone bought him. He did Al's dirty work until Uncle Sam sent the mobster to the West Coast. At that time, Redman fell in with Jim O'Toole. Unlike Al, Big Jim wanted people to know when folks had been taken out. And that gave Redman a chance to develop a certain style. He essentially signed his work."

"How so?"

"He'd get to know the marks, make friends with them, become their buddy. Once they were comfortable, Redman would take them out for drinks and drug them. When they came to, they'd be tied to a chair. He'd spend the next few hours working them over. If they passed out, he'd take a break until they woke up. Finally, when the game ceased to amuse him, he'd put his gun to the back of their head and execute them. The body and weapon would always be left where the cops could find it, but there was never any evidence tying Redman to the job. No witnesses, no prints—nothing. He got arrested a few times, but they couldn't hold him."

Lancelot considered the gruesome news, pushed away from the table, and walked over to the fourth-floor window. As he looked down at the city streets, he posed a question. "Why are you feeding me the information? After all this is your exclusive story."

"Because Redman's disappeared, and I don't know where he's gone. I know he's no longer in Chicago. When Redmen took out a member of the city council, O'Toole moved him to the West Coast in 1933. The cops don't work too hard on cases when you take out other hoods, but they tend to do their jobs when you start killing government officials. There were three hits carried out in Los Angeles using Redman's method, then he must have moved to San Francisco for a few months. After that it was Salt Lake and Denver in 1936. I believe he totaled, at least, seven hits over those three years. There were probably more."

Lancelot turned back to Goodwin. "Was he still working for O'Toole?"

"Yeah, he was." The reporter pulled a cigarette from his pocket and lit it. "But as you likely know, O'Toole disappeared in thirty-six and Redman fell off the planet at the same time."

"What do you think happened?"

"I don't know, but I have a couple of guesses."

"Care to share?"

After enjoying another draw from the Camel, Goodwin continued, "When someone like O'Toole goes missing, it means a rival has rubbed him out. I'm guessing that Redman took that as a sign to drop out of sight. I figure he had a pile of money socked away, because he was supposedly paid well, and so he likely had what he needed to live well. But if he's alive, he will resurface."

"Why do you say that?" Lancelot asked.

"Most hitmen look at their murders as a job. They never get to know their victims. For them it's not personal. They have no problem walking away from their work when they have financial security. That's why they're rarely caught. But Redman enjoys it. He gets close to those he kills. I think for him it's less about the money than about the experience. It's like a drink to a wino. So if he's alive, there will be more."

Goodwin snuffed out his smoke in an overflowing ashtray and shrugged. "Does that help?"

"Yeah, it does."

"And, as you're doing this research, you and Meeker must think he's alive."

Lancelot shook his head. "We don't know. The case we're working on is from the late thirties. His name just happened to intersect with a guy who's serving in the army."

"If you find out something," Goodwin asked. "I mean, if you discover when and how he died, will you let me know? I've been wanting to write this obituary for a lot of years."

"If there is an obit to write, I'll make sure you get the exclusive."

Goodwin smiled, turned, and left. Once again, Lancelot was alone but not quite as lost. Now he had a way to better track Redman, but it still gave him no link to the man using his name.

Lancelot walked over to the phone, got an outside line, and called the long-distance operator. It took five minutes to connect with the hotel in Alamogordo.

"You've reached Helen Meeker."

"It's Napoleon. What are you doing?"

"I'm packing and about to head home. Do you have something?"

"I've traced Redman to Denver in 1936."

"How did you manage that?" she asked.

"As a hit man, he had a pattern. Once he began working for Big Jim O'Toole in 1931, the pattern never varied. He got to know his victims. Once he had their confidence, he tied them to a chair and beat them. After he grew bored with knocking them around, he killed them execution style with a single shot to the back of the head."

"Whoa," Meeker whispered. "This changes everything."

"What do you mean?" Lancelot asked.

"Something I thought wasn't important is now vital. Here's an update. Teresa is on her way back to Waco to visit one more time with our shy hero, but what you just told means I need to find out a lot more about a murder victim here in Alamogordo. He was killed the Redman way back in the summer of 1936. And I know for a fact that Redman was in town when it happened. Now I must figure out why a WPA worker named Jenkins was executed and who placed the hit on him."

"What do I need to do?" Lancelot asked.

"Nap, we need to find out what happened to a banker named Taylor Owen. He was in Alamogordo for a few months running First State Bank. I was told it was owned by a group in Santa Fe. He supposedly returned to Santa Fe when the bank shut down. I need you to get to Santa Fe and see if anyone up there knows where Owen is now. We also need to find a guy named Horse."

"Horse?"

"Yeah, he's likely dead, and his body is out in the desert. Owen could, at least, tell you something about him."

"I'll grab a train there tomorrow."

"Thanks."

Lancelot pulled his notes off the table and stuffed them into his briefcase. He was not looking forward to the long trip, but being on the ground was the only way to find out who owned that bank, who employed Owen, and what became of a man named Horse. Besides, New Mexico was one state he'd never visited. Might as well add it to the list.

CHAPTER 8

Tuesday, September 28, 1943
11:41 a.m.
Waco, Texas

"He's gone," the sergeant explained. "When someone volunteers to go back to the fight, the Army doesn't waste time. Redman caught a train Saturday night."

Teresa Bryant frowned. She'd literally wasted two days. At Holloman Army Base in New Mexico, she'd caught a military plane headed for Texas. After several stops and a change of planes, she landed in Fort Worth and rented a car. Except for a stop for breakfast in Hillsboro, a place she'd driven through not that long ago, she wasted no time. And none of it mattered. The man she'd hoped to talk to had taken a powder.

"Did you see his orders?" Bryant asked. "Do you know where he was headed and when he was shipping out?"

"Redman didn't take the conventional route," the young man explained. "He wanted to get back to England so fast that they sent him to Houston. He caught a plane headed east from there. By now he's probably on a ship in the Atlantic." The sergeant reached into his pocket and retrieved a slip of paper. "Are you Teresa Bryant?"

"Yes."

"Then there's a message for you."

"Thanks," a disappointed Bryant whispered as she glanced at the typed communication. She was hoping the soldier who she now believed was Red Cloud had left her something with a bit more explanation, but this note was from Meeker. She had stayed in Alamogordo and Lancelot was on his way to Santa Fe. There was no explanation as to why plans had changed or a directive for what she should do next. So, Bryant was apparently on her own.

"Anyone here at the base know Redman very well?" Bryant asked her escort.

"No one knew him at all. He didn't talk much, didn't get any mail, never made any phone calls, and even when you ate your meals beside him, it was like he wasn't there. He was the most guarded person I'd ever met."

"That's what I was afraid of," Bryant answered. "Thanks for your time."

Exiting the building, she strolled quickly to her rented Chevy and slid behind the wheel. Setting on the dash was something she hadn't left there. She studied the white, folded paper for a few moments and then picked it up. Like the message the sergeant had given her, this one was typed.

DON'T TAKE THIS ANY FURTHER. LEAVE REDMAN ALONE.

The threat was far too polite. The writer had spelled out no consequences if she failed to comply with the directive. So, this read like a wish rather than an ultimatum.

"Having problems with the car?"

Bryant looked up as a captain approached her vehicle. He was tall with salt and pepper hair, likely about forty, and his accent hinted at midwestern roots.

"Have you been in the parking lot very long?" Bryant asked.

"Actually, I have been," he admitted. "A buddy from high school is being shipped out to the Pacific today. We went to town, grabbed an early lunch, then sat in the car and visited."

"Did you see anyone who might have dropped off this note?" she asked.

He nodded. "Yeah, I did. Why? Is it important?"

"Maybe."

"He wasn't proposing?" the officer teased. "There has been a lot of that going on, and you are a beautiful woman."

"Not that kind of proposal," Bryant explained. "But I need to talk to him."

"His name is Jim Watson. He's getting some time stateside after serving in England."

Watson was the officer who had submitted Redman's name for the Medal of Honor. Perhaps her trip hadn't been for nothing.

Bryant stepped out of the car and smiled. "Can you take me to him?"

"Sure. And I'm Hank Wilfong. And, just to be upfront, I'm not married or engaged, and I don't have a steady girlfriend. And just so you know, I haven't proposed to anyone for three weeks. And I knew she wouldn't accept anyway."

As she stepped away from the Chevy, Bryant grinned. "And my name is Teresa."

"Terri?"

"No, I don't really like Teresa that well, and Terri is a name I don't like at all."

"Teresa it is. Follow me."

Wilfong led Bryant across the parking lot, through a maze of buildings, and to the officer's quarters. The one-story structure was new, clean, but cheaply constructed.

When the war was over, it would likely be knocked down. After passing three open doors, the captain knocked on a fourth. A tall, good-looking man in a perfectly pressed uniform answered. He was obviously not happy to see the guest.

"Thank you, Hank," Bryant said. "I can handle it from here."

"Yes, ma'am."

Once the officer exited the building, Bryant held up the piece of paper and asked, "Do we talk about this out here, or do I go get your superior?"

He stepped aside. Once she had cleared the door, he closed it.

Bryant began by declaring, "If you're going to threaten me, do it to my face."

"You weren't supposed to know who left that note."

"Then be more careful. Now what's this all about?"

"Redman is a private person."

"Yeah, I've talked to him twice, I know that. And I also know you're the man who started the ball rolling on him getting the Medal of Honor."

"He doesn't want it."

"Why?" Bryant demanded.

"He wouldn't tell me."

Bryant frowned and pointed her finger in Watson's face. "Ruffin Redman is not his name. He just used it when he enlisted. The real Ruffin Redman is actually a hitman."

She watched the captain's knees buckle. "You mean, he's a profession—"

"No, your friend isn't that at all. He's a member of the Seminole tribe, but for reasons I don't understand, he took the name of a hitman. As long as he has that name, he can't get the recognition he deserves. I have to find out what this is all about so I can open the door for this Indian to bring honor to his tribe."

Watson eased down onto the bunk. "Why would he use a criminal's name?"

"I wish I knew. Maybe it's some kind of deal with the devil. Maybe Redman had something on Red Cloud and forced him to switch identities. Maybe it's just a coincidence, but you and our hero aren't helping me clear things up. And I'd like someone to start cooperating. I'm tired of being stonewalled."

Watson looked up and studied her face. "Who are you?"

"The world knows me as Teresa Bryant, but that's my White name. My Caddo name is Morning Song."

"Bryant." He snapped his fingers. "You work with Helen Meeker. You're a pretty big deal."

"Whatever! Now, why did the man you know as Redman tell you he didn't want the Medal of Honor?"

Perhaps it was knowing who Bryant worked with, maybe it was because she was so forceful, or perhaps it was finding out a hitman was named Ruffin Redman, but Watson suddenly opened up. And when he did, his words fell out of his mouth like water running over Niagara Falls.

"He didn't give me a reason. But on the night he went off on that suicide mission, he told me he had nothing to go home to but trouble. He gave the impression he was far better off dead than alive. And while it had to be serious, I got the idea whatever he was alluding to had not been his fault. He's a good guy, I can't imagine him doing anything wrong."

Bryant nodded. "That's what I took away from our meeting too. Did he ever mention a man called Horse?"

"No, he never talked about his private life."

"Okay." Bryant wadded up the note and tossed it to Watson. "Next time you want to warn me about something, have the guts to do it in person."

"You really want to find a way Redman—or whatever his name is—can get the award?"

"Yeah. And I'll do everything I can to protect him until I get this sorted out."

Bryant yanked the door open, exited the building, and marched back to her car. The confrontation had been worth it simply because it confirmed her gut instincts on their reluctant, publicity-shy hero. Now it was time to get back on the case. Returning to New Mexico was going to be a hassle, but if Helen was working on anything that had to do with Ruffin Redman, she wanted in on it. It was the only way to connect the dots in this matter.

CHAPTER 9

TUESDAY, SEPTEMBER 28, 1943
4:44 P.M.
ALAMOGORDO, NEW MEXICO

"You're back?" Hamilton Hodges asked as he looked up from his desk. He was obviously shocked. "I thought you said we had to handle solving this mystery on our own."

"Well," Meeker sighed. "It's a woman's right to change her mind. At least, that's what I've always been told."

Hodges pushed back in his chair and smiled. "I hope this is a fair question. What changed it?"

"For starters, I'm thinking the guy you buried might not be a WPA worker named Jenkins."

"Oh, this gets more and more interesting. Why's that?"

"Because I made a few phone calls, and it seems Jenkins now lives in Georgia and manages a dairy farm."

"What?"

"Yeah, he lost his billfold a couple of days before he finished his work here in Alamogordo."

"How do you know that?"

"Because I talked to him."

"Well, I'll be ..."

Meeker cut him off, "You could be a monkey's uncle or a hundred other things, but if what I believe is right, you also might be sitting on a story that'll solve a mystery that has confounded the FBI for seven years."

"You mean," Hodges laughed, "I could be the reporter who schools J. Edgar Hoover?"

"It's possible. And I'll let you do that. In fact, I'll help you. But I need some things first."

"What?" Hodges was eager to finally break a real story. His eyes blazed, and his body appeared poised to leap out of his chair.

Meeker crossed her arms and explained. "Those photos of the body that burned in the car—I need to see the one that has the clearest view of the jaw and teeth."

"Doc's got them—we can walk down to his office."

"Fine. Make sure he's there, and if he is, telephone the sheriff and have him join us."

Meeker watched as the publisher made the calls, then followed him the two blocks down the street to Doctor Edwards's office. By the time they arrived, the photos were spread out on a table.

"This is Jeb Kolb, our sheriff," Hodges announced as he pointed to the man in the gray uniform.

Kolb was about fifty, deeply tanned, five-ten, and straight as a broom handle. He wore the expression of a person who wasn't used to being in the presence of a woman who demanded to be treated as an equal. Meeker liked having that advantage and intended to use it.

"Nice meeting you Jeb. Good you could come down." Meeker glanced toward the doctor and demanded, perhaps a bit too assertively because she wanted to impress the sheriff, "Now, show me those photos."

Meeker shuffled through all of them before picking up the one that gave the best view of the jaw. This was what she needed. This blew everything wide open.

TIME WALKER

"Doctor Edwards," Meeker asked. "Would you come over here and look at this?"

"What do you want me to see?"

"This shot," she announced. "What do you notice about the teeth?"

Edwards leaned closer. "The back three on the bottom right, at the base of the jaw, are missing. The man is also missing one tooth on the upper right back side of his mouth."

"Now look at this wire photo of these dental records," Meeker suggested.

It took only a few seconds for Edwards to make a confirmation. "Yeah, these are a match."

After Kolb and Hodges had seen the photos and the X-ray, Meeker made an observation, "To make this official, we'll need to exhume the body and do another postmortem. Then we can say for sure who this man really is."

"And who is he?" Kolb demanded. "It seems obvious you already know."

Meeker smiled at the sheriff and nodded. "The guy who was executed and then cooked in 1936 was Big Jim O'Toole."

"I've heard of him," Hodges excitedly admitted. "He was a Chicago mobster."

"Yeah, and over time he expanded into many other cities," Meeker added.

"How did he end up here?" Kolk asked.

"It has to be tied to the robbery," Hodges suggested.

"Perhaps," Meeker agreed. "I'm more inclined to think there was something else that drew Big Jim here. A hundred grand was petty cash in O'Toole's world." She looked at Hodges. "I think, if you'll look through the photos you took of your 1936 summer festival ..."

"Frontier Days."

"Yeah," Meeker acknowledged. "If you look through those shots, I believe you might find one of O'Toole. If I'm right, that'll be the last photo ever taken of him."

Meeker turned back to the sheriff. "Could there have been something on the train besides the money? Something worth so much that O'Toole was lured out of Chicago to visit your little community?"

"Do you think there was?"

"I don't know," Meeker admitted. "But I called a contact at the FBI last night and had him look through the files on O'Toole. Twice, once in August of 1935, and then again in June of 1936, Hitler sent a couple of his SS officers to America. They met with Big Jim."

"There was something here Hitler wanted?" Edwards asked. "Really? I didn't know there was anything here anyone wanted."

"So," Kolb asked, "why was O'Toole killed?"

"I don't know the why," Meeker replied. "But I can tell you the who. The man who executed the crime boss worked for him. His name was Ruffin Redman. We're sure it was him because of the unique way he orchestrated his hits. And, as we have not heard of Redman since, this must have been his last job. That means he could have claimed what O'Toole was down here to get."

"Can I print this story in my paper?" Hodges asked.

"As soon as we confirm it by digging up the body," Meeker assured him. "But as it deals with another case I'm working on, please don't mention Redman's name. You can write this …" She paused and gathered her thoughts before dictating, "The authorities who are digging into the case have a strong indication the man behind the murder was a former close associate of O'Toole's." Meeker smiled. "If Redman is still alive, that might help bring him out into the open." Meeker then snapped her fingers and announced, "And I need to talk to the man who used to manage the First State Bank."

"Taylor Owen?" Kolb asked.

Meeker nodded. "In a day or two, I'll have an associate digging into that. Okay, gentlemen, we have some work to do. Let's get a judge to sign off on an exhumation and confirm what the photos seem to prove."

"And Jeb," Hodges chimed in. "While you do that, I'm going to see if I can find a picture of O'Toole visiting Alamogordo and write up a story that'll likely soon hit the wire and be in every newspaper in the country. Miss Meeker, you have made an old reporter's life worthwhile."

"Gentlemen," Meeker announced as she strolled to the door. "Let me know when you have confirmed what I believe. She paused as she reached for the doorknob. "Mr. Hodges, there two guys who you thought got some of the loot."

"Yeah, Zack Purdy and Dennis Michaels."

"Which one is still alive?"

"Purdy."

"He's in which branch of the service?"

"The Navy."

"Thanks."

Meeker exited and walked back toward the hotel. She was going to have to pull some strings to get Purdy back home. But she needed him. He might be the only way she could find out what happened to Horse.

CHAPTER 10

Wednesday, September 29, 1943
9:33 a.m.
Alamogordo, New Mexico

Helen Meeker was forced to make a dozen calls, ending with the President, to set the wheels moving so she could talk to someone in the US Navy who would listen to her request on Seaman Zack Purdy. As she sat in her hotel room, a polite Meeker made her case.

"I need him back in Alamogordo."

"Listen, I'm just a lieutenant, I'm not far enough up on the chain to have the President make calls for me like you did. I don't care if Roosevelt is in on this, I have to have real justification to get this guy on a flight back to the States. You do know we have this little thing called a war going on?"

"Is suspicion of murder enough for you?"

The man on the other end of the line paused. Things were suddenly so quiet, Meeker heard him lick his lips. Yet even the possibility of solving a murder hadn't yet freed his tongue. So, she opted to stop being polite and go into attack mode.

"I believe you said your name was Sanky."

"Yes, ma'am. Ben Sanky."

"Okay, Ben, Purdy is suspected of killing a possible witness to a robbery. The take on that job was a hundred grand. I don't know how they view that amount at the war office, but in Alamogordo, that's a lot of money. So, give me what you got on this guy, or you'll be scrubbing latrines, and I'll be talking to someone who wants your job. I can also have President Roosevelt call your office—don't doubt I can make it happen."

"Okay, I guess murder is a reason to release information I normally wouldn't. The records show Purdy's been in the Navy for eighteen months. When did this murder happen?"

"The summer of 1936, but the real facts of the case were buried until now."

"So, Purdy is guilty of all kinds of stuff?"

"I think so. But as bad as that is, what happened back then can be tied to a murder victim's working relationship with Hitler."

"You mean ..."

Meeker cut Sanky off, "Do you know of any other Hitler? Now, is Purdy on a ship? Is he at a base? Where is he, and how long before we can get him back in New Mexico?"

"He's at Pearl Harbor," Sanky explained. "With what you just told me, I think we can cut through the red tape and get him back here within a week."

"Keep him under armed guard," Meeker suggested. "I don't want him escaping."

"Yes, ma'am."

"Thank you, Lieutenant. Notify me when you get a timetable."

Meeker hung up the phone, glanced into the mirror, checked her hair, and left the room. She had just walked down to the lobby when she spotted a haggard Teresa Bryant stepping through the front door.

"Don't say anything," Bryant announced as she closed the distance between them. "I can't tell you the last time I slept."

"Aren't you in a wonderful mood." Meeker laughed. "You want some breakfast?"

"Yeah, then a bath and a bed."

After walking to the café and placing their order, Meeker caught Bryant up on what she'd learned since they'd headed their different directions. Bryant listened but didn't respond. In fact, she said nothing until after she consumed her order of pancakes, bacon, and eggs.

"Okay, Helen, what now?"

"I've got the paperwork started to get Zack Purdy back here. It should take a week. He might be able to answer the question of what happened to Horse. Nap is in Santa Fe digging through public records trying to find out where Taylor Owen is now. We know he worked in Santa Fe for a while after he left here, but then the trail dries up."

"What's left to do here?" Bryant asked.

"Well, how about some sightseeing."

"Or we could sleep. I vote for the latter. Seriously, why are we staying here? Why not just go to the West Coast and interview Purdy in San Diego?"

"Because, Teresa, my gut tells me the robbery was a cover for something else. A high roller like O'Toole wouldn't have been here for the cash. And when Hodges publishes the story in tomorrow's *Alamogordo Daily News*, I want to be here and see reactions. Perhaps someone's got some secrets they'll feel the need to spill."

Bryant was just finishing her coffee when an excited Hodges rushed through the front door, searched the café, and upon spotting the women, hurried back to their table.

"First copy off the press!" he exclaimed.

"Have a seat," Meeker suggested as she took the newspaper and studied the four-inch headline.

CHICAGO CRIME BOSS EXECUTED IN ALAMOGORDO

The story that followed read like pulp fiction. Hodges hit all the bases. The copy was so colorful and well-woven Raymond Chandler would have been impressed. He took readers back to 1936, set up what was going on, reminded them of the trainwreck and robbery, then introduced the cast of characters. He explained how Meeker and Bryant had spotted the car fire was not an accident but a murder. He concluded by pointing out the method O'Toole had been killed. The only thing he left out was Redman's name.

To the right side of the story was a photo, shot by the publisher in the summer of 1936, showing Big Jim O'Toole walking down the street during Frontier Days. In a separate story, Hodges asked if anyone knew Horse's real name and where he was from.

"So, what do you think?" Hodges asked.

After handing the newspaper to Bryant, Meeker nodded. "In newspaper slang, that's a great yarn. Is it on the street yet?"

"No."

"Let me warn you about something. Teresa and I are used to being targets. It comes with what we do. We've been shot at more than you can imagine. But by outlining the method of O'Toole's execution, you could be putting a target on your back. If Redman's still alive, he might be concerned your description links this crime to him."

"Listen," Hodges explained. "I've never gotten to cover anything big. In more than fifty years, I've never had a story that was even picked up in Roswell much less New York. If this goes coast to coast, then I can die happy. And it's all because of the two of you."

TIME WALKER

Bryant pushed her plate to the side and asked, "Did you discover any other pictures of O'Toole from that day?"

"I quit when I found this one," the publisher shot back.

"Could we look through the rest?" Bryant asked.

"I thought you wanted to go to bed," Meeker jabbed.

"I'll sleep better after I see the other shots."

"Let's go back to my office," Hodges suggested.

Five minutes later, Bryant was studying three, seven-year-old contact sheets. There were twelve photos on each one. As Meeker and Hodges looked on, Bryant tapped a middle shot on the second page and asked a question.

"Can you print a large copy of this one?"

"Sure, what number is it?" Hodges replied.

"It's fourteen, and I'd like an enlargement of twenty-two as well."

"Let me grab the negatives and get to the darkroom. How big do you need?"

"As large as possible."

"Eleven by fourteen it is."

"That'll be fine," Bryant assured him.

After Hodges left, Meeker picked up the contact sheet and studied the images. She was trying but failing to spot what was suddenly so important to her partner. Yes, there was another shot of O'Toole in fourteen, that was obvious. But the one Hodges had used with his story was much clearer. The other photo was just a street scene where about twenty people were watching a parade of wagons roll by. What could be so important about these two images?

"I don't get it," Meeker announced as she put the sheets back into the desk. "I see nothing!"

"My eyes are better than yours," Bryant replied. "You've told me that a hundred times."

"Are you going to explain what you saw?"

"What I think I saw," Bryant corrected Meeker. "Be patient, and we'll let things develop."

Meeker grinned at the pun and started to push for more elaboration, but when she glanced back across the room, Bryant had folded her body into a chair and was apparently sleeping. Granted she was tired, it made sense she'd she nodded off. It had likely been three days since she'd been to bed, but knowing the Caddo, she was probably feigning sleep to avoid any more prodding.

Biting her tongue and curbing her curiosity, Meeker walked across to the front window and glanced out on the street. Due in part to the nearby base, uniformed men were everywhere. Alamogordo was thriving because these soldiers were spending money in stores and restaurants. This was true of scores of places in 1943. For many towns, war was the best thing that had ever happened to them.

Quickly growing bored with the view, Meeker spotted a Zenith console radio set beside a row of filing cabinets. Needing something to take her mind off what she couldn't see in the contact page, she strolled over and switched it on. About forty-seconds later, the tubes warmed enough to produce a signal. Her timing was good. The national news had just come on.

> It's official. In Malta, the Italian government signed documents of surrender on the HMS Nelson. With General Dwight David Eisenhower's signature, one member of the Axis block has been eliminated from the war. While battles still rage in parts of Italy, now it's the Germans, on their own, that are facing the combined strength of the Allies.

Meeker smiled. Progress was being made. Yes, Mussolini was still alive, he hadn't been captured, but he was no longer Italy's dictator. How long he lived was now in

Hitler's hands. When the radio shifted to weather, Meeker flipped the dial to a station playing music, and the room was filled with Bob Wills and His Texas Playboys singing "San Antonio Rose."

"I like Western Swing," Hodges announced as he reentered. "Just hearing it makes me want to dance."

"Are you a good dancer?" Meeker asked.

"No, I can't dance a lick, but that music does make me wish I could." He held up two large photos, still a bit damp. "And though I don't know why, I have these photos printed and ready for viewing. As we won't want to touch them yet, I'll put them on my layout table." After setting them down, he flipped on a lamp suspended over the desk and swung it to where it fully illuminated the black and white images.

A suddenly awake Bryant silently rose from her chair and walked with purpose to the table. With Meeker hovering to her right and the publisher to her left, she studied the pictures.

"Okay," Hodges began. "I see O'Toole in the shot on the right. But it's a profile and that's why I passed on using it in the paper."

"I fully understand your reasoning," Bryant agreed. "We can only be sure this is O'Toole because we have already discovered he was here thanks to the photo you used in the newspaper. But except for the clothes he's wearing, even I'd be hard pressed to make a definitive identification from this shot."

"Then why print it?" Meeker asked.

"On the surface," Bryant explained, "this is a photo of O'Toole looking toward the street. That likely means nothing. But what makes it interesting is who he's talking to."

"There's no one in the photo but him," Hodges argued.

"Yes, the men are cropped out on the right side," Bryant agreed. "But look at the reflection in the window of the Western Auto store. It's not real obvious until you study it for a moment. But Mr. Hodges, when you look at what is reflected there—who do you see?"

Meeker offered her observation before the newspaper's owner could speak. "Even though I can't see his whole face, the guy on the right is Ruffin Redman. This ties them together. They were talking to each other on the streets of Alamogordo."

"And the guy on the left?" Bryant asked. "I can only see a part of his face." She glanced toward Hodges and asked, "Do you know who that is?"

"The suit he's wearing is a lot different than what folks around here have. It has more of a European cut. So, thanks to that, and being able to see a bit of his face, I know that's the bank manager, Taylor Owen."

Bryant smiled. "Look at the reflection. Owen is pointing at something—do you have any idea what it might be?"

Hodges shook his head, "Probably something in the parade. Maybe one of the antique wagons."

"We can figure that out later," Bryant suggested. "The mere fact those men are together leads me to believe they were all in on the bank job."

"If they were," Hodges asked, "why would Redman execute O'Toole?"

"It couldn't have been for the money," Meeker observed. "O'Toole had more cash than he knew what to do with. So, it had to be whatever was on that train. And that had to be so big Redman felt getting rid of the boss was worth the risk."

"And," Hodges suggested, "if that were the case, the hitman likely came into enough money to live like a king the rest of this life. Maybe that's why he disappeared."

"It's something to think about," Bryant admitted. "Now look at the other shot."

"It's a wasted photo," Hodges quickly explained. "I just took a picture of a wagon in the parade. My only reason was because Homer Ogden owned the wagon and paid me to get a picture of him driving it. It was nothing more than a way to make an extra five bucks."

"And I'm sure Homer appreciated it," Bryant laughed. "What interests me are the folks who are watching across the street."

"Just locals," the publisher pointed out. "I don't see how they tie into anything."

Bryant pointed to a person on the second row standing behind a heavyset woman wearing a pioneer dress and bonnet. "Who's that?"

Hodges took a quick breath. "It's Horse."

"That was my guess," Bryant added before turning to Meeker. "Helen, who's standing beside him?"

Meeker's dark blue eyes locked onto the man. "It's our hero."

"We have now put Redman and Red Cloud in the same town on the same day," Bryant explained, "along with the man called Horse, Jim O'Toole, and Taylor Owen. In this case, a photo is worth a thousand words ... or even more." Bryant looked at the shot for a few more seconds before asking, "Mr. Hodges, do you have any idea if these two photos were taken about the same time?"

"Let me look at my contact sheet." The publisher walked over to the desk and studied the printed pages before acknowledging, "They were maybe ten or fifteen minutes apart. The photo with Owen and Redman was taken first."

"Teresa," Meeker asked. "What are you thinking?"

"We know Owen hired Horse. According to Mr. Hodges, Horse was a nice guy, but not mentally altogether there."

"Around here, we call people like him half-wits," the publisher explained.

"Why hire someone like that?" Bryant asked. Before anyone could respond, she answered her own question. "Maybe because he would work cheap, or maybe it was because he had information Owen wanted. I can tell you this, Horse isn't Mexican, he's an Indian. If that's the case, this picture ties him to our hero."

"I'm not following all of this," a confused Hodges admitted.

"There are some things we can't tell you," Meeker explained. "At least not until we find out if Redman is alive."

"Miss Bryant," Hodges asked, "is the guy with Horse the soldier you showed me the picture of?"

"Yes," Bryant cut in. "But for the moment you need to pretend you never saw that picture or printed these two shots. Are they dry enough for us to take with us?"

"They should be."

Bryant pointed to the photos. "Mr. Hodges, let me pose a question. Could Owen be pointing toward Horse and our hero?"

Hodges studied the two shots and nodded. "Based on location, yes, he was pointing in their direction."

A suddenly assertive Meeker stiffened her lip. "Mr. Hodges, I agree with Teresa. You can't print these photos again and don't tell anyone about this. What we just learned must remain secret. There is far more at stake than you can imagine. Just play up the angle of O'Toole being murdered."

"You have my word," the publisher assured Meeker.

An enlightened Meeker picked up the photos, slipped them inside a copy of the day's newspaper, and exited the business. Bryant followed her out into the early afternoon sun. Neither spoke until they were behind a locked door in Meeker's hotel room.

"Did everything just get a lot muddier?" Meeker asked.

"Let me see. We have connected an American war hero to a hitman. We have a crime boss who has ties to Hitler. We have that crime boss being executed by the hitman. On top of that, we have a missing seventy-five grand, a Navy seaman who might have killed a man called Horse. And for some reason, we have our hero using the hitman's name. To me, this just sounds like one of our normal cases."

"Joke all you want," Meeker whispered as she sat on the bed. "I wasn't expecting this."

"Maybe it'll make more sense to me when I get some sleep," Bryant suggested. "Which room is mine?"

"The adjoining room. The door is unlocked. You don't even have to go out in the hall."

"And what are you going to do?"

Meeker shook her head. "I'll sit by the phone until Napoleon calls. Maybe he'll find out something in Santa Fe that'll make this mess a bit clearer."

"Only wake me if it's really good," Bryant suggested. "I might just sleep until tomorrow morning."

Once the door between the rooms had closed, Meeker stood at the window and looked down at the dusty street. Why was the hero, who Bryant had learned was likely Red Cloud, using Redman's name, and what was it Hitler wanted in Alamogordo? With what they knew now, there was no way to connect those dots.

CHAPTER 11

Wednesday, September 29, 1943
4:00 p.m.
Santa Fe, New Mexico

Napoleon Lancelot's five hours in the records office and newspaper morgue yielded a couple of interesting bits of information. The First State Bank in Alamogordo had been owned by the same group that ran the Savings and Trust Bank in Santa Fe. While the Security Partnership, which was the name of the ownership group for both banks, was registered locally, the actual stockholders were a bit harder to locate. When formed in 1932, the front man was a local defense attorney. J.J. Johnson was hardly the kind of person Lancelot would have trusted with his money. The lawyer had long been the go-to man for people caught in various types of illegal enterprises. Much to the consternation of the law enforcement, Johnson almost always found ways to get free passes out of jail for those who paid for his legal work.

When Johnson created the Security Partnership, it was initially used to purchase homes, ranches, and businesses who'd defaulted on loans or failed to pay taxes. Where Johnson got the funds to make those acquisitions was a question often asked but never answered. When he purchased a vacant bank building and started the Savings and Trust, there was a rumor the seed money had come from Chicago. This made even more sense when Lancelot visited the local newspaper and found a photo of Jim O'Toole at the ribbon cutting.

As he tried to make some sense of what he'd uncovered, Lancelot was sitting on a bench at a city park. Even though he was deep in thought, he was still fully aware when a tall, well-dressed Black man, about fifty, strolled down the sidewalk. Lancelot checked his watch. It was exactly four o'clock. The man also checked the time, pulled a newspaper out of his suit pocket, and sat on a bench that backed up to the one Lancelot was occupying.

That gentleman opened his newspaper and held it in front of his face. He spoke in a very low tone. "You have to be Lancelot."

"Yes. And you must be Frank Jones."

"The only Black banker in the city," came the quick reply. "I'm sorry I couldn't meet you in my office, but I don't need to be seen with anyone associated with Helen Meeker."

"I fully understand," Lancelot assured him. "How long have you worked for Savings and Trust?"

"Since it opened," Jones explained as he pretended to study the sport's page. "I was hired to make inroads with Negro and Mexican businesses."

"Kind of a risky move for a White banker to hire a Negro," Lancelot suggested.

"Not really, it was simply a good front. The bank was awash in accounts from places like Chicago, Denver, Los Angeles, and even New York. Essentially, Saving and Trust was a hiding place for mob money. Respectable people wouldn't be caught dead in our lobby. But while it might have not been created for or by honest businessmen when I was hired, the bank did offer folks from my part of town a place to go to for loans. That gave it a sense of legitimacy. 'The Bank that Cares for Everyone' was even painted onto the front window."

Lancelot smiled. Essentially, the bank was using minorities to make it appear as if it valued them. He was sure that wasn't the case, but minority businesses were smart enough to take advantage of the ploy and use it to their advantage. Frank Jones made decisions that gave those no one else cared about a chance to open a store, buy a home, or keep a farm going.

"There was a man named Taylor Owen," Lancelot said. "He worked at the bank in the mid-1930s. He also ran First State in Alamogordo until it collapsed. What can you tell me about him?"

"For starters, I didn't like him much. He was well-educated but just slimy—worse than even J.J."

As two women ambled up the walk, Lancelot went mute and turned his attention to a rabbit hopping across the lawn. Only when he was sure no one could hear did he pose another question.

"What else do you have on Owen?"

"He was transferred to Alamogordo for a few months. When that bank failed, he came back here. He was living high too. Spending a lot more money than he made, but no one cared. In early 1937, he moved to Los Angeles. One of the tellers moved out there with him. When she returns to town on vacations, she always stops in the bank and visits with her old friends. She brags about the people they know, the houses they own, and the places they go. So, Owen's evidently in the chips."

"Can you get me an address?"

"Tomorrow, I can. I know a couple of people who write to his girlfriend. I'll just make up an excuse about needing to send him an update on a friend of his."

Finding Owen had been easier than Lancelot expected, and the fact he was alive meant they finally had someone who was in Alamogordo in 1936 who might be able to give them some much needed information on what Hitler wanted there. As luck seemed to be on his side, Lancelot rolled the dice and posed a question that was seemingly out of left field.

"Does the bank have a customer named Ruffin Redman?"

"Not now, but we used to."

"So, he moved to another bank?"

"No, he changed the name on his account. He still comes in a couple of times a year, but he goes by Steven Black."

Lancelot couldn't believe his good fortune. Information never came this easily. "So, he's local?"

"No," Jones explained, "all his statements are sent to a post office box in Pittsburgh."

"Do you think he lives there?"

"I think he lives in a lot of places. Back in the bank's early days, I saw him with Big Jim O'Toole some. They'd come into town, hang out, and hit the local night spots. They seemed to be real close. Then O'Toole disappeared."

"What do you make of that?"

"We figured the government had the goods on him, so he changed his name and took a powder. Black, or Redman as you know him, told one of the bank's officers he thought O'Toole was in South America."

"He went south," Lancelot agreed, "but take my word for it, it wasn't that far south."

"Do you need anything else?"

"No."

Jones folded his newspaper, stood, looked toward downtown, and whispered, "I never talked to you."

Lancelot didn't move as the man walked off. Five minutes later, he stood, stretched, and ambled toward his hotel on the other side of town. After a good night's sleep, he'd catch a train to Alamogordo and tell Meeker and Bryant what he'd learned.

CHAPTER 12

Thursday, September 30, 1943
12:30 A.M.
Denver, Colorado

When a person is bored, the clock rarely seems to move. Today, the time between seconds felt like hours. Ruffin Redman knew he drank too much whiskey, but when it was the top shelf variety, pouring another glass seemed appropriate. Besides, he had nowhere to go and nothing to do, and being sober only served to make him much more aware of his sorry state.

Letting the amber liquid burn his throat, the middle-aged, red-headed man loosened his tie and collapsed onto the hotel bed. The overwhelming feeling of loneliness took root and with it came waves of depression. He had money but no home, no friends, and no plans. He aimlessly moved from place to place, all the time looking for a man who could have died seven years ago. Redman might have drowned in an ocean of loneliness if there hadn't been a knock on the door. Pushing off the mattress, he shuffled to the entry and threw it open.

"Been a long time."

The woman making that observation was thirty-five but appeared fifty. A cigarette dangled from her painted lips and a sense of profound sadness clouded her bloodshot, green eyes. She'd once been pretty with a figure that turned heads everywhere she went, but that was thirty pounds and a million smokes ago.

"Gladys," he snapped, making it clear this reunion was not wanted. "How did you find out I was here?"

"Louie at the Brass Slipper told me you'd been in there earlier. He also let it drop where you were staying. It seems he's been making deliveries of high-class liquor and says you tip real good." She smiled and spun, showing a body that spilled out a dress four sizes too small. "I thought you might want to relive some old times." She giggled and asked, "Aren't you going to invite me in?"

"Sure, there's a chair in the corner. You want a splash of whiskey?"

"I never turn down the good stuff," she announced as she wobbled across the room.

It seemed obvious Gladys Branch was drunk—a place she'd called home for years. Over that time, she'd given so much of herself away in exchange for booze there was nothing left anyone wanted. The dress she was wore was as faded as her memories. It had once been red, but now was much closer to pink. Her skin was yellow, her arms revealed needle marks, and her eyes were bloodshot.

"Here you go, babe," he announced. Her hand shook as she took the glass.

"No one's called me that in a long time. 'Babe.' I like the way it sounds. Do you remember that night in LA, or was it San Francisco? You told me I was a painted angel. I—"

"Where you been lately?" he asked as he sat on the corner of the bed.

"Here and there. To tell you the truth, I don't really remember. It's all kind of foggy."

He reached for his own glass, but after taking a second look at Gladys, he opted to abstain. Booze and cigarettes might have been cheap, but the toll they'd extracted from this woman was extremely high. That reminder convinced him it was time he laid off both of those vices.

"We had some good times," she announced, her words so slurred they piled into each other like a train crash. "I was your good luck charm. Whenever Big Jim gave you a job, you and I'd go out on the town. We always painted it red." She laughed before adding, "Just as red as the blood you spilled."

"I don't think we need to be talking about that," he suggested.

"Do you still spill blood for money?" she asked. "Or maybe that ended when Big Jim kicked the bucket ... or you kicked it for him. What does kick the bucket mean anyway? Who was the first who called death kicking the bucket?"

"Gladys, Jim and you were the only two who knew about those days, and we all agreed to never talk about them. So, you need to shut up."

She drunkenly wagged her finger, "No, we agreed to not tell anyone else about them. We didn't mind talking about them to each other. Those were fun nights."

"Why are you here?" he demanded.

She set the glass on the coffee table and smiled. "I need some money, baby. Mamma just can't make the dough she used to make. You used to brag about how people begged you not to kill them. You enjoyed being the god who could spare them but never did. I loved hearing how you tortured your marks, and you reveled in telling me about those executions. Do you still like reliving those moments?"

"I like living," he snapped.

"So do I, and I used to have what it takes to live good. Time is a killer."

She was right, because once she'd had that kind of beauty. But the days of employing her charms to rake in cash were long gone. Now she was someone to pity, not covet.

"How much you need?" He reached into his pocket and pulled out a dozen twenties. "Will this do?"

Gladys nodded. "Not even close. I want twenty grand."

"What?"

"You're getting off cheap. I know enough about you and what you've done to put you in the chair. And that's what the Feds have been begging me to do for years."

"So, you haven't sung yet?"

"No," Gladys chuckled. "I think you'll pay better than they do,"

"What took you so long to try to score the payoff?"

"I had to find you first. Tonight, I got lucky."

The years of booze had taken more than just a toll on Gladys's body—it had done a number on her mind. No one threatened Redman like this. She was signing her own death warrant.

He got up, crossed the room, opened the ninth-floor window, and looked out into the night. Denver was closed up as tight as a coffin. There was no one on the streets, and few of the windows in this area were lit up. He turned and studied his guest. She probably weighed about one-fifty. As drunk as she was, she'd be easy to control. A swift strike across her head with the whiskey bottle would knock her into next week. Then he could take her somewhere else and finish her off. It was almost too easy. Or maybe it would be better and easier to throw her out the window. Drunks committed suicide all the time.

"Red," she announced, her voice suddenly much clearer. "I'm not drunk, I was just pretending. Have you read tonight's late edition of the *Denver Post*? You need to. I've got one in my purse. Let me get it for you."

Redman watched as a now very steady Gladys pushed off the chair, reached into her bag, and retrieved the paper. She smiled as she tossed it onto the bed.

"If you don't want to take the time to read it," she announced with a smile, "I can summarize it for you. They exhumed that body in Alamogordo and figured out it was Big Jim. And while they don't say your name, it's pretty clear they know who pulled the trigger." She nodded and smiled. "I remember the next night back in 1936. I recall asking you if it was worth it. You told me then you were tired of being under Big Jim's thumb, but maybe being under his thumb was far better than being under the gaze of Helen Meeker. She and that Indian she works with have things figured out. And, if you don't pay Gladys, I can deliver you to them."

He glanced at the paper and shrugged. "No one knows I'm even alive. I've got nothing to worry about."

"Except me," she laughed.

"You never were too bright. You walked into the room of a man who knows how to take care of problems. I did that for years for both Al and Big Jim."

"Are you going to toss me out that window?" she asked. "Are you going to make it look like a washed-up dame with no future got tired of living and checked out?"

"You read my mind," he chuckled.

"That's really kind of sad. I thought you might tie me to a chair and shoot me like you did Jim and all the others. But that's not going to happen. I'm about to leave, and there's nothing you can do to stop me."

She smiled and headed to the door on steady legs. She was quick, but he was quicker. He grabbed her by the throat on the third step. He was reaching for the whiskey bottle when she whispered, "I have an insurance policy. If I don't come home, there's a lawyer who'll send a detailed story of your life to Helen Meeker. It will contain dates and the amounts of the payments. I got real specific on that federal judge you took out in Chicago. If you remember, I was in the room when you did it. Big Jim paid you fifty grand for that one. It was a big mistake to invite me along, but you just had to show off."

Redman loosened his grip on Gladys's throat. She stepped free and grinned.

"What do you want?" he grumbled.

"I already told you. But the money's not nearly as important as owning you. You used me, abused me, and then threw me away. You promised that after Alamogordo, we'd take the cash you'd gotten and see the world. But, until tonight, I never saw you again. Now, I'll use you like you did me. I'll bleed you until you have no blood left. And because of what I've written down, you can't stop me."

Redman sat on the bed. "Twenty grand?"

"For starters. Consider it a down payment." She reached into her purse, pulled out a slip of paper, and dropped it on the table. "Send it to this post office box. If it's not there by October 2nd, Meeker will be reading the story of your life. I think she'll find it very interesting."

"Fine, you win for now."

Gladys grinned before coughing four times. Once she cleared her throat, she posed a final question.

"Did you ever find Horse? I'll bet you forgot you told me about him."

"No."

TIME WALKER

She laughed. "You killed Big Jim to get to Horse, and you got nothing for it."

"Not entirely true," Redman replied. "I got access to a lot of Big Jim's accounts, and I got a lot of cash, enough to last the rest of my life."

"Yeah, if you don't mind staying in cheap joints like this. But if you'd found Horse, you'd be living in a palace. That's got to sting."

Gladys smiled, walked to the door, twisted the knob, and left.

Ruffin Redman had to do something about the woman. While the twenty grand would buy him some time, he wasn't going to let her bleed him forever. Glancing back at the bed, he noted the newspaper. Picking it up, he began to read the story. His name wasn't mentioned, but the writer seemed to know who was behind the hit. Maybe Gladys was right—Redman shouldn't have made the move on O'Toole.

Picking up the room phone, he waited for the operator.

"I need Crestview 4-1275."

"Just a moment."

"Hello." The voice on the other end was groggy. Considering the hour, that was to be expected.

"Sorry for calling in the middle of the night," Redman announced, "but this is an emergency."

"Who is this?"

"Steven Black."

"What do you need?"

"I need to take a trip south. I hear Brazil is nice. And I need to get there without attracting attention."

"How about a steamer out of Houston? If you pay enough, you'll be listed as a crewman, but you won't have to do any work. When do you need to leave?"

"I have to get my cash out of a few different banks and tie up some loose ends."

"Let me look at something."

As he waited, Redman read back through the story. There was no mention of the young man who'd prevented the hitman from grabbing Horse. If only he knew who that guy was, he might be able to live like a king in Brazil.

"Mr. Black, there's a cargo ship that's leaving Houston on the fifteenth. I can get you a place on it, but it's not cheap. I'll need ten grand to make sure no one asks any questions and to insure you are protected."

"I'm going out of town in a few days, but before I leave, I'll drop by your office with the cash. Thanks."

Redman looked out the window. His long-held dream of finding Horse was over. Still, there were a few things that had to be finished before he left the country. The first was right here in Denver.

CHAPTER 13

Friday October 1, 1943
Noon
Alamogordo, New Mexico

Helen Meeker met Napoleon Lancelot at the train depot. As they walked back to the hotel, he explained what he'd dug up. She was hardly surprised to learn Ruffin Redman had changed his name. In his position, who wouldn't? The fact he was still alive gave her an even greater incentive to move forward with the case.

"Nap, I can't figure out what was so valuable Redman would kill a man who paid him so well. O'Toole was his bread and butter; the crime boss kept the hitman in the chips. Is there anything we've missed that justified such a dramatic move?"

"It wasn't the money," Lancelot announced as they walked toward the café that had become Meeker's most frequent haunt the past few days. "My contacts indicated Redman had a nice bank account in Santa Fe. And we know that he didn't take over the mob upon O'Toole's disappearance. So, it must be something we haven't found yet."

"Something that was on the train," Meeker suggested. "Teresa's waiting for us in the restaurant. With her help, perhaps we can figure out our next move."

The café was crowded, Meeker had to wade through a mass of hungry GIs before spotting her partner at the back of the room.

"Good to see you, Nap," Bryant announced as the pair took their seats. "I trust your work in Santa Fe produced something we didn't know."

"Redman has changed his name to Steven Black," Lancelot explained as he picked up a menu, "and Taylor Owen is living in Los Angeles. But I'm like Helen, I have no idea what was so valuable that Redman felt taking out O'Toole was a smart move. And what in the world would Hitler want in this town?"

"Has anyone contacted Owen?" Bryant asked.

"No," Meeker answered. "I think we need to take him by surprise. Which means Nap and I will be headed west as soon as I can secure some plane reservations."

"What about me?" Bryant asked.

"You need to stay here and question Purdy. We must find out what happened to Horse. If Owen doesn't know, Purdy might."

"When's he coming in?" Bryant asked.

"They told me it would be Sunday morning."

"So, two days with nothing to do. I'm not good at having to kill that much time."

"It might just be the moment to find a new hobby," Meeker joked. "Perhaps you could take up knitting."

"Not likely."

"Well, you like to read, and there is a library here."

"I'll get a card," Bryant grumbled. "Give me a bit more on what I can expect when Purdy gets here."

"They'll put him in the local jail, and you can interview him there. Do whatever it takes to get him to talk about Horse. I've already made the moves and touched base with the folks needed to cut some deals. So, tell Purdy we can give him immunity for taking the stolen money and save him the death penalty if he cops to killing Horse. But to earn that, he must give us everything he knows. He can't leave anything out."

"Hi, I'm, Pam," a fresh-faced teen announced, "What can I get for you?"

Meeker smiled. "Do you have burgers today?"

"We sure do."

"How does that sound guys?" Lancelot and Bryant nodded. "Okay, give us three burgers, some fries, and Cokes."

Pam jotted down the order and strolled toward the kitchen. When she was out of earshot, Meeker leaned over the table. "I figure Purdy or Owen can give us, at least, a part of what we're missing."

"Helen," Bryant whispered, "I've thought a lot about what Red Cloud might feel is so important he'd willing to die rather than have his heritage revealed."

"And?" Meeker asked.

"If he were White, the options could be wide open, but as a Seminole he couldn't be swayed by wealth or power. So, greed doesn't play into this. And I believe if he had committed a crime, even murder, he would have told me. He must be protecting something that has to do with his culture and his tribe."

Lancelot shrugged, "What's left to protect? I mean, their lands have been taken, and the people have been moved to places that are all but worthless. The tribes have had their way of life erased. They have no rights. They get no respect. What is left that is worth anything?"

"You don't have to tell me that," Bryant admitted. "I've lived it. But if Hitler was interested in something on that train …"

Meeker shook her head and waved her hands. When she did, Bryant stopped mid-sentence and waited for some kind of insight. Once Meeker had her arms around a new theory, she leaned forward and explained.

"We've been looking at this all wrong. It wasn't what was on the train, it was who. There had to be someone who knew something so valuable they were the target. That's all that makes sense."

"So," Lancelot asked, "you're saying it was a person who Hitler wanted? Why?"

"I can only guess," Meeker suggested. "Maybe he had some kind of plans for a weapon that the Nazis wanted."

"But that was three years before the war in Europe," Lancelot pointed out.

"True. But having a super weapon would've made the war so much easier and quicker. Hitler might have won before we ever got involved. And if I'm right, then a weapon like that in the hands of either side could still determine the outcome of the war."

"If you're right," Bryant suggested, "then what we're doing would seem to be counterproductive."

"Explain."

"Horse had an addled mind. He wouldn't have recognized that kind of person, so how does he figure in? And, I have to believe Red Cloud would quickly spill the beans on a story like that."

Lancelot countered, "Perhaps Red Cloud doesn't trust our side with that kind of knowledge. Perhaps, he knows who the guy is and is trying to protect him because he fears whatever this is could be misused by us."

"That makes more sense than anything else," Meeker agreed. "And if Red Cloud has to remain in hiding while using an alias and refusing the greatest honor this country has, then Owen and Redman likely know who the missing man is. And maybe Horse did too."

"You've just given Red Cloud an even greater reason to keep his secrets."

"In your judgment," Meeker asked, "is Red Cloud the kind of man who would give up his heritage and fame to hide this kind of weapon from the world?"

Bryant shrugged. "Nap might have hit the nail on the head. He was torn from his family by White men and placed in a school where everything about his life was deemed worthless. They gave him a different name and tried to erase who he was. Yet, he couldn't forget he and all those like him were hunted, abused, and murdered by White men. Their lands were stripped from them by White men. Why would anyone who had experienced that want to see a White man in this country or a White man in Germany have access to a weapon that would kill tens of millions?"

The concept was so overwhelming, and the history so uncomfortable, the voices around the table grew suddenly silent. Not another word was said until the meal was finished and the plates taken away.

"So," Meeker asked, "do we need to let this case die?"

"I don't think we can," Lancelot argued. "I see Teresa's point. If she's right about Red Cloud, I fully understand why he's bent on going to the grave with what he knows. But if there's a man out there with that kind of information and those kinds of plans, we must find him before Hitler does."

Bryant posed the question she figured Red Cloud would ask if he were at the table. "Can you trust the United States with that kind of power?"

"More than we can trust Hitler," Lancelot suggested.

"Then I guess the case continues," Bryant grimly replied. "But I want us to consider something. If we find this guy, and he has what Helen thinks he might, is it better for us to protect that secret or turn it over to our government? You don't have to answer now, but please, at least, think about it."

"You have my word," Meeker agreed. "Now, let's get back to the hotel so I can arrange a trip to Los Angeles."

CHAPTER 14

Saturday October 2, 1943
1:15 p.m.
Denver Post Office

"Can I help you, sir?" the post clerk asked.

"Yes," a weak, trembling voice replied. "I need to mail a package to Gladys Blanch. I was given a post office box number. Am I at the right place?"

"Is this the package?"

A disguised Ruffin Redman nodded and slid the shoebox-sized parcel across the counter.

"Let me weigh it, and I'll get you a price for shipping."

Redman smiled and stepped back. Out of the corner of his eye, he noticed a mirror. Turning, he studied the person reflected in the glass. The gray wig, wire-rimmed glasses, and fake beard would have fooled even his closest associates. Rather than the muscular, middle-aged man he'd been an hour earlier, he now looked close to eighty. Being able to disguise himself had been a part of Redman's life since his mid-twenties. While he'd occasionally dressed like a woman, he most often took on the guise of an old man. His reason was clear—old people were simply ignored. In his trade, that was a very important quality.

"Sir," the clerk announced. "This will cost $1.45 to mail. Is that all right?"

"Perfect," Redman agreed as he turned back to the desk. After retrieving change from his coin purse, he stayed in character, carefully counted it out, and handed it to the clerk.

"Do you need any stamps?"

"No, thank you."

Redman smiled and waddled off. Once he was out of sight of the clerk, he began to search the boxes. The one he wanted ... 11042 ... was around the corner. He walked over to a bench against a far wall, sat down, and waited.

An anxious Gladys Blanch strolled in just over an hour later. She quickly worked the combination lock, slipped the drawer open, and smiled. Pulling the package out, she tucked it under her arm and headed toward the door. Redman followed her step-by-step as she hurried down 19th Street, only slowing to enter the Regency Drug Store. She moved quickly past the counter, a display of soaps and beauty aids, and to a bank of phones. When she entered a booth, Redman strolled through the business and slipped into the booth beside where Blanch was making the call. He picked up the phone and pretended to dial but was listening to the woman instead.

"Operator, I need Wilkes and Miller Law Firm. What? Oh yes." After digging into her purse, she deposited some coins. It was thirty seconds before she spoke. "I need to speak to Mr. Wilkes." Another thirty seconds passed before she spoke again. "Mr. Wilkes, this is Gladys Blanch. I received what I needed, so don't mail the file. Just put it back in the file cabinet for future use. I'll drop off your fee on Monday morning."

Redman emerged from the phone booth first. Taking up his unstable old man gait, he moved to the exit. Just before he got there, an anxious Gladys pushed past him. Once outside, she signaled for a cab. Redman stood by the curb as she slipped in, then waved for his own taxi.

"Where to?"

"Just go straight until I tell you to turn." Redman answered.

"Is this going to be a long trip?"

"I doubt it, but I'll pay you quite well."

"How much is quite well."

Redman waved a bill. "Twenty dollars."

"For that, I'll drive you to the mountains if you want."

"Let's just go straight for right now."

As they rolled down 19th Street, Redman could see Glady's head framed by the rear window. His gut told him she wouldn't be able to wait until she got home to count her cash. She glanced to her left and right before looking down. He figured she was making sure no one was watching, and it was safe to open the package. In less than a minute, his guess was confirmed.

The blast that tore through the Checker Cab scattered metal and glass in all directions. The explosion was so loud it rattled windows on both sides of the street. At one moment, there was a car and the next, there was nothing.

"Did you see that?" Redman's driver yelled as he slammed on the brakes.

"Yes. I wonder what happened?"

As fire destroyed the cab, traffic in all directions stopped. For the moment, the crowd was too shocked to be angry about having their travel interrupted.

"I don't guess we'll be going anywhere for a while," the driver announced.

Redman nodded and pushed the twenty toward the driver. "I'll just put my trip off and run some other errands."

"Sure. I can't believe what I just saw. I knew that cabbie—he was good guy."

Redman stepped onto the sidewalk and made his way to the nearest phone. Once in the booth, he searched the white pages for the law firm of Wilkes and Miller. After memorizing the address, he turned left and headed back to his hotel room. He needed to connect with a man who was known for being able to open any door in the world. It was going to be a late night.

CHAPTER 15

Sunday October 3, 1943
1:13 a.m.
Denver, Colorado

The Wilkes and Miller Law Offices were on the third floor of the Hoover Building. Based on the location and the furnishings, this wasn't one of Denver's premier practices. The door had been so easy to pick Ruffin Redman kicked himself for hiring outside help.

"What are we looking for?" Ralph Cantus asked. He was a small man, about forty, who'd been picking locks and cracking safes since his teens. He was good but careless. The fact he didn't pay close attention to wiping away fingerprints had led to a couple of prison stints. Why was so much talent wasted on a man like that?

"First, we need to find Wilkes's office," Redman explained as he shined his flashlight around the reception area.

"It's the one on the left," Cantus observed as the light hit the lettering on the door.

"So, it is. If it's locked, you can go to work. If not, then we walk in. And keep your gloves on."

Redman strolled over to the door, grabbed the knob, and twisted. It sprang open. Pushing through the entry, he shined his light around the room. A desk, two chairs, two legal bookcases, and a row of five, four-drawer filing cabinets filled the twelve-by-twelve-foot cubicle. As there were two outside windows, he figured it'd be best to not turn on any lights. After walking around the desk, Redman studied the file cabinets. They were wood, likely oak, and locked. It was time for the hired help to go to work for the second time.

"Open this one," Redman announced while patting the third drawer in the first cabinet. "I need to search the *Bs*. And don't make any marks. I can't afford to call attention to the fact anyone was here."

Cantus nodded, and after pulling out his picks, asked, "Can you shine your light on the lock?"

"Sure."

"This won't take any time at all." True to his word, the underworld's best locksmith had the drawer open in less than thirty seconds. "Do you need anything else?"

"Just step aside."

Redman thumbed through the files until he came across one labeled, "Gladys Branch." Retrieving the folder, he sat it on the desk.

"Is that what you wanted?" Cantus asked.

"I'll know in a second."

The first few pages were receipts for payments. The fifth was a typed letter from the firm agreeing to never open the manila envelope, but in the event of Glady Branch's death to forward it to Helen Meeker. Behind that was the sealed envelope. Redman picked it up and turned it over. The tape had not been tampered with. He was now completely confident no one at the firm knew what they had been holding. He smiled. There was no reason to leave the country now. He could cancel that planned trip to South America. This had been far too easy.

Sliding the folder under his arm, Redman pointed to the cabinet. "Relock it, and we'll get out of here."

Five minutes later, they were back on the street. Without speaking, they casually walked two blocks to a 1938 Oldsmobile. After setting the file folder onto the seat, Redman started the car.

"Ralph, it's time for a drink. There's a bottle in the glovebox."

Cantus hurriedly opened the door, took the fifth, and offered it to Redman.

"I'm driving, you enjoy it until we arrive at the warehouse."

"Warehouse?"

As he placed the car into first gear and turned onto the street, Redman explained. "I have a place I keep stuff I don't want others to see ... like this file. My cash is hidden there too, so we need to go there to get your payoff."

Cantus took a long draw from the bottle and smiled. "I need the grand. I'm at the end of my rope. Honest folks won't hire an ex-con, especially a guy who specialized in what I did. This buys me some time. I really appreciate it."

After making a left turn, Redman offered an observation. "This world is made up of people who tie up loose ends and those who don't. It's the loose ends that always trip you up."

"Tell me about it," Cantus agreed. "My times in stir were because I always overlooked something." He took another drink. "You have a reputation—everyone knows what you do. I'll bet the FBI is aware of almost all your hits. And they can't lay a finger on you. You've never left anything that could be tied back to you. Here's to no loose ends," he announced as he took another drink.

Redman nodded, pulled the car off the main street and into a warehouse district alley. Except for a stray dog, it was void of activity. He parked the car in front of a door and left the lights on. As he exited the vehicle, he looked at the safecracker and barked, "Bring your tools, I forgot my keys."

Cantus laughed. "That's one loose end you missed." He grabbed his kit, opened the car door, and wobbled out. "Boy, that booze is hitting me. Must be good stuff."

"High octane," Redman suggested. "Can you pick that door?"

"I can do this one even while plastered," he bragged. Within seconds, the door snapped open.

"Good job," Redman announced. "Time for the payoff."

Cantus turned and laughed. "You don't have your file, aren't you going to put it up?"

"I'll get it in a second. You step on in and find the light switch—I need to turn the car off."

Redman took a final look up and down the alley, killed the motor and the lights, strolled into the building, and closed the door. He turned and observed Cantus marveling at everything in the now-lit room.

"Wow," he announced, "there are racks of clothes, car parts, furniture, and even a few canoes. And this place goes on forever. This is all yours? It must be worth a fortune."

Redman pointed to a chair by a desk. "You're pretty drunk Why don't you sit down before you fall down."

Cantus nodded and staggered over to the chair. "I didn't drink that much. I can't believe how hard this stuff hit me."

Once he'd collapsed into the seat, Redman pulled a five-foot long section of rope from his pocket, strolled behind the safecracker, and before Cantus knew what had happened, he was bound to the chair.

"What are you doing?"

"No loose ends," Redman announced, as he pulled out more rope and secured the captive's wrists. Once Cantus couldn't move, Redman explained, "The file we stole tonight was my loose end. Or, at least, the woman who created that file was a loose end. When I destroy it, I'm free and clear. Unfortunately, if I let you live, then you know what happened. That would be a loose end."

"I won't tell anyone," Cantus screamed as he struggled with the ropes.

"Gladys always said the same thing. But people's promises seem to dissolve when times get tough. Gladys's hard life caught up with her. Suddenly, her looks couldn't pay her bills. You just admitted no one will hire you. Maybe not today or tomorrow, but when you'd run through the grand, you'd realize what you did tonight would be worth some money."

"Please."

"I hated blowing Gladys up," Redman explained. "That's not my style. It's Tom Sears who uses bombs for hits. It was a shame I couldn't have worked it out where she could have exited like Big Jim O'Toole and so many others." He laughed. "I do like to sign my work." Redman strolled behind Cantus and pulled out his gun. "And just think, Ralph. When they find you, they'll know who did it. It'll be obvious by the drugs in your system, the way you're tied, where the wound is, and what kind of weapon was used, but they won't be able to prove it. You see, I made sure there are no loose ends."

Cantus was sobbing as Redman aimed the Smith and Wesson 45. He studied his trembling victim for a few seconds, and then, it was over.

Redman set the gun on the floor. There were no fingerprints to wipe clean, he'd worn gloves even when he loaded the gun. And there was no way to trace the weapon to him. And as he never kept a gun he used on a hit, not even the FBI lab could prove he'd pulled the trigger tonight or any those other times.

"No loose ends," Redman whispered as he strolled across the warehouse, flipped the light switch, closed the door, and disappeared into the night.

CHAPTER 16

SUNDAY, OCTOBER 3
12:07 P.M.
ALAMOGORDO, NEW MEXICO

Teresa Bryant rarely approached anything like Helen Meeker. Meeker charged in, but Bryant was a student of the situation. Successfully won battles were measured when the earth was not disturbed and only those with keen eyes could read what had happened. This took planning. Instinct was only used when there were no other options. Today, she read the room, and not having to worry about how long it took to get the information she needed, she played the game her way.

Seaman Zack Purdy was outfitted in his dress blues. He was tall, a touch over six-two, lean, and not bad looking. While the military file listed him as cocky, the way he fidgeted in the chair, placed just a few feet in front of Sheriff Jeb Kolb's desk, reflected a man who knew he was in trouble but wasn't sure why.

As was a part of the plan Bryant had outlined, no one had said a word to Purdy since he'd entered the jail. During the first hour, Sheriff Jeb Kolb stood against the building's lone jail cell, his arms folded, looking out the window. The

MP who'd driven Purdy to Alamogordo was stationed by the door. Bryant, standing five feet behind the desk, just stared at the sailor. Her gaze never left him, her eyes rarely blinked, and she showed no sign of emotion.

"Isn't anyone going to say anything?" Purdy finally moaned. In a completely unexpected move, he confessed to an offense that must have been haunting him for years. "You have me," Purdy pleaded, "I'll admit it. I robbed Evans's Dry Goods Store right before I entered the service. I got twenty dollars and some change. I'd been drinking and did it on a dare. Besides, the door was unlocked. If I pay it back, can I go back to my ship?"

Bryant looked over at Kolb. Her plan had worked. She hadn't even had to open her mouth to upset Purdy enough to talk.

The smiling sheriff was shaking his head. From across the room he asked, "Anything else you want to get off your chest?"

"No."

"I think there is," Bryant suggested as she moved to the sheriff's desk and eased into a chair. "Zack, my name is Teresa Bryant, but you will call me Miss Bryant. I work with the President."

"Roosevelt?"

"I don't think I missed an election, so, yes."

"You mean FDR has good looking babes like you on his staff?" Purdy's eyes were hugging her curves, although pretty well hidden by a gray jacket and skirt.

"I'm an agent," Bryant countered.

"Like a G-Man?"

"Something like that." Bryant leaned forward and looked deeply into the confused man's eyes. "Let's go back to 1936. I want to talk about the bank robbery."

"I didn't rob First State Bank. You can't pin that on me."

"No," Bryant agreed, "but you got the money, didn't you?"

Purdy's face momentarily froze, then his eyes shifted, and locked onto the sheriff. He knew he'd been caught, but he wasn't ready to admit it.

"Let me explain something," Bryant cut in, pulling Purdy's attention back to her. "It just so happens the statute of limitations for robbery is seven years. So, even if you did it, we can't touch you for it."

"I didn't rob the bank," Purdy muttered. "I'd admit it if I did, statute of limitations or not."

"But," Bryant continued. "You did get some of the money. Let's talk about that."

Purdy took a deep breath. After a few seconds of suffering under the woman's unrelenting gaze, he opened up. "I was on the search party for whoever robbed the bank. I was working with a friend I'd known since high school. His name was Denny Michaels, but everyone called him Jip. We were in my Model A truck and came upon a burning wreck. About ten feet from the car was a bag of cash. Jip wanted to take it, but I talked him out of it."

"That's a nice clean story," Bryant suggested. "We know you got the cash, or at least some of it, so your story is too convenient. You see, we also know the guy in the car was not the bank robber."

"That's not what they told me," Purdy argued.

"At the time, we got it wrong," Kolb volunteered.

Bryant nodded. "It was actually a Chicago hood named Jim O'Toole. He was awash in cash, so he wouldn't have robbed the bank. And O'Toole didn't die in the crash and fire. The whole thing was staged. He was murdered. Single shot through the back of the head. So, the simple story you just told puts you at the scene of a crime with no statute of limitation." She paused and smiled before adding, "That crime is murder. So, unless you start telling me the whole truth, you might be on your way to the electric chair."

"I didn't kill him." Purdy was now frantic.

"But where did you find the money? We know you got away with some."

Purdy shook his head and sighed. "Jip and I found what we kept along a desert trail about five miles north of the wreck. We were driving back when we spotted the wreck and noticed the cash that was there. And we left it there. That one was the only bag at the wreck."

"How much did you find on the trail?"

"Fifty grand."

"How did you happen upon it?" Bryant demanded. "I mean, just taking off into the dessert and walking into the cash sounds pretty far-fetched."

Purdy was sweating through his uniform. His gaze was darting to each corner of the room. Even though he had to know there was no escape, he was still looking for one.

"Why were you on that trail?" Bryant asked.

"There's an old cabin in a draw not far from that spot. We thought the robber might have holed up there. At that point, I knew my truck wouldn't make it, so we got out and walked."

"I am guessing then the money was in the cabin rather than on the trail?"

"No, we found the bag when we were headed back."

As the statute of limitations had already saved his skin, why did Purdy keep changing his story? There was absolutely no reason not to tell the whole story. Bryant leaned closer and studied the anxious man's face. She could read trouble in his eyes. Something about this memory had him rattled. She looked toward Kolb and then the MP. They didn't seem to want to get involved, so she sat back and considered what had Purdy so frightened. Whatever it was, she had to know. This might very well be the key to the whole mystery.

"What did you find in the cabin, Zack?" she demanded.

"There was no one there," he explained, his eyes looking out the window. "We called out a few times before pushing the door open. There's only one room. In the middle of that room was a chair. On the floor was blood and what looked like other stuff too."

"Like brains?" Bryant asked. "There were still pieces of rope on the chair where it looked like someone had been tied up, weren't there? Was there a gun beside the chair?"

Purdy, his face ashen white, nodded.

Bryant turned to Kolb. "Do you know this place?"

"Yeah, no one has lived there since the twenties when Grant Winters died. He had no relatives, so the property was just left to rot."

"We found the place when we were in high school," Purdy volunteered. "We used the cabin as a place to go and drink. We knew we could stash our booze there, and no one would find it. We always told our folks we were camping out."

"Is it still there?" Bryant asked.

"I haven't been there in a decade," Kolb volunteered. "So, I don't know."

"It's still there," Purdy whispered. "Jip and I went to the cabin a few days before we left for the service. Nothing had changed. The gun, chair, and ropes were still there."

"And you didn't touch them?" Bryant asked.

"We didn't get any further than looking inside."

It was all but impossible to believe a crime scene where Big Jim O'Toole was murdered might be undisturbed after all these years. She turned to Kolb. "Why did Winters live so far away from everything?"

"The rumor is he found a small gold nugget in a draw not far from that creek. He spent the next twenty years looking for more. That area's where the mountains begin. Some say the whole region is haunted by Indian ghosts. I know he didn't find any more gold, but I wouldn't be surprised if he didn't meet some ghosts."

"When we get finished here," Bryant suggested, "we need to go up there."

"Okay."

"Zack, what about Horse?"

"What about him?"

"He disappeared the day you found the money. Did you kill him?"

"No," Purdy announced. "He wasn't all there, but he was a nice guy. I kept others in our group from making fun of him. I felt sorry for him."

Bryant nodded. If true, that was a noble display of empathy she hadn't expected from this guy. Still, her gut told her there was something Purdy wasn't telling her. It was time to find out what his secret was.

"Zach, you saw Horse that day, didn't you?"

"I didn't kill him. The last time I saw him, he was alive."

"Where did you see him?"

"On the trail coming back from the cabin. He had blood on his forehead but didn't appear to have a cut or anything. He was carrying two bags of money. Jip pulled out a rifle and demanded he give us both of them. Horse told us he'd just found the cash and wanted to get it back to the bank."

"Where was he coming from?" Bryant demanded.

"The direction of the cabin."

"I believe you didn't kill him," Bryant assured him, "but what about Jip?"

TIME WALKER

"I think he would have," Purdy admitted. "But when he lifted his rifle to his shoulder, a voice behind us told him to drop it to the ground."

"Who was it?"

"I don't know. The guy had been in town for a couple of days. He'd been hanging out with Horse. I think he was an Indian."

"What happened then?"

"The Indian took Jip's rifle and gave us some orders."

"What were they?" Kolb chimed in.

"He told us we could never tell anyone we had seen them. If we kept our mouths shut, we could have the cash. Don't forget, we'd seen the blood and stuff in the cabin, so there was no way we were going to open our mouths. We figured this guy would have no problem doing the same thing to us. Besides, we were smart enough to know if we kept the money, we couldn't talk anyway. We'd have been hanging ourselves if we did. I think the Indian knew us taking the bank's money would buy our silence."

Bryant stood, walked to a table, opened her purse, and pulled out a photo. Reversing her steps, she held the black and white image in front of Purdy. "Is this the guy you saw?"

"Yeah, that's him."

Bryant waved to the MP. "You can take him. When he pays the twenty-two bucks he stole, send him back to the ship."

A suddenly relieved and grateful Purdy stood and dug into his pocket. He quickly fished out a twenty and a five. "Will this cover it, Mr. Kolb?"

"Sure, kid."

The MP grabbed Purdy by the arm, spun him around, and marched him out of the office. After considering what she'd learned, Bryant turned to face the sheriff.

"I need to go to the cabin."

"After all this time, you expect to see something out there?"

"If the gun hasn't been moved, there could be prints. And maybe there were some other things left as well."

"Miss Bryant, why would Redman take O'Toole there to kill him?"

"Let me ask you a question before I answer yours."

"Okay."

"How would those two men have known about the cabin?"

"I can tell you. In 1936, during Frontier Days, the newspaper ran a story on the life of Grant Winters. When he wrote the article, Hodges told the legend of the gold. The locals all laughed—none of them would have cared about going out there to see where a man had wasted his life. But as the article did give directions to the cabin, maybe someone like O'Toole or Redman would." Kolb paused before asking, "Now answer my question. Why would Redman kill O'Toole there? That's a lot of effort when the job could have been done much closer to town."

"From what Nap told us," Bryant explained, "Redman became friends with those he killed. They trusted him. Like you said, he probably read the story in the newspaper and convinced O'Toole this would be a fun way to spend an afternoon. As far as the cabin was from anything, the location was the perfect spot for a murder and a place to hide the loot from a robbery staged to draw attention away from something else. I'm betting Jenkins left his wallet at the bank. Owen likely showed it to Redman, who might have promised to find a way to get it back to Jenkins. But in fact, he had already planned to use it to cover up killing O'Toole."

"It sounds complicated," Kolb suggested.

"Actually, his plan was really simple and practically perfect. Jenkins is framed, but because everyone assumed he died in the wreck and fire, no one looks for him. O'Toole disappears, and the rumor is he has gone to South America to evade prosecution. And as O'Toole still has loyal gang members, this is one hit that Redman wants to make sure no one finds out about. Even with what Michaels and Purdy took and what you recovered from the wreck, there is still at least twenty-five grand missing. Redman could stay out of sight for a long time with that kind of loot."

"I guess that makes sense. So, you want to see the cabin?"

"Yeah, let me change from this suit into slacks and a shirt, and I'll meet you back here in thirty minutes. It might be wise to not tell anyone where we're going."

"What about Hodges?"

"Okay, let him come along. There's no reason for him not to collect information for a story, if he will go along with us on what he can and can't release.

"He will."

CHAPTER 17

MONDAY, OCTOBER 3, 1943
2:00 P.M.
LOS ANGELES, CALIFORNIA

The Hollywood Hills section of Los Angeles was growing rapidly, and though he didn't live in one of the movie star mansions that were springing up in this area, Taylor Owen had a nice, two-thousand-square-foot, ranch-style home constructed of white brick, featuring a red tile roof, gardens filled with shrubbery and flowers, and a recently manicured lawn. At the end of the driveway was a separate two-car garage. The open doors revealed a 1940 Lincoln on the left and a 1941 Cadillac on the right.

Napoleon Lancelot, who knew Los Angeles very well, observed, "Quite the digs for a man who had no visible means of income. You need to be walking in high cotton to afford this kind of place."

"Financial stability," Helen Meeker suggested, "can be achieved by hard work, through lucky birth, or by knowing where the bodies are buried." She parked the rented 1939 Dodge at the curb and stepped out into a perfect Southern California fall day. After adjusting her fedora, she added, "From what we've learned, Owen has never worked hard and wasn't born into money, so I think we can assume his wealth has come from knowing the location of bodies. And as we dug one of them up, we just might be able to apply some pressure."

In the time he'd worked with Meeker, Nap found her straightforward manner spoke the loudest. She didn't couch anything. She wore her emotions on her sleeve and usually voiced her thoughts without any filters. Yet the woman's open nature was sometimes confusing. Unlike Teresa Bryant, whose approach was almost always based on considerable thought, Meeker was more about instinct. Now, minutes before they were to meet Owen, he still had no idea as to her plans.

"How are we playing this?" Lancelot asked as he got out of the car and retrieved his hat. "I want to make sure we're on the same page. Is the big guy, me, going to scare him, or is the beautiful woman, you, going to charm him?"

"He's not going to volunteer anything," she suggested, "so we must look for an opening and exploit it. Let me take the lead. Our advantage lies in the fact I'm a woman, and you're a Negro. As a wealthy, White male he will surely feel superior to both of us. We can use that against him."

Meeker led the way up the walk, knocked on the door, and waited. When the entry swung open, a very tanned Owen appeared. His smug look clearly defined his inflated ego. After scanning Meeker from head to toe, he smiled and asked, "What movie set did you step out of?"

"What genre did you want?" Meeker shot back.

"I'm thinking romance."

"I'm thinking horror film," she said, pulling his gaze from her legs to her face.

Owen grinned and announced, "Whatever you're raising donations for, I'm giving."

Lancelot turned his face toward the street to hide his smile. Owen clearly thought he was in control. He had no idea how hot the fire was about to get.

"My name is Helen Meeker," she announced. "My associate is Napoleon Lancelot. We work for a man you may have heard of ... Franklin Roosevelt."

Meeker's name dropping worked, the lust on Owen's face immediately faded. It was replaced by utter confusion.

"Mr. Owen," Meeker continued, "We're here to interview you about something that happened seven years ago in Alamogordo, New Mexico. As I don't think you will want your neighbors to hear this conversation, can we step inside?" She smiled before adding, "And even if you say no, we will be coming in."

A now compliant Owen waved and moved to the side. Meeker nodded at Lancelot who entered first. She then signaled for their host to follow. Finally, she closed the door and brought up the rear.

"The living room is to the right," Owen announced.

"That will work," Meeker assured him. "Before we get comfortable, Nap, pat him down and make sure he isn't carrying a weapon."

"I'm clean."

Meeker smiled. "We'll make sure anyway."

Lancelot quickly ran his hands over the man's slacks. There was no reason to check the shirt, it was far too tight to hide anything. Satisfied Owen had shot straight, Lancelot stepped back and let Meeker take over.

"Owen, take the green leather chair," she suggested. "Nap, you've got the couch, and I'll ease down into this wingback."

For the next few minutes, Meeker took a page out of Bryant's playbook and stared at Owen while saying nothing.

At first, he tried studying her, but her intense glare quickly pushed him to turn his head and look out the window. As the silence continued, he crossed and uncrossed his legs three times. He then took to rubbing his brow. Only when sweat appeared on his forehead did Meeker finally break the silence.

"What happened to Big Jim O'Toole?"

"Who?" he asked, his voice cracking.

"He owned the bank in Alamogordo. The one you managed for a few months. You did such a great job it went under."

"I just took the job," Owen offered. "I never actually knew who owned the bank. And I never met O'Toole."

Meeker reached into her purse, retrieved a photo, and handed it to Owen. "Look in the reflection in the window. You'll see yourself pointing something out to that man you've never met."

He glanced at the image. "What does this prove? Maybe he wanted directions. How am I supposed to remember?"

Lancelot looked at Meeker. She nodded. With that signal, he stood and approached Owen. After cracking his knuckles, he made a suggestion, "Let's stop playing games. I've been to Santa Fe. I know you worked at the O'Toole-backed bank there as well. I know Saving and Trust was a depository for mob money. I know you still have an account there. I know your girlfriend still goes back there."

"She's my ex," Owen cut in. "That happened in the last few weeks. She's living with a movie director now."

"Okay," Lancelot replied, "we know your ex worked there. So, now we've established that, why don't you answer Miss Meeker's questions?" He leaned forward until he was nose to nose with the smaller man. "You see, if you don't answer her, you'll have to answer to me. And I'm not the kind of teacher who grades on the curve. I think you know what that means."

Owen fidgeted for a moment before nodding. "You don't have to get rough, I'll come clean. Of course, I knew Big Jim. You have to believe this, when he hired me right out of college, I didn't know he was an underworld figure. I thought he was a bank owner. But when I found out, I didn't let it bother me too much."

After Lancelot moved back to the couch, Meeker asked, "Why didn't it bother you?"

"The money was real good. Is that honest enough for you?"

"I'll buy that," she replied. "Now what happened to Big Jim?"

"Everybody wants to know," Owen suggested. "Last I heard, the FBI couldn't answer that question."

Lancelot smiled. It appeared their host didn't bother reading the newspapers. If he did, he would have seen the stories the wire services had picked up on the mobster's death.

Meeker pulled out a second photo and tossed it Owen's way. He glanced at it, frowned, and dropped it face down on the coffee table.

"That's O'Toole," she announced. "He was executed a couple of days after the photo of you and him had been taken. Right after the bank was robbed. By the way, who was the other man reflected in the window in that shot?"

"Do you know?" Owen asked.

"I know," Meeker assured him, "but I want to know if you know. Your answer better be the right one, or Mr. Lancelot will be doing some after school tutoring."

"He worked for O'Toole. His name was Redman."

"Do you know what he did?" Lancelot asked.

"I was told he was a magician."

"What?" Meeker asked.

"Redman made people disappear." Owen looked out the window as if thinking back to another time and place before adding, "Are you sure he killed Big Jim? I thought they were really tight."

"No doubt Redman murdered O'Toole," Meeker answered. "Now, why would he do that?"

"I don't know."

Meeker looked over at Lancelot and nodded. He stood, moved over to Owen, grabbed his shirt collar, and grinned.

"Wait a minute," Owen cried out, "there's no reason to get rough. I'm sure we can work something out."

"What will loosen your tongue?" Meeker asked.

"I don't want to go to jail."

Meeker nodded, and Lancelot dropped Owen back into the chair. Once he'd pulled his shirt down, the former banker looked back at Meeker.

"Will you give me a stay out of jail card?"

She nodded. "As long as you didn't kill anyone."

"I didn't."

"Then, once again, why would Redman kill O'Toole?"

"It was long before the war, but Big Jim had been offered some big bucks to get something for Hitler. The American press was still pretty much in Hitler's corner, and no one was talking about war back then, so working with Hitler wasn't poison. With a chance to make some easy cash, Big Jim signed off on the deal."

"What was the deal?"

"I don't know. I really, really don't know. I'm being straight with you on that. I'd been working in Chicago, and with no warning was moved to New Mexico. They just wanted me to go down there and charm the town. I did what they asked."

"Did the train wreck have anything to do with this?" Meeker asked.

"No, in truth, it complicated things. I thought the bank in Alamogordo was opened as another place to put underworld loot. But that never happened because the train robbery put First State under an FBI spotlight. After that, we closed it pretty quick and blamed it on the locals not trusting the institution due to the publicity created by losing a hundred grand. But the real reason was we couldn't use it to move mob cash around."

Meeker glanced over at Lancelot. As he had more knowledge of O'Toole's banking empire, it was time for him to take the lead.

"I need to know something," Lancelot queried. "What did they tell you do at the bank before the robbery?"

"I was supposed to meet everyone in the community, spread some money around to various charities, organizations, and churches. And that was about it."

"Was that everything?" Lancelot demanded.

"Everything that mattered. I mean I hired staff, made a few speeches at local clubs, and greeted customers."

"What about Horse?"

"What about him?"

"Why did you hire him?" Lancelot pushed. "I mean he wasn't the brightest bulb."

"I was told to give him a job," Owen claimed.

"Who told you?" Lancelot barked.

"The word came down from O'Toole, though the order came from his secretary."

"Why?"

"I don't know. I really don't. I was told to give him a job and keep him close. Big Jim had an interest in the kid. Maybe he just wanted to help a guy who didn't have anything going for him. I mean, Horse was nice, just not very bright. He had real problems talking."

"In that first photo I showed you," Meeker said, "you were pointing to something. What was it?"

"If I remember right, Big Jim asked me to point out Horse to Redman. Horse was watching the parade from the other side of the street."

Meeker looked at Lancelot and shrugged. He was as confused as she was.

"Listen," Meeker opined, "the hundred grand was not what Hitler was interested in. So, what was O'Toole after?"

"They never let me in on that."

"Why were O'Toole and Redman at Frontier Days?"

"There was a deal working," Owen assured Meeker, "but I don't know anything about the deal."

"Let's go back to Horse," Lancelot suggested. "If you pointed him out to O'Toole and Redman, they didn't know him. So, why would O'Toole take such an interest in a kid he'd never met?"

"I never thought of that," Owen admitted, "but I have no idea."

"There was another guy with Horse that day," Meeker observed. "Do you know who he was?"

"Horse introduced me to him. He was an Indian. I think they were old friends. I got the idea this guy came into town just to see Horse."

"Do you remember the guy's name?" Meeker asked.

"Red Hawk or Red Sky, I don't recall. I never paid much attention to Horse. But I do remember that was the day I figured out he wasn't a Mexican but an Indian."

Lancelot leaned closer. "Besides the money, was there anything else taken off the train and stored in the bank?"

"No."

"What happened to Horse?"

"I assumed he grabbed some of the loot, wandered into the desert, and died." Owen paused before adding, "And that's all I know. I can't figure out how anything that happened in Alamogordo has anything to do with Big Jim trying to get something for Hitler. Don't get me wrong, I knew Big Jim was trying to work with the Nazis, I admitted that to you, but I was never given any information on it. There was no reason for Redman to take out the boss."

"Where did you get all your money?" Lancelot demanded. "This place costs a fortune. You have expensive cars and clothes. And you don't work. So, where did it come from?"

"I was paid off when I left Santa Fe."

"If," Lancelot observed, "O'Toole was dead or missing at that time, who funded your move west and gave you enough to live without working?"

"Okay, fine, I did some playing with the books. For a few years, I'd been skimming off some of Big Jim's money and funneling it into my own accounts. When he disappeared, I dipped pretty heavily into his accounts and got out of Santa Fe. Let's face it, having O'Toole gone was the best thing that happened to me."

"Okay," Meeker announced as she stood. "For the time being you have nothing to worry about. But if we find out anything you told us is a lie, our deal's off."

"It's the truth," Owen assured her.

"Let's go," Meeker commanded.

A relieved Owen stood in the doorway until Meeker pulled the car away from the curb. It was obvious he was happy to have dodged a bullet.

"He was shooting straight," Lancelot suggested.

"I've got that feeling too. But he's wrong on one thing."

"What's that, Helen?"

"I think whatever Hitler wanted was in Alamogordo in the summer of 1936. I sense that because of the connection between Redman and Red Cloud. Something the Indian discovered on his visit is why he joined the Army under an alias, and he has been hiding ever since."

"But Helen, why hide under Redman's name?"

"My theory is as follows. Red Cloud figured out the reason Redman executed Big Jim. He used the hitman's own name when he enlisted because he thought it would be the last name Redman would ever look for. If you think about it, it's brilliant. For all these years, Redman has been searching for Red Cloud, and Red Cloud had become Redman to keep him from finding him. And until we discover where the plans are hidden, we can't stop that masquerade. There's too much at stake."

CHAPTER 18

Sunday, October 3
4:00 p.m.
Alamogordo, New Mexico

The cabin was almost twenty miles northeast, into an area where the mountains replaced the desert. The landscape was still barren and stark, but there was something hauntingly beautiful about it as well. It was a place that never changed, a land where nature still triumphed over man.

A thousand years before, natives called this often-foreboding land home. The Mescalero Apache had been hunters, skilled trackers, and courageous warriors. They dominated this region for centuries. But now, the tribe that once wandered for hundreds of miles in all directions was confined to a small reservation that offered little hope and even less inspiration. Being so near a people who had been all but wiped out by the greed of a culture whose thirst for gold and power trumped their sense of compassion and empathy, plunged Teresa Bryant into such a deep pool of depression, she barely noticed the roar of a 1939 Diamond T truck struggling along the long unused trail. And for the moment, she'd forgotten there were two men riding in the truck with her on this trek into nowhere.

"It's just around this next bend," Sheriff Jeb Kolb announced, shaking Bryant back into reality.

"I was here once," Hodges observed from the far passenger side of the truck. "It was just as barren then."

From her place in the middle of the front seat, Bryant looked through the windshield and over the vehicle's long hood. It was time to shake old images and concerns out of her mind and focus on the mission at hand. As Kolb made a hard left, she spotted the tiny, wood and clay structure that had once served as home for Grant Winters. Calling it humble would have been a vast exaggeration. It couldn't have been over three hundred square feet. It had two tiny-paned windows on the front and likely two more on the back. One of those was broken. It had never seen a paint brush, the tin roof was rusty, and the roof over the porch leaned toward the north.

"How long did he live here?" Bryant asked.

"About thirty years," Hodges explained. "Winters moved here from the east. He was educated, had a degree in history, and I was told he'd been a college professor. I once asked why he left Baltimore, and his answer was kind of numbing. His wife and kids had died from influenza. He told me he was running from their memories. He only meant to stay for a few months, but he discovered a gold nugget. He built this shack and wasted the rest of his life looking for a fortune. If he had found gold, he likely wouldn't have enjoyed what it could buy. After all, it wouldn't have healed his broken heart."

"So," Bryant asked, "he got gold fever?"

"That never made any sense to me," the publisher opined. "He wasn't the type to see money as the answer to problems. I don't think he cared about wealth. So, I don't have an answer as to why he stayed here. I mean, he was ten miles from his nearest neighbor."

As Kolb pulled up to the cabin, Bryant made a bleak observation. "These mountains and deserts are filled with sad stories. Winters's troubled spirit is not alone."

The trio got out of the cab and silently studied the scene. While she couldn't know what the men were thinking, Bryant was immersed in a great sense of desolation. She was a loner by nature, but living here would've even driven her crazy. How had Winters stayed sane? Or had he? Maybe someone who lived this far from everything and everyone was crazy.

"Miss Bryant," Kolb announced, "as this was your idea, I'll yield to you. What do you have in mind?"

"Odds are not in our favor that we'll find anything of any use," Bryant suggested, "but let me go in first. And, when you do join me, don't touch anything. Let's treat this just like a fresh crime scene."

Bryant was once more focused. Her vision and purpose were back as she walked across the clay-brick front porch and pushed on the door. It slowly creaked open. According to Purdy, this was as far as he and Jip had gotten in 1936, and on initial viewing, it appeared neither the two of them nor anyone else had gone any further since that day seven years ago.

Even though there was a thick layer of dust, Bryant could make out the blood stains on the floor's wooden planks. The ancient oak captain's chair still had pieces of rope attached to the arm. Most importantly, the gun—a Smith and Wesson 45—was on the floor. This was a crime scene that had remained stuck in time.

Reaching into a pocket, she pulled out a large handkerchief, strolled to the chair, leaned down, used the cloth to pick up the weapon, and dropped it into her purse. After dusting the chair with her gloved right hand, she took a seat.

This would have been Jim O'Toole's last view of the world. When he was shot, he was likely looking at a 1936 calendar issued by the bank he owned. It appeared blood, flesh, and brain matter had sprayed the entire month of July with a fine mist. She moved her gaze to her left. There was a bed, a cowhide-covered chair, and a small table. On the table was what appeared to be a Bible. To her right was a threadbare couch and floor-to-ceiling shelves filled with books. Further back was an iron stove, likely used for both cooking and heat. A small cupboard held cans, pots, and pans. Against the back walls were some picks and shovels used for mining.

She got up and moved to the rows of books. Winters appeared to be a reader of only nonfiction. Most of the volumes dealt with history.

"Miss Bryant."

She looked back at the door and waved. "Come on in."

As she continued to study the books, the men shuffled around the small cabin like bored children. It was Hodges who broke the silence.

"Did you find anything?"

"I picked up the gun," Bryant announced. "By looking at these books, I can get a sense for who Winters was. But my gut tells me there's something I'm not seeing." She glanced back toward the calendar and then the front window beside it. The glass was gone. She strolled over to study it more closely.

"Do you have something?" Kolb asked.

"The window frame is stained with blood. So is the calendar." Bryant snapped her fingers. "Do you remember

Purdy told us Horse had blood on his forehead but didn't seem to have any injury?"

"Yeah," Kolb answered.

"I'm guessing he was standing on the porch, looking through the window, when O'Toole was killed. He probably ducked to avoid the glass, but some of the blood landed on him. He would have been so frightened; he wouldn't have taken the time to wipe it off. So, that means if Horse is still alive, we might have a witness to Big Jim's execution."

"But don't you think his being alive is a long shot?" Hodges asked.

Though she offered no explanation, Bryant shook her head. Horse had to be alive or Red Cloud would have no reason not to take the Medal of Honor. He was hiding Horse from Redman. But where?

She walked back to the entry, turned around, and once more studied the room. "There's not enough here," Bryant suggested.

"What do you mean?" Kolb asked.

"A person who spends more than a decade searching these hills, digging holes, walking through dried up streams, collects things. Winters read books on history, archelogy, and ancient civilizations. Therefore, if he'd found an arrowhead or a spear tip, he would have kept it, brought it home, and studied it. But look around, you don't see one thing he dug up."

She turned and hurried outside. What she observed behind the cabin brought a huge smile.

"What is it?" Hodges asked.

"A huge pile of dirt," Bryant explained.

Leaving the two men wondering what she found so intriguing about a mound of sand, she returned to the cabin and studied the one thing she'd missed. A four-by-four piece of carpet had been placed in front of the shelves. She hurried over, grabbed it, and tossed it to the side, revealing a trap door.

Bryant retrieved a flashlight from her purse, and as the now curious men stood in the doorway and watched, she pulled the door upward. There were stairs leading down into a dugout basement. She wasted no time using them. She was slowly shining her light around the room when Kolb came down holding a lit lantern. Their two lights revealed piles of stuff, including ancient weapons, blankets, and coats in every corner. Some of it was surely centuries old.

"My Lord," he whispered, "how many bodies are down here?"

"Don't worry," Bryant suggested, "you aren't viewing a murder scene."

"What is it then?"

"Look at the pottery, the clothing, and the bones. Winters didn't find gold, he found burial grounds. And rather than leave the graves alone, he brought everything back to this hidden room."

"Now this is a story," Hodges suggested as he climbed down the stairs. "This basement is four times the size of the cabin."

"This was what was missing," Bryant explained. "If it had just been the gold he was looking for, he would have given up and left a few years after he arrived. But as a historian, he couldn't leave this. The past had him by the throat, and he had to continue looking for more of the ghosts from another time."

Noting books setting on an old ceremonial drum, she walked over and picked up one of them. After leafing through several pages, she announced, "Gentleman, he wrote in detail about every artifact he found. As misguided as stealing from graves was, he considered this his life work."

Hodges studied the room for several moments before observing, "But it's still a waste. Indians make this stuff on the reservation and sell it to tourists. I mean this is much older, but he didn't find anything of any value. There is no jewelry, no gold, no silver."

Bryant shrugged and continued to read through the first journal. After scanning a dozen more pages, she closed the volume and picked up the other six.

"Gentlemen, we don't tell anyone about this room and the stuff that's down here. At least, not yet. Our focus has to be on the crime that was committed upstairs. If word gets out about the cellar, then people will be pouring out here messing up our crime scene. Let's cover everything up, hide the trap door, and get back to town."

"What can I write about in my story?" Hodges asked.

"We found the gun. And as what we found will be sent to the crime lab, you can write your feature on how modern technology might just be the key to identifying a killer whose crime is seven years old."

"I like that angle," Hodges laughed. "I think I'm about to have another story that will go coast to coast." He looked at Bryant and asked, "What's next for you?"

"I need to make a call to England and see if an associate we work with can talk to a hero no one knows. Then I get to wait on lab results."

CHAPTER 19

WEDNESDAY, OCTOBER 6, 1943
8:00 P.M.
LIVERPOOL, ENGLAND

It's never easy to find one specific American in England—there are just too many people from the United States in the UK at any given time. In 1943, as Allied Powers geared up to invade Europe, it was all but impossible locate a private who didn't want to be found. For two days and nights, OSS operative Russell Strickland had a team making calls across the island nation. There was one roadblock after another. By noon on Wednesday, Strickland was sorry he'd agreed to do this favor for Teresa Bryant, yet he didn't give up. Finally, Ruffin Redman was located on a base outside of Liverpool. Once orders came through from command, he was taken to a two-hundred-year-old cottage on the outside of the city. He was waiting in the small home's parlor when the agent arrived.

The tall, athletic Strickland was a no-nonsense interrogator. As his job was to get information out of enemy agents, he had to operate that way. But this was different. Bryant had shared Redman's story, or what she knew of it, and this soldier felt the secret he kept was more important than his own life. On top of that, he wasn't the enemy, he was a legitimate hero. In cases like this, how could Strickland push the buttons to obtain the needed information and not feel guilty? So, he dreaded this interview. But a promise was a promise, and Meeker's team was doing something vital for international security. If Redman knew something that Hitler wanted to know, then the Allies needed to learn it too.

"Private Redman," Strickland announced as he entered the room and reached out his hand, "my name is Russell, and I work for the OSS. Sometimes, I also cross the line and help England's MI6."

As they shook, Redman was polite if not enthusiastic. "Nice to meet you, sir."

"Let's just sit down and talk," Strickland suggested. Once they'd found chairs on either side of a stone fireplace, the OSS agent continued. "First of all, I was a part of the team who interviewed the two women you helped save in France. The information they gave us has proven to be very valuable. Needless to say, the plans you helped us obtain are very important as well."

"Then," Redman replied, "whatever our team went through was worth it."

"Without you, everyone on that team and the two French women would have likely died or been captured. This mission was a success because of your actions."

"No, it happened because the team worked together. The mission was successful because of leadership. It happened because of luck too. I was just a part of all that. I did the job that needed to be done because I had the least to lose. Still, there were three good soldiers who died during that mission. Worst of all, they didn't die fighting the enemy."

Strickland nodded. "If war isn't hell itself, it opens the door so people can see it." He paused, leaned closer to the fire, and frowned. "I understand you want to get back into an active unit. It doesn't matter where, but you want it to happen now."

"The sooner the better."

"Do you enjoy killing?"

Redman shook his head. "No, I'd never killed anyone until this war. I'll admit there were times I wanted to, but something always held me back."

"What was that?"

"You've talked to Teresa Bryant, haven't you?"

Strickland shrugged, "She and I have worked together in the past. I respect and like her."

"So, she hasn't dropped her desire for me to get a piece of metal pinned to my chest."

"She can't," Strickland countered. "She has a job to do."

"Her job has nothing to with a soldier deciding not to accept an award. That's my choice."

"And she agrees. Though she thinks the Seminole people would benefit from having one of their own accept the Medal of Honor, Teresa will let that pass. But there's something else she can't let go of." He paused until the two men were looking at each other directly in the eyes. "Why did you blow up that bridge?"

"To save lives and help us win the war."

"That's why Teresa can't let it go." Strickland folded his hands together and gazed into the fire. "Let me share something with you. Teresa has a thousand reasons not to help the United States. She once admitted this to me. American men in uniform killed her parents, and an American government took her from her people and placed her in a horrible school. That school had one goal—to erase every bit of the Indian from her being."

"My parents weren't murdered," Redman countered, "but the Whites did the same thing to me. My father died a drunk, and it was due to life on the reservation. My mother's heart was broken when he left this earth. So, my life hasn't been a piece of cake."

"And yet you fight for the same people who took away your land."

"No," Redman solemnly announced, "I fight against a system, one led by Hitler, that's even worse than the one in Washington. Consider this, sometimes the need to fight against something is a far greater motivator than the need to fight for something."

"That's a good line, but it's mostly rationalization. You joined up long before the war began. There was nothing to fight for back then. So, you must have been running away from something."

Redman glared at Strickland. Though he said nothing, obviously, a rage was building in his gut, and even though he didn't want to, the OSS agent took advantage of it.

"If you were running from something, you might have been displaying the signs of cowardice."

"No," Redman spit. "I had to do what I did."

"Entering a military that was going to discriminate against you, serving under officers who were going to treat you like a dog, being called a redskin and worse repeatedly, how was that the answer? If this was the best thing for the Indian, then all those men on the reservations would have joined."

"It wasn't about me," Redman argued.

Strickland nodded. "No, it wasn't."

Redman frowned. "How do you know? After all, you just called me a coward."

"I didn't call you a coward. I just said if you were running from something you needed to face, it was cowardly behavior."

"Ah, White man, you can dissect words and then put them back together in ways that favor your objectives and points of view."

Strickland smiled. "I deserved that. But now I will level with you. Here's what Teresa and Helen Meeker know. You joined to protect a man called Horse. That young man is not all there. He has problems connecting thoughts and speaking, but he's a good person. Bryant believes Horse saw a murder. If you want, I can even tell you where, when, and who. And you saved his life when he was threatened by two men. Then you found a way to hide Horse from a killer and joined the Army so no one could get to you."

"Let's say that's true," Redman agreed. "Let's say that's the reason I can't accept the medal. Isn't that my business?"

"That man Horse saw executed in 1936," Strickland explained, "makes it more than your business. His name was Jim O'Toole. He was in Alamogordo because of something Hitler wanted. Meeker's team hasn't figured out what that was, but they're pretty sure the Nazis don't have it yet."

"Who was O'Toole?"

"He was a big crime boss out of Chicago."

"Why did someone kill him?"

Strickland took a deep breath. "Our guess is to make their own deal with Hitler."

"Do you know who that guy was?"

Strickland smiled. "Have you heard the statement there is no honor among thieves?"

"Who hasn't?"

"O'Toole was taken out by a hitman he'd employed for years. But I think you know that. I think you're just fishing for how much we have learned."

"What makes you say that?" Redman demanded.

"Teresa has talked to your people. She found out your name is Red Cloud. Now, let me ask you a question. Why did you choose the name you chose when you enlisted? As we know all about you, it's not going to hurt you to, at least, tell me that."

Redman chuckled. "There's no mystery. Teresa guessed it before I even admitted it. You can go to any Hollywood western and my people are always called red men. So, when I joined, I just used that moniker. I considered it my way of ribbing or making fun of the White man."

"Seriously, that was your reasoning?"

"Yeah."

"What about Ruffin?"

"I had a teacher at the Indian school who was from Kent, England. He was in America because he cared about us. I was the peacemaker between the boys at the school. If there was a fight, I found a way to settle it. So, he called me Ruffin, which in Old English means 'one who settles disputes.'"

Strickland's jaw dropped. What were the odds? He quickly shifted his eyes from the floor to his guest. "Did you witness what Horse saw?"

"Yeah, I did. He wanted to help find the stolen money, so I went with him. He knew of some caves in the area. We searched a small one not far from a vacant shack and found two bags. We headed back to town to turn it over to the sheriff when we heard arguing in that same shack. When we looked in the window, a stocky man shot another man who was tied to a chair. At that point, we hightailed it out of there, and then hid out for a day before moving on."

"Did you know either of those men? The executioner or O'Toole?"

"Horse knew O'Toole. He'd met him at the bank where he worked, but he'd only seen the other one. He didn't know him by name. I'd never met or seen either of them."

"Then you ran into the other two White men—Michaels and Purdy."

"The next day, I had Horse wait on the trail and cut back around to see if anyone was following us. When I returned, the two were holding a rifle on Horse. I disarmed them, gave them the bags of cash, and we moved on. Neither Horse nor I went back to Alamogordo again."

"Why not go to the authorities?"

"We were Indians, and they needed scapegoats. Besides, the guy who killed O'Toole was surely going to want to silence us. So, I got Horse to safety, then went to Tulsa and enlisted in the army. You know the rest. And now you should understand why it's more essential than ever for me to not get any attention. I have to protect my friend."

"Let me stun you."

"With what I've been through in life, I don't shock easily."

"Try this on for size," Strickland suggested. "The hitman's name was Ruffin Redman."

"What?"

"Of the hundreds of millions of names in the world, you chose the same one as the man who's after you."

Red Cloud laughed. "Maybe that was the Great Spirit's way of protecting me. I mean who would look for someone whose name was the same as theirs?"

Strickland considered the irony. The choice of that name did seem on the divine side of the spectrum.

"May I call you Red Cloud?"

"When we are alone, but not beyond these doors."

"What happened to Horse?"

"If you're asking why he couldn't talk right or had problems with his head, which I'm sure you know about, he had been a stubborn kid who was really smart. He wouldn't conform. So, a bull of a teacher beat him into a coma with a baseball bat. He was out for a week but somehow lived."

The image of a child being assaulted in that fashion brought tears to Strickland's eyes. He replayed the scene several times before asking the most important question of the night. "Where's Horse now?"

Red Cloud shook his head. "He's safe. But that's all I'm going to tell you."

"Is Horse his name?"

"No, just one a White man gave when he wandered into Alamogordo. But I think he kind of liked it."

"And you're not going to tell me his real name either?"

Red Cloud shook his head and smiled. "You know far more than you did, but you've learned all you will from me. I've confirmed I'm Red Cloud. If what you're looking at is in the national interest, then inform Morning Song, or Teresa Bryant as you call her, to keep digging. But tell her not to look for Horse, and assure her I won't accept the medal. May I leave?"

"Sure, thanks for your time. And let me assure you, I don't think you're a coward."

In silence, both men pushed out of their chairs and moved to the door. After twisting the knob, Red Cloud paused and made an offer. "Tell Morning Song if she and her team kill Redman, I'd owe them. That would mean my pledge to Horse would be met. At that point, maybe she and I can speak openly." He smiled before adding, "And now I know why Morning Song was talking about Chicago the first time we met. Imagine my choosing an alias that is the name of the man who wants to kill me."

Strickland nodded and watched as the door opened, and the reluctant hero walked out. This visit had brought some light to the darkness. Was it enough to help Meeker and her team get closer to why Hitler was so interested in something in Alamogordo, New Mexico? Somehow, he didn't think so.

CHAPTER 20

Wednesday, October 6, 1943
10:35 p.m.
Alamogordo, New Mexico

Teresa Bryant had been all by herself in Alamogordo for five days. Some of that time had been fruitful, but a lot of it had just been spent waiting. And how she hated waiting. According to a telegram, Helen Meeker and Napoleon Lancelot would be back in town by midnight. She was hoping they had something to go with what she'd uncovered.

To pass time, she fell back onto her hotel bed and picked one of Grant Winters's journals. While she had to admit what this man had found was remarkable, what he'd done was disturbing. He had not only violated sacred burial grounds, but he'd also stolen from them. There weren't just artifacts, there were bones too. And he had documented every bit in minute detail. In journal after journal, she'd read about caves filled with bodies and all the things buried with them. The more she read, the more the ghosts cried out to her. Why was the White man so arrogant only the graves of his people were to be left undisturbed? Why were the rituals and paths of others mocked and dismissed? Why was there no value in being something other than White?

The one thing Winters had not spelled out—where to find what he'd discovered. There were no maps to the locations. Though she searched through every page several times, there were no directions to his discoveries spelled out. This should have brought her some comfort, but it didn't. She surmised the reason there were no maps is someone had ripped those pages from all the journals. If that were the case, then perhaps the burial caves could have been located and looted. So, what Winters discovered could find its way into the hands of collectors who had no regard for the artifacts' sacred nature. Maybe that was why the ghosts were crying out to her. She sensed they wanted her to protect their slumber. But perhaps it was already too late.

As she was drawn deeper into a story of betrayal, as the sins of Winters caused her heart to weep, there was a knock. She should have been grateful to whoever was calling. She needed to turn the page and change the subject, but in her world, the wolf was at the door far more than a friendly face. Rather than rush to the entry, she retrieved her gun.

"Who is it?"

"It's the night clerk. An envelope was just delivered for you by an Army officer."

Considering what she'd discovered and what Hodges was printing in his newspaper, this could be a trap. Even with a lethal weapon in her hand, she wasn't spoiling for a fight.

"Could you slide it under the door?" she called out.

"Sure."

A few seconds later, a large manilla, almost flat envelope appeared, so it contained very little. After retrieving it, she tore it open at the small table she'd been using as a desk . There were four pages, all typed. She scanned through the first one.

> Teresa, I opted to send what I found out in my interview with our hero via an OSS radio letter. As you have access to our latest encryption, I'm sending it in code. I think you will find what I discovered very interesting, but there is only one thing likely to surprise you. RS

After retrieving her latest code book, she began to mark up the pages. When she'd finished, she knew exactly what was supposed surprise her. The name Red Cloud was using—Ruffin Redman—had no ties to the man who'd shot O'Toole. That completely blew her theory on why Red Cloud had chosen that name. Thankfully, it had served him well.

She read on. The fact he hadn't given the name nor the location of Horse was no shock, but the reason for the man's reduced mental functions hit her with the force of a Sherman tank. Now she was sure if she had been in Red Cloud's position, she'd have reacted in much the same way. This also made finding out what happened to Redman even more important.

She set the papers to one side just as her phone rang.

"Bryant," she announced.

"It's Collins from the FBI."

"Did the lab find something?" she asked hopefully.

"No, the gun was clean. But I can tell you that during the early to mid-1930s, we know of at least a dozen murder scenes arranged in the same way as the one you found. The victim was tied up, executed with a single shot from behind, and there was aways a Smith and Wesson 45 left at the scene. And never were there any prints."

"Obviously a signed hit," Bryant suggested. She asked the next question, not because she didn't know the answer, but because she wanted to learn how much the FBI knew.

"So, who was the artist?"

"A hitman named Ruffin Redman, but there was never a single bit of evidence nor a witness that tied him to the executions."

"So, if I'm hearing what you're saying, the hit on O'Toole in the summer of 1936 was the last?"

"Maybe. Until you discovered Big Jim had been Redman's work, we thought he'd disappeared in April 1936."

"And what happened to him?" Bryant asked.

"We figured he messed up and was at the bottom of a lake somewhere."

"If he's dead," Bryant said, "then I can inform someone he can quit hiding."

Collins took a breath so deep Bryant could hear it over the phone. "A week ago, I'd have told you to give your man the good news. But on Sunday morning that changed. A small-time hood in Denver was executed the same way Redman always did his jobs. And the day before, Redman's old girlfriend, Gladys Branch, was murdered in a cab explosion. Someone put a bomb in a package she picked up at the post office."

"Any witnesses?"

"The clerk who took that package described an old man as the sender. Back in the thirties, we were told that Redman often disguised himself in that way. So, I don't think there's any doubt that Redman is still with us. I've got to believe he has now come out of hiding. Sorry I couldn't give you better news."

"Actually, you gave me some very good news. Thanks."

As she set the phone back in the cradle, she grimly smiled. Perhaps it was the writing by Hodges that forced Redman back into the open. After all, the wire services had picked up those stories and that meant they were being read from coast-to-coast. If the small-time hood in Denver and the old gal pal read them and knew about O'Toole, they might have forced Redman's hand. Meaning Horse and Red Cloud needed to stay out of sight. Perhaps it was just as well Strickland didn't find out any more than he did.

Bryant was staring at the ceiling, guessing where Redman would go next, when there was another knock at the door. A voice she knew well called, "We're back!"

It was time to bounce some ideas off Meeker and Lancelot as well as find out what they learned on the West Coast. This might turn out to be a very long night.

CHAPTER 21

Thursday, October 7, 1943
9:10 a.m.
Alamogordo, New Mexico

"So," Teresa Bryant asked as they finished breakfast, "are we going to leave Red Cloud in England? Let me say, I think that would be best for him and Horse."

"He stays overseas," Meeker agreed, "but he's not going to be shipped to any combat zones. The military wants to keep him out of harm's way until he agrees to accept the Medal of Honor. Without realizing it, the Army is doing us a big favor."

"Unless we solve this case," Lancelot suggested. "Unless we take Redman off the streets and put him behind bars, Red Cloud might have to stay hidden until 1960." He drummed his finger on the café's table and asked, "More importantly what do we do now? How do we find Redman? Everything has come down to that."

"Nap, you're going to Santa Fe," Meeker announced. "Talk to your banker friend again. The easiest way to locate Redman might be to follow the money. If he's taking money out, where is it being sent? If he is depositing money, where's it coming from?"

"Okay. I'll leave right after breakfast."

"Take the car," Meeker suggested. "I'll pick up another one for us."

"And what are we going to do?" Bryant asked.

"I want to see that cabin," Meeker explained. "Other than what you shared last night, is there anything else important in those journals?"

"There is something unusual. Winters never wrote about anything of value. I mean museums or wealthy collectors would love the artifacts, but there's not one thing in the inventory made from precious metal."

"Is that so strange?" Meeker asked

Bryant leaned forward and explained, "The ancient natives in this area created certain ceremonial items out of gold and silver. Some of them should have been in those tombs. I don't understand why they aren't mentioned."

"This Indian history is fascinating," Lancelot announced, "and I'd love to view the artifacts, but we're no closer to understanding what O'Toole was getting for Hitler. We need to be concentrating on that."

"Which is why we need to find Redman," Bryant suggested. "If anyone knew, it would be him. My gut tells me that's why he bumped off O'Toole."

"No one has used the First State Bank building since it was closed in 1936." Meeker pointed out. "What do you say we take a look at it. I'm betting our newspaper publisher can get us in. Though the odds are against us, maybe we can find something there. Now, if everyone has finished eating, let's walk next door and talk to Hamilton Hodges."

"Y'all go ahead," Lancelot suggested, "I'm going to grab my bags. I need to get on the road. I have lots of things to accomplish in Santa Fe, and it's a long drive."

As Meeker paid the check, Bryant glanced at the latest issue of the *Alamogordo Daily News*. The lead story continued a theme centering on O'Toole's execution and the need to find and prosecute the killer. Hammering on that might have been fine when Redman was off the radar, but with the hitman back and working—it was a dangerous subject—one the publisher likely needed to put to rest for a while. Though he probably wouldn't listen, she felt compelled to warn him the fire was getting too hot.

"You ready?" Meeker asked when she joined Bryant at the door.

"I need to talk to Mr. Hodges. I'm now having some concerns about how hard he's pushing this story."

As the two exited, an elderly man brushed past them, slightly knocking Bryant to the side.

"Excuse me," he meekly offered.

"No problem."

After she and Meeker strolled the forty feet to the newspaper office, Bryant looked back and observed the man sliding into a 1940 Mercury coupe. Upon starting the car, he pulled out of the parking space, made a U-turn, headed east, then took a right and disappeared.

"What are you looking at?" Meeker asked.

"Look at the street. It's filled with people, half of them men in uniform who had no connection to this area. What had once been a place where everyone knew everyone is now a community where a stranger draws no attention. No one is asking 'Where are you from?' or 'What are you doing here?' There're simply too many people who are from too many places all doing too many things for the war effort to make those questions viable."

"The war has changed things," Meeker admitted "I'm betting a lot of the locals don't like it."

"I can understand that too. Helen, a few years ago, this was a place like most other small towns where people stopped and visited with each other. Now they just hurry around like ants. Before the base was located here, that guy who bumped into me would've likely stopped and we'd have gotten to know each other. Might have learned each other's name and talked about the weather or sports. This place is now so crowded, and there are so many strangers that the old man is probably in a hurry to get someplace where there are sounds rather than noise. For him, all of this is probably unnerving."

"Teresa, you might be overthinking."

"Maybe." After taking a final look at a place completely changed by events taking place a half a world away, Bryant followed Meeker into the newspaper office.

"Mr. Hodges," Meeker called out. There was no answer. Meeker looked back at Bryant and shrugged. "Maybe he's out covering a story."

"His life has changed as much as the town," Bryant suggested. "For five decades, no one outside of Alamogordo noticed Hodges, and now his name is appearing in newspapers all over the country and beyond. In a very real sense, he's a celebrity. People are hanging on to each word he writes. In death, Jim O'Toole made an old publisher famous. Perhaps someone is buying him breakfast."

"And he's loving it," Meeker laughed. "Everyone needs their moment in the spotlight."

"Except Red Cloud," Bryant observed.

Meeker shook her head before again calling out, "Mr. Hodges."

Bryant pointed toward the ceiling. "Why don't we check upstairs. Maybe he's taking a nap. After all, he's been burning the midnight oil a lot."

Meeker nodded, walked across to the back wall, and led the way up the steep staircase to the second floor. Bryant had just stepped onto the landing when Meeker's body went stiff. Looking past her partner toward the center of the living area, Bryant also froze. Hodges was there, but he was not asleep. The publisher was tied to a chair, his chin resting on his chest, blood had pooled in his lap and was dripping onto the floor. Her eyes moved from the dead body to the room. There was blood splatter on the far wall with a Smith & Wesson 45 on the floor.

"Redman's been here," Bryant whispered.

"Shot from behind execution style." Meeker observed as she pulled her Colt from her purse. She covered the four steps to his body and put her hand against the man's cheek. "He's not cold, so this likely happened while we were eating breakfast next door. That means Redman had to use a silencer."

Bryant nodded, retrieved gloves from her pocket, and pulled them on. She then picked up the phone and made a call.

"Sheriff, it's Teresa Bryant. Helen Meeker and I just got to the *Daily Times* office and found Hodges dead. He's been executed. He's up in his living quarters."

"What?"

"We're with the body. Get here as fast as you can." She put the phone back in the cradle.

"When the sheriff takes over the crime scene," Meeker suggested, "we need to circulate posters of Redman."

"It won't do any good," Bryant replied.

"Why?"

"Because, Helen, we saw him. He was the old man who bumped into me. He got into a green Mercury and drove away. Collins from the FBI told me that was Redman's favorite disguise."

"Okay, we track the car."

"That a good idea," Bryant agreed, "but this guy is a pro. I think we'll discover the car will be dumped outside of town. We'll surely find that it's been stolen." She looked back at the lifeless publisher and frowned. "The next huge story out of this town will be the death of the man who broke the first big story out of this town." She sighed, "We should have left this alone. If we had, Hodges would be alive."

"What do you mean *left it alone*?" Meeker demanded.

"Red Cloud didn't want the medal. He had his reasons. None of this happened until we tried to find out what those reasons were. That's what brought us here. It's why Hodges met us and got dragged into this mess."

"There was something of great value Hitler wanted that is associated with this too. He was working with O'Toole to get it. We couldn't leave it alone." Meeker argued.

"That was 1936, and Hitler didn't get it, so why would he be able to get it now? Redman stayed underground until we started digging, and now at least three people associated with him or this case no longer have any need for air."

Meeker's eyes were on fire. "Are you blaming me?"

"I not blaming as much as I'm questioning what we're doing. I'm a part of this too."

"Okay, partner, what do your instincts tell you we need to do now?"

Bryant shook her head. "We must find Redman. He must pay. Which means we start by locating the Mercury he was driving." She paused and clinched her jaw before adding, "He made a big mistake. Redman killed the messenger. That's what Hodges was. He was the man telling the world what we had uncovered. And there will now be other messengers coming from all over the country to cover this story. Redman is going to understand he has to get the people who dug up the facts in this case. Helen, we're the next targets."

CHAPTER 22

Thursday, October 7, 1943
11:09 a.m.
Alamogordo, New Mexico

Bryant and Meeker sat silently in the Sheriff's Office as Jeb Kolb made a series of telephone calls. After setting the phone down, he angrily pounded his fist onto his desk.

"He was a fool for doing those features," Kolb screamed. "That reporter in Chicago, Goodwin, gave him all that information on Redman's style and background, and Hodges just had to use it. And that cost him his life."

"What about the car?" Bryant asked.

"The state police found the Mercury parked on Highway 54, just outside the city limits. Based on what a hitchhiker told them, an old man got out of that car and drove away in another vehicle that was parked there. All the witness could remember was that it been a dark sedan. It had so much dust on it he couldn't make out the color. It could have been blue, black, brown, or dark green."

"Was the Mercury stolen?" Bryant asked.

"Yeah, from an old woman, Charlotte Baker. She lived about a half mile from where it was left. It seemed she always parked the car in her drive and never took the key out. Until the state cops knocked at her door, she didn't even know it was missing."

"Meaning, Redman came to town, then drove around in his sedan until he found a car to borrow. Was there anything missing at the newspaper office?"

"One thing," Kolb replied.

"The file on the O'Toole case," guessed Bryant.

"Bingo! Miss Bryant, the old man who bumped you, was he wearing gloves."

Bryant paused, grabbed a breath, slowed her heart, and took herself back two hours. To save time, she verbally recalled everything she'd seen. "He was about five-six to five-eight, gray suit, white shirt, and no tie. He wore a fedora and glasses. I remember he had something stuffed under his arm. It must have been the file. His eyes were green, his lips thin, and he had far more gray in his goatee than the hair that was showing from under his hat. As I think about it now, while his gait appeared to be that of a man seventy-five or more, when he entered the car, he moved like a person much younger. When he pulled away from the curb, I saw his hand on top of the wheel as he made his U-turn. He was wearing black gloves."

"So," Kolb suggested. "No use looking for fingerprints."

"There's only one thing we need to be looking for," Meeker suggested.

"What's that?"

"Redman himself. Sheriff, what's in the direction where he was headed?"

"Nothing on a direct path. He could cut over onto 380 and go to Roswell, or make a left and head to Albuquerque, then there is Clovis or Tucumcari."

Bryant walked over to a map of New Mexico hanging next to the door. She studied for a moment and tapped Santa Fe.

"He still has a bank account there. He likely knows people who would hide him. Put out alerts for every place you mentioned, but Santa Fe is the most likely destination."

"I'll get Nap working on that when he checks in with us," Meeker volunteered, "but even if we find him, we still have a problem. We can't arrest or hold him."

"He killed Hodges," Kolb argued.

"We know that," Meeker agreed, "and we know of a dozen other people he took out. He signs his work, so we know each time he kills. But we have no evidence and no witnesses."

"Miss Bryant saw him on the street."

"No," Bryant cut in. "I saw an old man. Was it Redman? I think we are sure of that. But it wouldn't stand up in court. And on top of that, I didn't see him leave the newspaper office. We have no reason to arrest him even if we figure out where he is."

"We're back to one thing." Meeker snapped. "There was a witness in the O'Toole murder, and he won't talk nor give us the name or location of the other man who saw that execution."

"There was a witness?" a shocked Kolb gasped.

"Oh, yeah," Meeker continued, her tone displaying intense frustration, "but he won't step forward."

"Why not?"

Meeker turned and stared at Bryant. "Do you want to tell him?"

"He claims he's protecting someone. But I think that's only a part of the story. I think those two witnesses know what O'Toole was looking for. I think they're not coming forward because if they do Hitler might get his hands on what he wanted back in 1936." Bryant crossed her arms. "Ask any military expert, and they'll tell you the tide has turned in Europe. We are going to win this war."

"Unless Hitler gets some kind of super weapon," Meeker argued. "So, you believe this is about keeping that out of his hands?"

Bryant nodded. That really wasn't fully what she believed. Her instinct told her that Red Cloud didn't want anyone to find what Hitler wanted. He wanted it to remain buried forever.

"I'll get the state police working on what we need in Santa Fe," Kolb promised.

"I'll get the FBI involved," Meeker added. She looked toward Bryant, "You think we need to get back to the hotel?"

"I think we need to borrow a truck," Bryant suggested. "Can you get us one, Sheriff?"

"You can have mine."

"Thanks."

"Where are we going?" Meeker asked.

"Once we change clothes, we're going on a wild goose chase."

CHAPTER 23

Thursday, October 7, 1943
3:25 p.m.
Outside Alamogordo, New Mexico

Teresa Bryant's expression grew grim as she and Helen Meeker got closer to Grant Winters's cabin. This wasn't a place she wanted to return to, but a troubling hunch demanded she drive out of Alamogordo and toward the mountains. The closer she got to her destination, the more she wanted to turn back.

"You haven't said anything since we left town," Meeker announced as Bryant pulled off the road onto what might generously be called a trail. "Are you still angry because I kept digging?"

"There's a difference in your kind of investigating and mine," Bryant explained, her tone calm and controlled. "We allow people to be who they are and who they want to be. So many Whites try to make everyone who isn't White act and respond as if they are. Your missionaries are a classic example. They were trying to get us to worship a man who was born in the middle east by demanding we become little White Americans. Jesus wasn't White. He looked more like me than he did you."

"I don't know what—"

"Let me finish," Bryant demanded as she drove the truck up a rocky, steep, hill. "I'm sorry if you're tired of hearing it, and believe me, I'm not blaming you, but the Whites put us in Indian schools to teach us how not to be an Indian. When we graduated, we were sent back to reservations and told to stay in the Indian world and not interact with Whites. It was like the government wanted us where people could watch us but not have to associate with us. And the goal was to keep us humble and poor."

"What does this have to do with this case?"

"I'm getting to that. A part of it is Red Cloud feels that protecting his friend is far more important than being singled out and honored."

"I understand," Meeker admitted. "And if this didn't involve something Hitler desperately wanted, I'd let him have his wish."

"But, Helen, have you considered it might be more than that? What if Red Cloud doesn't want a Medal of Honor because he doesn't want to be paraded around this country as the good Indian? That's what would happen. The Whites would point out how Red Cloud was the pride of America, but when the war ended, they'd still send him back to the reservation. Maybe Red Cloud just doesn't want to go through that charade. He doesn't want to be lionized one moment and dismissed the next."

"Is that what we do?" Meeker asked.

"Yes. Those in charge tell us if we dress and act like Whites, we will be accepted. But we never are. We lose what we were without gaining anything at all."

"I don't treat you that way," Meeker argued.

"No, but a lot of the White world does. And while you might allow me to have my own ideas and make my own decisions, you don't feel that others like Red Cloud have the same rights."

Meeker didn't reply. Bryant didn't know if her silence was fueled by anger or shame. At this point, it didn't matter. So, for thirty minutes they rode along in silence that was uncomfortable on every level, from physical to psychological. Thus, the half hour seemed to stretch out forever.

"If I remember correctly, the cabin's just around the next bend." Bryant explained as she wrestled the truck along the trail. "There it is."

Meeker didn't reply.

Bryant pulled the truck to a stop about sixty feet from the front of the shack. Normally she would have jumped out and gotten to work, but something didn't feel right. After a few seconds of studying the scene, she reached into her purse and pulled out her pistol.

"Why are we going in armed?" Meeker asked.

"Just a hunch," Bryant explained as she slid out of the truck. Though a chill ran down her spine and her heart threatened to leap from her chest, nothing seemed out of order. The cabin looked the same way as when she'd last been inside. So, why were her instincts screaming for her to run for cover? Talking a deep breath, Bryant whispered, "Just follow me."

"Care to explain what we're looking for?"

"Did you read all the stories Hodges wrote about the O'Toole murder?"

"Yes, I even went through the ones I missed on my trip. Why?"

"I asked him not to mention the cabin. I didn't want anyone coming back and looting the artifacts Grant Winters had stored here. So, no one should know about this place."

Bryant studied the dirt about twenty feet in front of the entry. "Yet those tire tracks prove someone has been here."

A suddenly wary Meeker pulled her Colt from her pocket and looked toward the cabin. "Is anyone here now?"

"I don't think so but stay here and give me cover."

Bryant creeped up to the entry, turned the knob, and the door swung open. With her weapon leading the way, she stepped in. There was no one there.

"Come on in," Bryant yelled out.

Bryant was standing by the cookstove when Meeker entered. She was just as concerned as she had been outside.

"That's the chair where O'Toole sat during his execution," Meeker observed. "And by the way, you still haven't told me why we're here."

"Hodges forced Redman's hand. We know he came back to Alamogordo to stop the publisher from writing any future stories. But that didn't end his work in the town."

"What do you mean?"

"Redman needs to kill you and me. We were the stars of the story he's not enjoying reading. We were the ones who pointed out it was no accident. We identified the killer. Redman must believe we have some kind of proof, so he'll be gunning for us as well."

"I hate to sound redundant, then why are we here?"

"Because if we're in Alamogordo, Redman has to stick around to finish his work. He isn't going to stray very far. The cabin was not mentioned in the stories, so he has to believe this is a safe place to hide."

"I don't see him," Meeker pointed out.

"The stove is warm, so someone used it. If we opened it up, we'd likely find some coals under the ashes. And, as no one disturbed this place from 1936 until I was here the other day, that leads me to think Redman is the person who has been here."

Bryant's observation made an impact. Meeker's body tensed as she asked, "Then where is he now?"

"Perhaps, back in town in another disguise looking for one of us," Bryant explained. "As there's no car around, we're probably safe. Still, why don't you wait in the cabin while I scout around the area."

"Teresa."

"Yes."

"I get what you were saying in the truck. I'm as guilty as anyone of thinking everyone needs to adopt my culture."

"Helen, let me ask you this. When you say your culture, does that mean the ways of America and Europe?"

"I guess so."

"Believe me, I know deep down you recognize a person's character, value, and worth are not defined by the color of skin or having a common origin. You have proven that over and over again. We just need to get others to see that too. Until we do, then a lot of the world will be shut off from Nap and me. Now, I'm going to take a hike and see if I can spot anything suspicious in the area. Be on guard."

With that thought hanging in the air, Bryant walked past Meeker and out the door. Once outside, she considered the lay of the land, put her gun in her belt, glanced at her watch, and starting walking east.

There was rugged beauty about this country, but it was also unforgiving in many ways. There were snakes whose bite could kill you and wolves that might see you as prey. There were times when it was impossible to find water and other times a person could get caught in a sudden flash flood. This was a land that could kill a person with both heat and cold. On top of that, if you were caught in a firefight, there were no places to hide. And then there were the ghosts who seemed to walk in this place, their voices howling in the wind.

Bryant's twenty-minute easterly hike revealed nothing but a cold and unforgiving environment. Turning north, she walked along a dry gulch for another twenty minutes. Again, she came up empty. The only sign of life was a coyote. After searching along a ridge, she decided to come up to the cabin from the back side. She figured that would present a complete view of the land. She had gone ten minutes to her west when she saw something along a hillside. A short jog revealed the opening to a small cave. After pulling out her gun, she entered.

To the untrained eye, there was nothing to see. It was just a room about twenty-by-twenty, with a ceiling sixteen feet over the floor. Pulling her flashlight out of her purse offered a bit more illumination. At the back corner someone had painted something on the smooth rock wall. Bryant carefully crossed to the spot to get a better look.

"It's a map," she whispered.

It wasn't one like Whites used—whoever drew this was a native. It showed a trail around what seemed to be three mountains, and at the end were stick figures of hundreds of people. Why would someone put the map here? What purpose did it have? She pulled out a piece of paper and did a rough drawing of the wall art before leaving the cave and continuing to backtrack toward the cabin.

Bryant was five minutes from where she'd started her trek when the sinking sun caught something in the shadow created by a hill. She retrieved her weapon and eased down a rock slope. Parked at the bottom was a dusty 1939 Desoto. She stopped, searched in all directions, and listened for any signs of life. She saw and heard nothing, so she moved closer.

The car had not been deserted here. The tracks leading to the parking spot were fresh. There was even luggage in the back seat. Beside the suitcases were the clothes she'd seen the old man wearing earlier in the day. In the floor was a wig, glasses, and a fake beard.

A chill ran down Bryant's spine. Redman might have been hiding the car when they arrived. While she'd been scouting the area, he could have made his way back to the cabin and found Meeker. This was not the time to walk. She had to run.

CHAPTER 24

THURSDAY, OCTOBER 7, 1943
5:45 P.M.
OUTSIDE ALAMOGORDO, NEW MEXICO

Initially, when left alone at the cabin, Helen Meeker examined and reexamined the crime scene. She found nothing new. As the sun fell lower in the sky, Meeker lit one of the oil lamps and wandered over to the bookshelves. Perhaps she could uncover more about the man who once lived here, if she knew what he read. She began at the top left. In an hour, she flipped through four books on the history of American natives, three on the times and people of the old west, and a couple covering Greek and Roman mythology. A Bible, printed in New York in 1910, was next. A few of the passages were underlined. As she read those, she got the idea Winters was looking for answers. He'd lost his wife and children, and from his notes it seemed he was trying to find something in this book that assured him he would see them again. Intrigued, she took the lamp and Bible back to the chair, pulled the table over, placed the old-fashioned light on the table, and eased down into the place where Big Jim O'Toole had taken his last breath.

Grant Winters's search for Heaven took him from Genesis to Revelation. Meeker was several pages into Matthew when she found something she hadn't expected. Tucked into the pages, as if it was a bookmark, was a hand drawn map. In this drawing, the center point appeared to be the cabin, from there lines led to three different locations. As there were only typographic references, she had no idea how far the locations were from where she sat. But, if Winters had spent so much time creating this map, it would have been important. Written on the bottom of the page was, "Seek and you shall find."

The map had been torn out of a notebook or journal. Was this one of the missing pages from the books Bryant had studied? She was about to dig deeper when a voice caused her blood to run cold.

"Helen Meeker."

She glanced toward the door she'd left open to keep the shack cooler and provide some afternoon sunlight. The man now filling the entry was holding a gun. When he strolled to where the light from the oil lamp caught his face, Meeker recognized the visitor.

"Ruffin Redman," she whispered as she glanced toward the bookshelves. She'd been so intent on studying the books, she'd carelessly left her gun there. There was no way she could get it now.

"So, you know me," he chuckled.

She tried to cover her apprehension with humor. "I've seen a few pictures. They didn't do you justice. You're actually uglier than I expected."

He laughed. "I've been reading about you for years. Even in jeans, a flannel shirt, and a baseball hat, you still look like a movie star."

He was dressed in slacks, a blue shirt, and tan coat. As he stepped toward Meeker, he pulled a rope from his pocket. "Put your hands behind the chair," he barked.

She knew she was being set up, but there was no reason to argue. If she put up a fight, she'd die immediately. If she played nice, Teresa Bryant might have time to return.

"What do you call this game?" Meeker asked as she felt the rope tighten around her chest.

"Life and death," Redman explained.

Once he had her secured, he yanked another piece of rope from his coat and tied her left hand to the chair's arm. He repeated the action on the right side. He was good. His knots were so tight it was cutting off blood flow. Even when she had been in Germany, looking into Hitler's face, she hadn't felt this helpless.

With his target immobilized, Redman circled the chair until he was standing six feet in front of her. His grin proved he was enjoying the moment far more than Meeker wanted.

"I've been following your career since you tied Big Nose over the hood of your yellow Packard."

"That was a lifetime ago," Meeker suggested.

"I always admired your brains and spunk. The last thing I ever wanted to do was kill you."

"Then, let's forget about everything and become pals."

He smiled and nodded. "You're just like I pictured you, tough and funny till the end."

Meeker tried the ropes. There was no give. He'd done a really good job. Of course, he'd had a lot of experience.

"I don't know how you learned about this place," he quipped, "and I'm at a loss as to how you figured I might come here. In truth, I don't care. I just want to offer my thanks for making this easy. I was about to go into town and start observing you to figure out when I could make my move. I appreciate not having to do that."

"We figured out the old man disguise," Meeker announced.

"I have several others you don't know about," he assured her. He leaned close enough she could smell peanut butter on is breath. "Helen, I find you interesting. I've read everything that's been printed about your exploits. Although, I'd love to spend the night visiting with you about them, there isn't time for that."

"Why not? We're the only two here. I'd love to tell you about some of my adventures behind enemy lines in Europe. You know I once came face-to-face with Hitler. He isn't as tall as I thought he was."

"You can quit stalling," Redman advised. "Everyone tries it. They all search for subjects that they can engage me in. It's never worked before, and it won't work now."

Meeker smiled. "My life is far more interesting than your other victims."

"No doubt."

He ran his gun's cold barrel over her cheeks, across her lips, and down her neck. She wondered if this was another part of the ritual or if this element was just for her. Perhaps this was his perverse way of flirting.

"I'd so love to continue this," he whispered, "it makes me feel so alive. But I'm sure you told someone where you were going. So, I need to get well away from here before they come looking. I trust it will be some comfort knowing you will be found."

"I'm celebrating that," Meeker snapped, "I'm sure you can see the joy written all over my face."

"Usually, I have to drug those I kill. That means the newspaper guy didn't even know what hit him. He was out like a light and feeling no pain. This is far better. I'll get to watch you as you consider your last few moments of life."

"You're sick."

"I just enjoy my work," he argued. "My father always told me to find something I loved to do and to stick to it." He laughed. "You know, here's an interesting fact, I've never killed two people in the same place. Imagine that. You're making history. It was right here, in this very spot, when Big Jim O'Toole begged for his life. Are you going to beg?"

"What good would it do?"

"You're a wise woman. And you have enough courage for a marine platoon."

"Before you blow my brains out," Meeker suggested, "why don't you satisfy my curiosity."

"What you do you mean?"

"Tell me why you killed O'Toole."

"That's fair." His green eyes glowed in the lamp light as he shared the story. "He cut a deal with Hitler to get him something the Nazis wanted. Hitler didn't care who he paid, so I decided I'd be the one who would take over the deal."

"What did you sell him?"

"I didn't," Redman admitted. "The deal fell apart because of the bank robbery. But I did the next best thing, I took over a few of O'Toole's business dealings. You know, I was happy to have lived out a modest life with the profits I made from selling Big Jim's legitimate businesses until you gummed things up."

"What did Hitler want?"

"Wants," Redman corrected her, "he's still looking for a way to get it."

"Get what?"

"No one needs to exit this world having all the answers. I figure you need one mystery left unsolved. But I'll assure you of this—if the United States knew about it, they'd want it just as badly as Germany. When I find it, Uncle Sam will pay me what I want and give me a pass for all those I've sent to the next life."

"It's that big?" Meeker asked.

"Even bigger. When I find Horse, I might be able to help reshape the whole planet. Now, I've wasted enough time. Start saying your prayers."

Meeker knew from previous close calls with death that time slowed down when you were near the end. As Redman moved behind her, the world seemed to all but stop. Between each one of his steps, a dozen memories came and went. The first burst of snapshots from the past covered everything from Christmas when she was five to reconnecting with her sister, Alison. Between his next steps, she considered the fact she'd never gotten married or had children. A step later, she was thinking about those she'd lost. Then she felt the gun's barrel at the back of her head and the memories abruptly stopped cascading through her mind.

"Where do you get all the Smith & Wessons?" Meeker asked.

"That's a funny question."

"Just curious."

"Haven't you heard? Curiosity killed the cat." He laughed hard enough, the gun's barrel bumped her head. He finally stopped chuckling and announced, "But here's the story. A decade ago, I ordered a hundred of them at a shop outside of Chicago. I figured that if I used a different gun for each hit, they could never trace any of the bullets to me."

"Didn't you figure the gun dealer might talk?"

Redman laughed, "Sure. I was worried enough about having him connect me to my work that he was the first kill."

"And Hodges was your last," Bryant announced from the open door.

Though Bryant would not have approved of the analogy, Meeker felt as if the cavalry had just arrived. All that was missing was the bugle call.

"Ah, the Indian sidekick," Redman quipped as he fell to one knee behind Meeker. His tone displayed no apprehension, fear, or panic. "I should have known you'd be here too."

"She is not, nor ever has been, my sidekick," Meeker announced. "We are equals."

"Whatever," Redman muttered. "I can assure you of this. If the Indian even flinches, I'll pull this trigger and you'll be dead. So, you little squaw, if you don't let me walk out the door, the Lone Ranger dies. What is more important to you? Helen Meeker's life or having the satisfaction of taking me out?"

Bryant stepped through the door and inside. As she did, Redman moved around Meeker, all the while continuing to crouch and employ her as a shield.

"I think we have a standoff," Redman suggested.

As he moved toward the door, dragging the chair with him, a frustrated Meeker called out, "Shoot the devil, don't worry about me."

Before Bryant could respond, Redman reached his gun around Meeker's head and fired. The bullet whizzed by Bryant's head, struck the metal stove, and ricocheted back toward Meeker, ripping into her arm, causing blood to splash up onto her face. Using the distraction, Redman knocked the chair over and raced through the door.

Through half open eyes, Meeker watched Bryant push off a knee and look outside.

"Go get him," Meeker barked.

"Are you all right?" Bryant demanded.

"No! But go get him anyway."

As Meeker's world suddenly grew dim, Bryant moved quickly out the door. Meeker heard a shot before sliding into a warm dark pool. Then everything disappeared.

Chapter 25

Thursday, October 7, 1943
8:19 p.m.
Outside Alamogordo, New Mexico

Teresa Bryant had done all she could to stop the bleeding, wrapping and rewrapping Helen Meeker's arm with torn pieces of blanket, but it didn't seem to help. Meeker was still unconscious. Worse yet, her pulse was weak and her breathing shallow. She needed medical attention, but that was a long way away, and driving that trail at night would be impossible.

"Someone in there?" a voice called out from outside.

Anyone who was out in this forgotten place at this time of night had to be trouble. Could this day get any worse?

Bryant picked up her gun and crept toward the door and shouted. "You can see the light. So, it should be obvious people are here. Who are you?"

"A man on a walk."

The voice was male, and by the tone and strength, she guessed he was young. At this point, Bryant would have preferred a visit from one of the ghosts who'd been haunting her dreams.

She cracked the door and yelled, "Strange time and place for a walk."

"Maybe," the voice agreed, "but my people have done solitary spiritual walks for years. I haven't had much time for that recently."

Bryant opened the door, stepped to one side where she was hidden from view, and barked, "Come on up here where I can see you."

"Is that an order?"

"Let's call it a strong request. The last visitor we had today shot my friend."

"I'm unarmed," he answered.

"Raise your hands, walk up here, and prove it."

Ten seconds later, a thin man, likely in his twenties, with black hair and piercing eyes approached. He was dressed in dungarees, a pullover red shirt, and buckskin jacket. He didn't wear shoes, instead his feet were covered with moccasins.

"I have no gun," he assured her.

"Then come on in."

The man entered and sized up Bryant before looking at the bed. "She was shot?"

"Yeah, I stopped the bleeding, but she hasn't come to."

"Can I look at her?"

Bryant shrugged. "Are you a medicine man?"

He shook his head and frowned as if he'd been insulted. "No, we don't use those anymore. Though some of the ancient cures still work. I'm an Army medic. I'm on a two-week leave after spending over a year in the Pacific."

"Apache?" Bryant asked.

"Yes. And you?"

"Caddo."

"My name's John Melton."

"Funny name for an Apache."

"My father is White. That's his last name. He's dead, and my mother's family lives on a reservation not far from here. What do they call you?"

"The Whites gave me the name Teresa."

"Okay, we'll start there. Teresa, do you mind if I look at the patient?"

"Please do, but I've got a gun on you, so don't try anything."

"I've had lots of guns not only pointed my way but fired at me too. I'm used to it.

He moved to Meeker and unwrapped the homemade bandage. After studying the wound, he checked the pulse, and finally looked into Meeker's eyes. He then rolled her head to one side and nodded.

"You find something?" Bryant asked.

"Did she hit her head?"

"She might have. She was tied to a chair as the man who was bent on killing us pulled it over onto the floor."

He nodded. "That makes sense. She has a knot the size of an orange on the back of her head. What's her name?"

"Helen Meeker."

His jaw dropped. "Then you're Teresa Bryant. Meeker is your White sidekick."

"That would be funny," Bryant assured him, "if I knew she was going to be all right."

"She's got a concussion. She likely needs to get to town and have an X-ray. But I think she'll be fine. I left my backpack outside—do you mind if I get it?"

"Only if I search it first?"

"Help yourself. I'll stay with Miss Meeker."

Bryant ran outside, picked up the Army-issued backpack, and returned. After opening it and spotting nothing suspicious, she tossed it to Melton. He took it, reached inside, pulled a small jar out, and held it under Meeker's nose. In three breaths, her eyes were open.

"What is that stuff?" Bryant asked.

"Pepper juice."

"Helen," Bryant called out. "Are you okay?"

"My head assures me I'm not," she replied. "Someone has crawled into my brain through my ears and is doing some blasting." She rubbed her face and spotted their guest. "Who's he?"

"That's an Army medic making a house call. He assured me you're going to be fine."

"If this is fine," Meeker quipped, "I don't think I want it." She turned her face toward Bryant and demanded, "Did you get Redman?"

"No," Bryant admitted, "he made a clean break."

"I heard a shot right before I went under."

"He killed one of our tires."

"How long has it been?" Meeker asked.

"About two hours. Now that he knows he's been spotted, Redman's likely headed north. With you among the living, I'll go out and put the spare on the truck. At the first sign of light, we need to drive back to town and have a doctor check you out."

"I'll put the spare on," Melton offered. "You stay here."

"Thanks, my White sidekick might need me."

"Sidekick?" Meeker asked.

"That's what my people call you," Melton laughed. "Now, give me a flashlight, and I'll fix that dead tire."

Bryant followed Melton to the door. "You know the area well?"

"Yeah, as well anyone. I've hiked all over the desert, hills, and mountains."

"Are there burial mounds in this area?"

"No, but there are stories of caves that hold bodies of those who walked this land long before my mother's people. Some call them the ancients. They lived and died without seeing anyone whose ancestors came from Europe."

"Where are those caves?"

"I know of no one who has ever seen one of them. They're hidden. But I've heard stories about them since childhood."

Bryant nodded. "Tell me, do the stories say there is anything of value in those tombs?"

"You mean like gold or silver?"

"Yeah."

"No, the legends are about ghosts not riches. And those stories will keep you awake at night. Rumor has it, if disturbed, those spirits have the ability to kill the living. Now you know why no one is looking for the burial grounds."

"Thanks."

As Melton walked to the truck, Bryant returned to Meeker's side.

"I don't like losing Redman," Meeker announced.

"We're still alive," Bryant offered. "At this point I prefer to live and fight another day."

"You see the Bible on the floor?" Meeker asked. "Get it and open it to Matthew."

"Are you looking for a prayer?" Bryant asked as she crossed the room.

"Just look."

Bryant picked up the book and thumbed through it. When she got to Matthew 7, she saw what Meeker had found.

"Does it mean anything?" Meeker asked.

"It's from one of Winter's journals. I was right, he drew maps. In fact, I saw this map on a cave wall today."

"Where do you think those lines lead?"

"It would have to be tombs," Bryant suggested, "and I'd like to see them. But from what Melton just told me, there's no reason to go until after we get Redman. What's in those places is just more of what's downstairs."

"So, nothing to do with what Hitler wanted?" Meeker asked.

"I doubt it."

CHAPTER 26

SATURDAY, OCTOBER 9, 1943
9:45 P.M.
LIVERPOOL, ENGLAND

Red Cloud was frustrated. The Army continued to refuse to place him in any kind of combat situations. He was obviously being protected because the man the military knew as Ruffin Redman was a hero, even if he didn't want to admit it. One day of menial duties followed by another and another was driving him crazy. The only saving grace was living in a city that didn't see the color of his skin as a detriment. He could walk in the front door of any store, café, or pool hall he wanted. Perhaps, when the war ended, he would just stay in England.

Tonight, the boredom had been relieved for a while as he enjoyed a dinner. Johnny's was a restaurant that offered typical American fare. The menu featured hamburgers, hot dogs, fries, and even apple pie. His former commanding officer, Captain Jim Watson, had invited the private to this feast, and Watson was sitting directly across the table from Red Cloud. To the left and right were the two French underground women they'd rescued on their mission behind enemy lines. As the quartet polished off the last of the dessert, Watson lifted his glass of Coca-Cola and proposed a toast.

"To three people who have done so much to help us win this war."

Red Cloud shook his head and added, "No, to two people, Marie and Sylva, who've spent the last three years gathering information and risking their lives. They are the only real heroes at this table."

"No matter, Ruffin," Watson argued. "None of us would be here without you."

"That is true," Marie echoed, her accent giving her words even more impact.

Marie was in her late twenties, slim, not more than five feet tall with black eyes, dark hair, and perfect, white teeth. Sylva, across the table, was blonde and stood almost five and a half feet in her bare feet. She was blessed with light-blue eyes, a long neck, and a voluptuous figure. Unlike Marie, whose smile was easy, Sylva was almost always serious.

During dinner, Red Cloud wondered who the women had been and what their lives were like before the war. It seemed those questions would remain unanswered because, like him, Marie and Sylva didn't talk about their past. Thus, except for Watson, everyone at the table remained as tightly closed as a bank vault. Watson was a different egg. During the meal, the captain spilled his life story. The other three knew everything from his exploits on a college gridiron to what happened to the trio of women who'd broken the big man's heart. Best of all, each of those stories ended with laughter. When Watson wasn't leading a mission, he was just the kind of guy who made people feel good.

"I hate to turn out the lights on such a lovely evening, don't you, Ruffin?" Watson asked. "But I guess it's time we get these women back to the OSS."

"Yes, sir, I think you're right." Those words were sincere. For a few hours, the worries that had possessed his mind and influenced his every move had been forgotten. He had enjoyed ignoring the war, his true identity, and his concern over the safety of a man called Horse. He'd also found the company of two beautiful women as refreshing as a dip in a mountain stream.

As the quartet exited Johnny's, the air was brisk with a hint of possible rain. There was the smell of the sea and the sounds of a church bell peeling the hour. Thankfully, there were no Nazi bombers or lingering smoke.

"Come on," Watson called out as he pointed to a taxi. "Let's get Marie and Sylva home."

With smiles on their faces, the four piled into the cab. As they settled into their seats, the driver turned and greeted them with a pistol. A second later, another man entered the front seat and closed the door. He was armed in the same fashion.

"No one speaks," the passenger barked as the driver pulled away from the curb.

"If this is a robbery," Watson offered, "you can have everything we have. We won't put up a fight. I'll even give you my watch."

There was no reply to that or any of the dozen questions that followed. The four were completely in the dark, and until that dynamic changed, they were at the mercy of two men who had them outgunned.

It took twenty minutes for the city to give way to the countryside. The rural road they were speeding down was narrow and winding. Then the rain started, making what had been a dark night even more foreboding.

Red Cloud was pinned against the driver's side of the vehicle. The women were between him and Watson. They bounced along for another thirty minutes when the captain finally lost his patience. With no warning, he jumped forward and reached for the passenger's gun. A roar and a flash of fire filled with car, the strong smell of cordite followed, and Watson fell, face down in the floorboard. There was no reason to check his pulse. A man who'd survived a mission behind enemy lines had been killed in an English cab.

The stage was reset by the American's impulsive actions. The kidnapping quickly and unexpectedly evolved into murder. Thus, there was no longer a reason for patience. The smoke was still clearing when Red Cloud lunged like a panther toward the gunman who killed Watson. As the men wrestled, Red Cloud pushed the pistol toward the ceiling with his left hand while using his right to slam the kidnapper's head against the door glass. At that same moment the gun discharged for a second time, sending a slug into the killer's throat, the driver lost his composure, the car jumped off the road and bounced through a field toward a wooded area. A few seconds later, the windshield cracked, and one of the headlights was broken by a bush.

While trying to steer the car back onto the road, the driver shoved his Lugar toward Red Cloud, but he was a second too slow. The American seized the driver's wrist, jerked it backward, gave a twist. When two bones snapped, the gun fell into the front seat. The car was now completely out of control, and the man who had once been driving the vehicle was in far too much pain to notice. There was nothing left to do but hang on and pray.

The Austin ran through a ditch and across a creak before hitting a century-old elm tree. The impact sent the driver through the windshield while Red Cloud flew over the front seat and struck his head on the dash. With darkness rushing into his mind, freeing him from all bounds of the world, he passed out. It was the smell of gasoline and smoke that caused him to wake up in a panic—the car was on fire!

Pulling upright, he crawled back to the rear seat, kicked open a door, and rolled out onto the wet grass. The cold rain helped revive his senses. Turning, he reached into the car, found one of the women's arms, and yanked her out the door. Taking a deep breath, he picked up Sylva and wobbled a dozen steps before dropping her onto the ground.

The flames were spreading, but the fact his face and uniform were now soaked offered some resistance to the heat and flames as he returned to the car, jumped into the smoke, and found Marie. There was no time to be gentle. Grabbing whatever he could, he tugged backwards. Once they were out of the taxi, Red Cloud tossed her over his shoulder, and shuffled away. He was just lowering the woman onto the ground when a car drove up and stopped.

"Did you have an accident?" a middle-aged man yelled as he got out and studied the scene.

"Not exactly," Red Cloud answered.

"Is anyone still in the car?"

"Yeah, but they're dead."

"I'm a doctor, would you like me to examine the women?"

Redman wiped the rain from his forehead and nodded. As the good Samaritan bent to offer aid to Marie and Sylva, a woman stepped out of the vehicle and approached. "William, is there anything I can do?"

"Drive into town, call the police, and get a couple of ambulances. We need to get these women to the hospital."

Satisfied the situation was under control, and he'd done all he could, Red Cloud looked back at the taxi.

The flames were now shooting a dozen feet into the air, scorching the elm tree's lower branches. He felt nothing for the kidnappers, they deserved their fate, but his heart ached for Watson. Somewhere in that car was a good man who deserved to get through this war and go home. Now, that wouldn't happen.

CHAPTER 27

Sunday, October 10, 1943
6:15 a.m.
Liverpool, England

Russell Strickland was roused from bed with the news of the abduction, murder of an American officer, and the resulting deaths of the two men behind the crime. He would've allowed his underlings to sort things out if he hadn't been told Ruffin Redman was involved. That news assured the OSS agent there was something here that had huge implications. When he discovered the American soldier was all right, he arranged to see him at the same location they'd used on their first visit. Once that meeting was set up, Strickland went to the crash scene, examined the evidence, assigned operatives to dig into the kidnappers' past, and then traveled to the hospital to talk to the former underground members and their doctors. By the time he arrived at the house in Liverpool, he possessed a fairly clear snapshot of what had happened and even a partial understanding of why the crime had been committed.

"Private Redman," Strickland announced as he entered the parlor, "or should I call you Red Cloud?"

"In case there is someone listening, I suggest Redman."

The soldier looked exhausted. His eyes were bloodshot, his hair ruffled, his uniform smudged with mud, and he smelled like smoke.

"You've had a rough night," Strickland suggested. "I read the interview you gave MI6. Sounds like you saved the lives of the French women ... again."

"I think Captain Watson deserves most of the credit. He got things rolling. If he hadn't acted, I wouldn't have had the chance."

"Maybe."

"Why did they do it?" Red Cloud asked. "And while we're at it, who were they?"

"Answering those questions is all but impossible. After all, dead men don't talk."

"Believe me, I couldn't take them alive."

"I'm not blaming you. Have a seat, and I'll tell you what I know." Once Red Cloud eased into a chair, Strickland shared what he'd discovered. "The men who pulled the jobs were both Germans. So, they were doing something they had been ordered to do."

"Did I get Captain Watson killed? Were they gunning for me because of what I saw all those years ago? After all, you told me O'Toole was doing something for Hitler."

"Trying to do something," Strickland corrected. "I don't think that had anything to do with it. I just believe you and Watson were at the wrong place at the wrong time. In my view, the targets were the two women. Here's my theory. The Nazis had once trusted the women. In fact, those women had entertained many high-ranking members of the German military and the SS. The Nazis never guessed Marie and Sylva were working for us. So, it makes sense they'd want to kidnap them, get them back to Germany, find out what they'd told us, and then take them back to Paris. And in order to scare other members of the underground, they would have probably been the stars of a public execution."

"And that's it?"

"Maybe not everything. You and Watson might have been a bonus. You two were responsible for getting the women out of France. The Nazis could have wanted to torture you as well. After all, the information you brought home involved everything from plans for a plane to the names of enemy agents. No matter the reason, this wasn't just a kidnapping, it was an act of war."

"That doesn't make Watson's death any easier. The captain was a man of character and courage."

"He thought you were too, which is why he nominated you for the Medal of Honor."

Red Cloud paused and looked at the fireplace. His sad eyes reflected the flames as he spoke. "What if they knew about me and Horse? Hitler wants to know what Horse knows."

"You think?"

"I don't know, but it's worth considering. I don't care about me, but I will not let my friend down."

"As no one knows where Horse is, that shouldn't be a problem."

"Will you protect Marie and Sylva?"

"They won't be able to get to them again," Strickland promised. "Now, there will be someone here to pick you up and take you to a safe location very soon. You see the man at the door. His name is Larson. He works for me. He'll escort you to your ride. Do not go anywhere without him."

"Okay."

Strickland shook Red Cloud's hand and hurried to his car. His driver, one of the top MI6 officers in Liverpool, handed him a note. He nodded.

"Okay, Basil, we need to get back to London. Let's plant a story that everyone in the car was killed in a robbery attempt. Write up a tribute to Watson, Redman, and the two French women. Give it to the media. That's the best way to handle their safety right now. It'll also convince the Nazis they should stop looking for them."

"So, it was about the women?"

"Maybe, but it could have been about getting to the man our solider is trying to protect in the United States. Thus, we must keep Red Cloud—"

"Red Cloud?"

Strickland had made a slip. Now he had to cover it. "Yeah, Red Cloud. That's our code name for Private Redman. We must keep him so far undercover that even our side has problems finding him."

CHAPTER 28

Wednesday. October 13
10:51 A.M.
Santa Fe, New Mexico

Diamond Drug was a full-service store. The diamond pattern was everywhere—from the floor tile to the walls. Even the staff wore uniforms embroidered with diamonds of all colors. Beyond prescriptions, it had cosmetics, candy, nuts, a soda bar featuring a menu ranging from stew to sandwiches to ice cream, and a large selection of household items. While customers walked in the front door for a wild variety of reasons, most didn't rush their shopping experience. They sauntered through the entire store before hitting the checkout counter.

The morning was sunny, the fall temperature already in the high sixties. And while Helen Meeker was sore, bloodied, and bruised, she no longer needed the sling. She almost had full range of motion in her arm. The bump on her head had subsided as well. She sat alone in a back booth of the Diamond Drug store, sipping on a Coke while reading the local newspaper. As she studied the news, she kept an eye on the front door. She hadn't seen her associates in two days, and it was time for a meeting. What they'd been able to uncover would determine the team's next move.

She'd made her way through the headline stories, editorial page, fashion section, and was working a crossword puzzle when Meeker spied Teresa Bryant glancing in through the plate glass windows. Employing her athletic stride while exhibiting a determined focus, Bryant went directly to the entry and quickly made her way to the booth. Meeker didn't have time to put down the puzzle before her partner began shelling out information.

"Redman didn't show up in Alamogordo again. The sheriff has had everyone looking for him. There are pictures of Redman on every store window. I'm pretty sure he couldn't have slipped through those nets. I talked to the FBI office in Little Rock today. My contact assured me there would be posters with Ruffin Redman's picture at every post office in the United States by the end of next week. It seems that going after you put the hounds on the trail. As I literally know what that's like, I bet he's not going to be able to surface anytime soon."

"Is the FBI offering a reward?" Meeker asked.

"Ten grand."

Meeker was disappointed. "That's all?"

"If they knew what we know, it'd be higher. Where do you think he is?"

Meeker put down her pencil and shrugged. "Redman is good at being lost. He successfully stayed hidden for the past seven years. That must mean his pockets are deep, and he has the contacts and resources to remain out of sight, but I think he's like a drunk. When he came out into the open and took a life, he once again got that taste of blood. What has been the focus of the last seven years will drive his need to satisfy that thirst. I found out at the cabin he enjoys what he does—I think he loves it. He wants whatever it is that Horse knows, and he will kill anyone who gets in his way."

"But we don't know what Horse knows or where he is. Did you get the message on what happened in Liverpool?" Bryant asked.

Meeker nodded. "Yeah. And for the moment Red Cloud's safe."

"What do you think? Did they want *him* or the women from the resistance?"

"By the tone of your voice," Meeker suggested, "I sense you have an opinion."

"Strickland communicated with our old friend, Hans Holsclaw, and the Dutch underground leader told him the Nazis wouldn't have kidnapped the women, they would have just assassinated them. Which means Red Cloud was the target, and they wanted him alive to dig for information."

"Hans is smart and well connected," Meeker agreed. "But my gut tells me it's just a hunch."

"It's not a long shot," Bryant argued. "They found an encrypted communication at the Germans' flat. They traced that message back to an MI6 operative. When deciphered, it gave them a location on Red Cloud not the women. They were sent to Johnny's Diner to kidnap our guy."

"So, a double agent in MI6?"

"Yeah."

"I have to believe he's off the job now."

Bryant smiled, "Actually, no. He's completely unaware they're onto him. They're going to use him to feed false information to the Nazis on the future invasion of Europe. The first lie they gave him was a bogus address for where Red Cloud is being held."

If Red Cloud would just spill what he knew, there would be a good chance to get this mess cleared up. But there was no use wishing for that. It was clear that until Redman was dead, Red Cloud would remain mute. In frustration, Meeker looked back at the crossword. She studied the empty boxes before asking, "What's an eleven-letter word for an emotion when you are unable to solve a problem?"

"What are you talking about, and what does it have to do with our case?"

"I'm working a crossword. Now, listen up, I need an eleven-letter word that describes your emotions when you're unable to solve a problem."

"Frustration."

Meeker smiled, picked up the pencil, and filled the spaces. "Thanks."

Getting the puzzle a bit closer to completion was at least something to celebrate, but having that word perfectly define her own emotions was a bummer. By all rights, she should be dead. And though she was still among the living, there was a target on her back. On top of that, she was dealing with the murder of a man she liked. So, her frustration was accompanied by a large dose of guilt. At this point, she hated her life.

Looking up from the puzzle, Meeker observed, "The last member of our team has arrived. Maybe Nap has a clue as to where Redman is hiding."

Taking the cue, Bryant moved to one side of the booth to give Lancelot room. Once he'd slid in, Meeker took charge.

"Please tell me you have something."

"I've dug up a few things that will interest you. Redman probably arrived in Santa Fe two days ago. That's when more than fifteen thousand was withdrawn from his account."

"Did he pick it up?" Meeker asked.

"No, the instructions for the withdrawal, telegraphed to Savings and Trust from the Chicago National Bank, were very specific. The amount, all in hundred dollar bills, was to be placed in shipping carton and sent to Jessica Roberts at PO Box 1793 in Santa Fe. Miss Roberts was to prove her identity and sign for the shipment."

"So," Meeker asked. "Do we know if she has picked it up?"

"A postal clerk told me," Lancelot explained, "an older woman showed up yesterday, produced two forms of identification, and took charge of the package. He said the lady was a bit over five-six, heavyset, dressed in dark clothes, and wore a large hat. He could see enough of her face to offer the following opinion—'She was ugly.'"

"So, another disguise."

"That's my guess," Lancelot quipped. "By the way, that same woman took a taxi to the train station. It took me a couple of hours of digging, but I discovered she bought a ticket on a westbound train that might take him as far as Los Angeles."

Meeker frowned. If Redman was a master of disguise, which it seemed he was, he was going to be very difficult to track. If the team couldn't follow him, perhaps they could draw him out. What they needed was the right bait. She leaned closer to Lancelot and Bryant.

"Redman's too smart to go after me again, at least not until things cool off. But thanks to our meeting, he's fully aware we know he cut himself in on the deal with Hitler. That means the clock is ticking, and he can no longer be patient. He will be under pressure to get possession of whatever it is the Nazis want."

"But who is Redman working for?" Bryant asked. "Is it still Hitler, or is there another party?"

Lancelot shrugged, "My guess is he's working for himself. If he gets his hands on whatever it is that's so valuable, he'll sell to the highest bidder."

"Why do you think that?" Meeker asked.

"Back in thirty-six, he told his family he'd found something that was going to make him rich. To me that means Horse has to be the key. If he wasn't, Redman would already have it and be swimming in money. I don't think he can find what he needs without Horse."

"What could a man whose mind was damaged by a severe beating and has problems communicating know what Hitler would be interested in?" Bryant asked. "I've thought a lot about that over the past few days, and I can't come up with anything that ties to the war."

"Besides," Meeker added, "There wasn't a war in 1936. Hitler wouldn't invade Poland for three more years."

"We aren't going to answer that question without Horse," Lancelot said. "Do we even know if he's still alive?"

"He's alive," Bryant assured the team. "If he weren't, Red Cloud would take the medal. As long as Red Cloud is protecting Horse, we know he's breathing."

Meeker looked at Bryant. "Do you still believe we need to call this off to protect Horse?"

"No, I don't. We're all in too deep. And with what has happened to Red Cloud in the past few days—"

"What was that?" a surprised Lancelot asked.

"The Nazis tried to kidnap him," Meeker explained. "Now, Teresa, finish what you were saying."

"We have to find Horse and protect him. I have a theory on where he is."

"We don't have to know where he is to protect him," Meeker suggested.

"What?" Bryant whispered. "I don't understand what you're saying."

"Let's pretend we have him."

"But we don't," Lancelot quipped.

"I know," Meeker announced with a smile, "but Redman doesn't know that. What if we announce we have Horse under protective custody? We don't mention anything about Hitler, we simply say we're hiding him because he witnessed O'Toole's murder and will be testifying before a grand jury in Chicago."

"Once again," Bryant said. "We don't have him."

"Teresa, we were in the cabin, which was the location of the hit. We ran into Redman there. Our story is we were investigating a crime scene we only knew about because of Horse sharing the location with us."

Lancelot chimed in. "So, we let Redman believe we've already found Horse, and he told you how to get to where O'Toole was killed."

Meeker smiled. "Doesn't that make sense? I think Redman would buy that. And if he thought we were hiding Horse in Chicago, he'd come back there to kill us and get Horse." She grinned. "Let's go back to the Windy City and make ourselves targets. I'm tired of being hunted. It's time we became the hunters."

"If we're the targets, I don't see how we can be the hunters. I think we'd still be classified as the hunted."

Meeker grinned. "Don't worry, I've got a plan."

CHAPTER 29

SUNDAY, OCTOBER 17
1:15 P.M.
LOS ANGELES, CALIFORNIA

Chief Detective Christopher Grimes of the Los Angeles homicide department had been having a quiet day, and he really liked quiet days. Quiet days gave him the chance to pretend that people had somehow matured and were solving their differences in civilized ways. Leaning back in his chair, he picked up an issue of *True Detective* and was about to begin a story called the "Santa Barbara Slasher" when his phone rang.

"Grimes."

"We have a really unusual murder in Hollywood Hills."

"Get the boys working on it, and I'll get over there. What's the address?"

"Johnson has it and is waiting for you at your car."

"Thanks."

Grimes hated to go to a crime scene blind, but that's where he was. He had no information on the victim, nor the method used in punching the ticket to the afterlife. He just knew it was unusual. What did that mean?

The drive to Hollywood Hills was uneventful. When Grimes and his partner arrived at the scene, he sadly shook his head. This was not the kind of street where people got murdered. Kids were playing in yards, people were coming home from church, and there was not a piece of trash or blowing newspaper anywhere. Stepping out of the 1940 Ford, he took a deep breath and studied an open front door. He knew as soon as he walked through the entry the peace he was witnessing would dissolve, and he didn't want to give it up that easily. He wanted to feel like he had in the office.

"The body's in the house," a lanky patrolman announced.

"You ready, Chris?" Andy Johnson asked.

He looked at his thirty-year-old, blue-eyed partner. "No. In truth, I just don't have the stomach for it today."

Grimes looked back to the patrolman. "What's your name?"

"Williams. I was the first on the scene."

"Tell me what to expect."

"It's a mess."

"Why don't you give me some details? Were they any witnesses?"

"No, no one heard a shot, and no one saw anyone enter or leave."

Grimes studied the homes on each side of the murder scene. The windows were open. That meant the killer must have used a silencer. He glanced back at Williams. "Who called it in?"

"The maid. She usually cleans on Sunday. She told us that's the day when no one is home. It seems the victim, a guy named Taylor Owen, has a beach house in Malibu and always leaves on Saturday afternoon to go there."

The house was one a middle-class family couldn't afford, so Owen had to have money, but where did it come from? The answer to that question might be the key to the whole case.

"What does this Owen do for a living?" Grimes asked.

"The maid didn't know and neither did the neighbors. From interviews I did, he didn't go to an office, so maybe he got his money the old fashion way—inherited it."

"Williams," Grimes asked, "how long had the guy lived here?"

"At least five years."

"What's your gut telling you?" Johnson asked.

"That I'm hungry," Grimes quipped.

The detective looked up and down the street one last time before strolling up the walk leading to the open front door. Voices led him through the foyer to the main living area. In the middle of that room was a wooden captain's chair. The man sitting there was dressed casually in sport shirt and dark slacks. He had been strapped to the seat by ropes. His chin was resting on his chest. As there was blood splatter on the floor in front of him, the single gunshot had come from behind. Grimes walked around the victim as four other investigators looked for evidence. The policemen seemed frustrated and that was never a good sign.

"In all of my twenty-two years on the force," gray-headed Walter Banyon observed, "I've never seen anything like this. This was brutal. The medical examiner just left and said this guy was beaten before he was finished off."

"When did Doc Simpson say he died?" Grimes asked.

"Yesterday afternoon."

"Everyone on this block would have been home," Grimes noted, "so, why didn't someone hear what was happening?"

"The guy next door said the radio was blasting away," Banyon volunteered.

Grimes nodded. "Williams told me Owen had no apparent job. Did you find out anything else on his background?"

"I made some calls. He used to be a banker back in New Mexico before moving here."

"Let me guess," Grimes offered, "he was employed at Savings and Trust in Santa Fe."

The sergeant raised his eyebrows. "How did you know that?"

"Do you remember Big Jim O'Toole?"

"Sure, what cop doesn't? Besides there's been a lot of press covering what happened to him in Alamogordo."

After taking another stroll around the victim, Grimes shared some old information. "About a decade ago, I had a case concerning O'Toole. I was trying to dig up something I could arrest him on. I discovered he owned that bank."

Grimes turned away from the body and walked outside. Banyon followed him step for step. When they were standing in the front yard, the sergeant repeated his question.

"How did you tie that to this mess?"

While continuing to look at the line of police vehicles parked on the curb, Grimes explained. "Do you remember the description of how O'Toole died?"

Banyon snapped his fingers. "Yeah, just like this guy."

"There were two hits I worked a decade ago. One was in 1932, and the next one a year later. We found the first victim in a hotel room and the second in a warehouse. They were both strapped to chairs." He turned to Banyon. "Did you find a Smith & Wesson 45 beside the chair?"

"Already bagged it for evidence."

"It happened the same way all those years ago too. It's the way a hitman named Redman worked. He settled scores for O'Toole. The guy considered himself an artist, and each kill became a portrait of death. But there was never a witness, never a fingerprint, nothing to tie him to the job. Even though we knew who did it, we couldn't prove anything. No police department anywhere ever has. Essentially, he mocked us."

"So, he never messed up?" Banyon asked.

"No, but for the past seven years, there had been no more hits. So, we thought he was either dead or retired. Last week, I got an alert from a friend in Denver there had been a murder fitting Redman's pattern. Some small-time hood had been extinguished while tied to a chair and there was a forty-five left behind. And now this. Redman has resurfaced, and it must be tied to the stories of him killing O'Toole."

"Why this guy?"

"Owen must have known something."

Banyon looked back toward the house. "I'm guessing we won't be finding out what he knew."

Grimes nodded. "It's a little late for that." The detective studied a gaggle of six reporters standing out by his car. It was time to give them their story. "Walter, tell the writers every detail but one. Don't mention the name of Ruffin Redman."

"Yes, sir."

Grimes walked back to his Ford and slid behind the wheel. As he drove away, the detective glanced into his rearview mirror. Banyon had walked over to the reporters and was sharing the story. The news of this murder would be on the streets in a few hours. Before that, Grimes was going to track down an old friend, a man the Los Angeles police force called the Black Knight. Helen Meeker's name had been all over the stories about O'Toole's body being found. She would want to know Redman was in Los Angeles and very much alive. And the Black Knight, Napoleon Lancelot, worked with Meeker.

CHAPTER 30

Monday, October 18, 1943
2:55 p.m.
Chicago, Illinois

Helen Meeker was not surprised by a story she found on page seven in the *Tribune*. Napoleon Lancelot had given her the details the night before. The fact Owen was dead meant Redman had been busy cleaning up loose ends. As always, the hits in Los Angeles and Alamogordo had been clean—there was nothing tying him to the murders. But he'd fouled up trying to kill her.

As she sat in the team's 13th floor offices at the Lincoln Hotel, she tapped a pencil on her desk. She honestly didn't figure Redman would come after her again. His targets were always people who were easy to isolate. She had a team, and he'd tasted a bit of the firepower of that team. But he also couldn't allow her or Teresa Bryant to live. They were the witnesses he had avoided in all his past hits. So, he was caught in a quandary. He either had to get out of the country or make a move. With Owen's execution, she was sure Redman had chosen to stay, even a few scores, and make another attempt to find Horse. Whatever it was

Horse knew had to be worth a fortune to illicit that kind of behavior from a man who had always been so careful.

A door opening caused Meeker to look up. Because she didn't hear any footsteps on the wooden floor, she knew it had to be Bryant. That woman's ability to walk without making any sound was uncanny.

"Look at this," Bryant announced as she rounded the corner. She tossed a piece of paper on Meeker's desk and waited for a response.

The photo of Redman on the wanted poster might have been more than a decade old, but people who saw him would still recognize the hitman. Having those posters, complete with the reward of ten thousand dollars, would add to the pressure she wanted. For the first time in two decades, Redman was not in control.

"Where do you think he's headed now?" Bryant asked.

"Where he thinks he's going is not important," Meeker suggested, "in one hour, when I have my press conference, I figure his plans will change. He'll be coming to Chicago."

"We aren't going to use a double for Horse?"

"No. Nap talked me out of it. The only photo we have of Horse is the one Hodges took. There is no detail in that shot at all. Redman has been close to the guy, he knows what he looks like, so using a stand-in wouldn't fool him. Instead, we pretend we are keeping him out of sight. I've got a warehouse we can use. The office has room for a bed, chairs, and anything else we might need. The three of us will work eight-hour shifts staying in that room. We will have food delivered, a patrolman will make regular walks around the outside of the building, and there are times we'll take a panel truck to the courthouse to convince anyone who is watching that Horse is testifying before a grand jury."

"The press won't know about the warehouse?" Bryant asked.

"No, we can't make it easy. The newspapers and radio reports will spell out the witness to the O'Toole murder is being kept in an undisclosed location. To fully sell this sting, we need Redman to have to work hard to find out where we are supposedly hiding the man he needs to have. His lust for getting what he thinks Horse has, or at least knows the location of, makes the reward greater than the risk. So, I'm banking on Redman stepping outside his comfort zone."

Meeker began tapping the pencil and continued to air her thoughts. "If Hitler wants whatever it is, then the United States will as well. So, as far as Redman is concerned, Horse is useful in many different ways. He's a witness to a murder who needs to be silenced, but if Redman can get the information he needs from Horse, that also gives him a get-out-of-jail-free card. My gut tells me Uncle Sam would trade a pardon and some cash to keep whatever Hitler wants out of the Nazis' hands. When we dangle the bait, Redman will bite. I'll bet my life on it."

"Okay," Bryant suggested as she eased into her desk chair, "but I need to warn you about something. You see a goal and then try to get to it as fast as possible."

"Yeah, I like to move, what does that have to do with this?"

"Helen, Redman won't hurry. He's not impulsive. He'll scout things out, take his time, and pick a moment when he has the advantage. And the longer this drags out, the better chance he has of finding the moment when we let down our guard."

Meeker studied Bryant. She really hated it when her friend was right. Redman would play this differently than most other people. After all, he'd waited seven years to find Horse. Even with the wanted posters all over the country, he wouldn't panic. He'd proven that in Winters's cabin. He'd given up what he wanted, which was to kill her, and found a way to get out with his skin. He was going to wait until the odds were in his favor. How long would that take?

"Teresa, we have to make it look real, and if it takes weeks or months, we have to keep it up."

Bryant frowned. "If this really was a grand jury, Horse wouldn't be testifying for months. For it to look real, it can only go for a certain amount of time. If Redman doesn't bite in a couple of weeks, we have to find another tactic."

"Okay. I get that. But what about the rest of the plan?"

"One patrolman is not enough," Bryant stated. "When I first heard your idea, I figured we'd be using as many resources as possible."

"Redman can spot a cop a mile away. The single patrolman will make sense to him. You add anyone else to the mix, and he will sniff out a trap."

The door opened again. This time Napoleon Lancelot entered. His footsteps were anything but silent.

"Well, ladies, things are set on my end. I've found out Redman still owns the family home and keeps the utilities paid. He even uses it from time to time when he comes to Chicago. If he rolls into town, he might check in there. I've assigned three operatives to watch the place."

"That's a good idea," Meeker agreed. "I noted you said if he comes to town. You don't think he will take the bait?"

Lancelot shook his head. "My gut says no."

"Why?"

"Redman's not a gambler. He plays his cards very carefully. He doesn't take risks. He fell into you and opted to take you out, but that's not the way he normally works. I'm sure he knows now he should have scouted out the cabin a bit better. If he'd seen Teresa, he would have waited."

"Your point?" Meeker demanded.

"My point is this. He knows us. He has, no doubt, studied our backgrounds."

Meeker nodded. "When he had me in the cabin, he admitted he'd followed my career."

Lancelot nodded and continued. "Redman might feel he could take on any of us one at a time, but I don't think he has the stomach to take all of us on at once. One gun against three is not his style."

If Lancelot was right, then the press conference Meeker was about to hold was needless. Yet, while Lancelot was focusing on Redman's intelligence, she was figuring on the killer's greed. He'd been waiting since 1936 to get his hands on whatever it was Horse knew. During that time, he'd never been able to find Horse. Meeker was betting if she gave Redman a location, he'd throw caution to the wind. The clock was ticking, and the FBI had reason to arrest him now. He could no longer afford to be patient.

She glanced at her watch. It was time to meet the press. By tomorrow morning, Redman would have the opportunity to read the news and decide if he wanted to take on a team that no one had ever brought down.

CHAPTER 31

Tuesday, October 19, 1943
8:15 a.m.
Somewhere in Nevada

"Your newspaper, sir."

Ruffin Redman, wearing a black wig, fake mustache, and an Edwardian suit, sat in the dining car of the Frisco Limited Flyer heading east through Nevada. He'd just finished a breakfast of eggs, bacon, and toast and was sipping on coffee while watching the barren desert fly by his window.

"Thank you, porter," Redman announced as he took a copy of the *Los Angeles Times*. He scanned the pages for the world news, read a bit about the war front in Italy, and noted a story from Chicago. He quickly digested the wire report before setting the paper to one side. Helen Meeker had done something he hadn't been able to do in seven years, she'd found Horse. Redman's mouth involuntarily formed a smile. The man he needed was alive and in the Windy City, a place he knew well. Yet, the news didn't open a door, it closed one. By finding Horse, Meeker was adding another chapter to her amazing career. Redman was on the run with wanted posters going up across the country, and though Meeker was the reason he was feeling the heat, he admired her. She had done something no one else could do. And based on what he'd learned in the past, she'd done the impossible a few other times as well. She'd even forced him to clean up a few loose ends and rebook a trip to South America. That journey would be a one-way passage. He would never come home again. But if he had to be beaten in a perverse way by anyone, he was glad it was her.

"You seem happy," a middle-aged man on the other side of the table observed. "Good news?"

"Yes," Redman admitted, employing a British accent, "someone I've been looking for has been found."

"A relative?"

"No, just an old acquaintance. The last time I saw the chap was years ago. I honestly thought he might be dead. But thankfully, the bloke is very much alive."

"He must mean a lot to you."

"At one time, he did."

The other man extended a hand. "I'm Jeff Reed. I work for the railroad as an inspector."

"Mr. Reed, I'm Charles Billingham. As you can tell, I'm not from this country."

"I'm guessing England. What business are you in, Mr. Billingham?"

Redman smiled, took another sip of coffee before announcing, "The business of life."

"Insurance?"

"In a way, yes. I deal with people who are on the edge between life and death. There are times I ease the transition from one place to another."

"That sounds like a doctor."

"Yes, you could call me a surgeon. At the moment, however, I'm just someone who's visiting your country in order to learn some new techniques."

Reed nodded. "There is no arguing that war's a horrible thing, but one of the results of combat injuries is the rapid advancement in medicine."

"So true. Just the other day I was with a woman I was sure had only a few minutes to live, and thanks to a timely intervention, she was given a second chance at life. She's making the most of it too."

"It must be gratifying to have that kind of power in your hands."

"It is," Redman assured him, "but, as a railroad inspector, you're also in the business of life and death. So, there's not that much difference between us."

"The man you found out who is alive," Reed asked, while pointing to the newspaper, "will you be seeing him?"

"I'd like to. You can't imagine how much I want to visit with him. We have a great deal to discuss, but I need to go to South America. When you work alone, you don't have as many options are others do."

"Will you be leaving soon?" Reed asked as he finished his coffee.

"As soon as I can. In this case, time is not my friend."

"Mr. Billingham, I'm fortunate. I have a team around me. When the job is too big for me, or I can't be in a certain place, I make a call. Soon, I have five sets of hands rather than just my own."

The porter approached the table, leaned over, and spoke to Reed. "Sir, you're needed in the baggage car. There's a postal inspector who wants to talk to you."

"Thank you," a gracious Reed replied before turning his attention to Redman. "I've enjoyed our visit. I hope you do manage to get to see the person you thought was dead. I'm sure you would have so much to talk about."

"I'm sure we would. It was a pleasure meeting you, Mr. Reed."

This unexpected meeting had been fortuitous. Without knowing it, the inspector had provided a possible answer to a puzzle Redman believed had no solution. While he was sure he couldn't take on Meeker and her people by himself, he wasn't going to risk doing that—even if it meant giving up a fortune. But perhaps he didn't have to. He knew other men in his business. While he'd always respected their work, he'd always seen them as competitors. At least until now. The visit with Reed had given him a new perspective. Perhaps a few professional killers might be interested in joining forces with him. The price would be high. They'd want a piece of the action. But if he could get Horse, and if that man would talk, then the shared profits would be huge.

Redman looked around until he spotted the porter and waved at him. A few moments later, the congenial man was by his side.

"Tell me, my good chap. Do we have a stop coming up? One that would be long enough for me to send a few telegrams?"

"Las Vegas is just ahead. We'll be there about twenty minutes."

"Thanks."

As he once again turned his attention to the desert landscape, Redman hatched a plan. He needed three other men. Tom Sears in New York always used bombs. He was clean, precise, closed mouth, and shrewd. People went through Wally Knuckel, a bartender at Bartles Pub, to visit with Sears.

J.J. Hooten out of Miami would be a perfect choice. His weapon of choice was an ice pick. He had the strength of a gorilla and had no vices. When not on the job, he dressed and presented himself as a preacher, quoting Scripture and singing hymns. Willie McGarron was the man who arranged for meetings with Hooten, and Redman knew him well.

Nic Ellis might be the person he needed to fill out the team. At fifty-five, Ellis was the old man in the profession. He most often used a scarf to stop his marks from breathing. No hitman in the world attracted so little attention. A woman named Nancy Hicks was the key to getting to him.

If none of those three were interested, there was always Santo Sappelli. He had no set methods, he just killed using whatever seemed the best at moment. Sappelli was a big, ugly, rude man who wore loud suits. He never went anywhere without a cigar in his mouth. He never lit it, just chewed on it. Redman didn't want to include this brute, but there were times when you had to do a few things you didn't like. So, he'd send him a wire as well.

"Las Vegas," the porter called out. "Feel free to get out and stretch as we'll be here for about twenty minutes."

It was time to send the telegrams. But where should those who were interested send the reply? Redman had seen the FBI posters. He needed to be somewhere he wouldn't be noticed. St. Louis was a city he knew well, but few there knew him. He could stay at the Park Hotel and continue his disguise as Billingham. When he got the team members he needed, he would then arrange a meeting in downstate Illinois. The objective was clear. He needed Horse alive, and he wanted Meeker, Bryant, and Lancelot dead. While he wouldn't even attempt that by himself, with a team of professional killers, he now felt confident the odds of reining in Horse were in his favor.

CHAPTER 32

WEDNESDAY, OCTOBER 27, 1943
12:05 A.M.
CHICAGO, ILLINOIS

It had been over a week, and nothing had happened. If Redman had come to Chicago, he hadn't been spotted. He hadn't visited his family home, hadn't been seen at any of the train stations or airports, and there were no signs of him at any of the hotels. During that time, Helen Meeker kept a close eye out each time she left her hotel to take her shift at the warehouse. She spotted no one. The bait she thought irresistible was evidently unappealing. Her other team members had experienced the same results. Still, the game continued.

Meeker, Bryant, and Lancelot all took different routes each day to come to the warehouse to protect their imaginary witness. They each pretended to be extremely careful while all the time leaving subtle clues for Redman. If he were in the Windy City, he was staying deep undercover.

Each time Meeker drove to the warehouse to replace Bryant, she spoke to whichever patrolman was on duty that day. They too had seen nothing. Just as Bryant had predicted, Redman was not in any hurry. Meeker had to acknowledge, if he did come, it wouldn't be forced. He would arrive only when he felt fully prepared. Just how long would that be?

After giving the assigned knock, she opened the warehouse door, strolled thirty feet across the main room, and walked up the stairs to the office. Bryant was there, sitting in a chair, her gun in her right hand. If she had anything on her mind, it wasn't revealed. Other than blinking, she showed no signs of life.

"All the comforts of home," Meeker quipped as she opened a small refrigerator. After pulling out a bottle of Coca-Cola, she popped the cap, took a sip, and wandered over to a worn-out couch. Its cracked and faded green leather cushions matched her mood.

"I thought sure this would work," Meeker sighed.

"Don't give up yet," Bryant stoically suggested. "As long as Redman thinks the grand jury is meeting, he can wait. He might think after an indictment is handed down, Horse will be on his own. If I were him, that's when I would make my move."

"I thought you believed White men aren't that patient," Meeker argued.

"Most aren't, but Redman has been waiting for seven years. A few more weeks might not matter to him."

A sudden and loud clang, coming from the warehouse floor, caused both women to leap to their feet. Maybe Redman wasn't as patient as Bryant believed.

"Someone's in the building," Meeker whispered. "Maybe, I gave up too soon."

To a casual visitor, the staircase would seem to be the only entrance to the office. But there was a closet in a small storage room hiding a ladder leading to another closet on the first floor.

"You stay here," Meeker whispered. "I'll take the ladder." She glanced over at the dummy that appeared to be sleeping in a bunk. "Make sure our friend is comfortable."

"Helen, if this is Redman, he's not going to be easy to find. There's a lot of places to hide in the warehouse. I think he's trying to lure one of us out."

"If it's Redman, he knows we're here. He was watching until he could get both of us at the same place. It's the perfect time for his move. Stay in the shadows."

Meeker nodded, hurried to the closet, scurried down the ladder, took a deep breath, and with gun in hand opened the door. Except for three exit lights, the building was dark. She remained still for a while, allowing her eyes to adjust to the lack of illumination. There were five rows of shelves. Once upon a time, they were used to store automotive and truck tires. Though now empty, the way the old wooden shelves were constructed allowed her to see about thirty percent of the floor. So almost three quarters of the building could be hiding a killer. After taking a deep breath, she glanced toward the office. She detected an all but hidden Bryant looking at the warehouse through a partially opened shade. Confident she was being covered, Meeker began to cautiously move down the first row. It was a hundred and fifty feet to the back wall, and with each step, she paused and peered through the shelves to the next aisle. Ten minutes later, she was at the back wall and had found nothing. The next three silent strolls up and down the aisles killed thirty more minutes and produced the same result. Now, it was time for the last one.

Redman had to be hiding somewhere along this row. He could see just as well as she could, but he had the advantage because he wouldn't be moving. If she saw or heard anything, she had to be ready to dive for cover. She also had to hope that Bryant was ready to lay down fire when trouble began.

After steadying her nerves, Meeker stepped around the corner. She caught movement in the deep shadows, and before she could aim her Colt, he rushed forward, knocking Meeker against the shelves. She hit so hard that for a moment she lost her ability to breathe. Awkwardly pushing away from the shelf, while attempting to catch her breath, she shook her head and searched the darkness. Though she couldn't see him, she heard someone running back toward the entry. Why was he running? Why hadn't he shot? He had had her right where he wanted her.

"Teresa," Meeker screamed, "he's coming your way."

As Meeker jogged forward, she kept searching for her attacker. Maybe she'd caused him to panic, maybe he'd dropped his weapon, maybe he was regrouping, or maybe he decided the odds were too long, and he had to retreat. No matter the reason, he surely had a gun out and was ready to fire when he caught her in the glow of an exit lamp. Was this his plan all along, to lure her into a trap where he had an easy kill? Or maybe he was setting things in motion to get Bryant on the warehouse floor as well. If he got them to bunch up, it would so much easier to punch both their tickets. There were too many questions, too much was unknown, and that always led to doubt. Slowing to a stop, she rethought the situation. There was one exit that was usable. The other two were padlocked from the outside. So, there was only a single route of escape. Turning, she raced to the back wall, ran over to the first row, and jogged toward the exit. If she moved quickly enough, she might beat him there.

With her heart in her throat and her Colt in her hand, Meeker stopped at the end of the shelves, and deliberately peaked around the corner. She fully expected to see Ruffin

Redman's Smith & Wesson aimed at her head. Instead, there was a man, face down on the concrete floor, his arms spread, and in the middle of his neck was Bryant's size seven black pump.

"I hope you don't mind I took care of the pest before you got here," Bryant announced as she added pressure with her shoe. "Would you turn on the lights, so we can get a better look at him?"

How had Bryant gotten to the door without making any noise? How had she taken the guy down so quietly?

A bit disappointed the glory hadn't been hers, Meeker walked over to the door, flipped the switch, and glanced back at the intruder. It wasn't Redman. This guy was thin, almost six feet tall, and dressed in dirty, worn clothing. His blond hair hadn't been cut in months, and the bottom on his shoes showed three holes.

"Shall I let him up?" Bryant asked.

"Sure."

As Bryant pulled her foot from the uninvited guest's neck, he pushed off the floor. His cheeks were hollow, his dark eyes bloodshot, and he needed a shave.

"Who are you?" Meeker demanded.

"Ben Krause."

"And just who is Ben Krause, and what are you doing here?"

He scratched the floor with his right shoe and shrugged. "I'm just a guy who needed a place to flop. I thought no one would care if I spent the night here. Except for the cat that knocked over the oil can, I thought I was alone."

Meeker glanced over to Bryant and asked, "Did you know we have a cat?"

"I've been feeding it," Bryant admitted. "I named him Yellow."

"That's original."

"Well, when you consider the cat is gray, I think it is."

Meeker raised her eyebrows before turning back to the man. "What do you do? Where are you from? How do you know Ruffin Redman?"

"Who?"

"Ruffin Redman."

"Never heard of him."

Bryant eased her weapon back into her pocket, walked over to a wooden crate, and casually sat down. She obviously believed this guy was not dangerous. Meeker wasn't so sure and kept her Colt ready. It was time to get to know Ben Krause a bit better.

"Okay, Ben. Looks like you don't have a job. Am I right? And your accent has a twang. I'm guessing you aren't a native of Chicago."

"Texas."

"With a war raging and jobs easy to find, why aren't you working?"

"I had a job," Adams offered, "but it didn't work out."

"And what was that?"

"I was in the Navy."

Meeker suggested, "I'm guessing you're AWOL."

"Yes, ma'am."

"How long you been on the run?" Meeker demanded.

"About six weeks."

"Why?"

"I'm scared. I miss home. I don't want to die."

Meeker could understand his thinking. How many times had she wanted to run away and hide since the war started? In her case, though, there were far more times than she cared to remember. It was only her sense of duty that had kept from turning tail.

"Okay, Ben," Bryant cut in, "look at yourself. You're hungry, dirty, and sharing quarters with rats. Which is probably why Yellow's here. You have no friends. You can't go home because the people there would be ashamed of you."

"But—"

"No," she continued, "I'm not saying you're a horrible person, I'm just pointing out that when we run from what scares us, we can't stop running. And our lives just get more miserable with each passing day. Are your folks alive?"

"Yes."

"Do you want to see them again? Do you want them to be proud of you?"

"Sure."

"The life you're living—if you call this living—is one that keeps you in the shadows. There's no hope to be found in the darkness. It's time you admit to the Navy you were scared, and you were wrong. You'll have to pay for this, but you still have time to turn things around, get right with yourself and your country, and be someone your folks are proud of."

"But I don't want to die!" he cried.

Bryant pushed off the crate and waved her hand toward the streets outside the warehouse. "The odds of you dying in the world you're living in now are far greater than dying in war. This area is filled with human rodents who will stab or shoot you if you have ten dollars. You won't survive a year in the shadows."

"You can't make me go back," Krause argued.

"Actually," Meeker announced, "we can. We work for the government. But, as my associate pointed out, it's really your choice. You're not equipped to survive in this world, but in the Navy, you'd at least be given the tools and training, along with a team supporting you, that would offer you the things you need to have a chance to come out of this alive." Meeker paused, smiled, lowered her weapon, and asked, "Were you in basic at Great Lakes when you ran away?"

"Yeah."

"Even in the guard house," Bryant pointed out, "you'd be well fed and clean. Doesn't that sound better than being here and starving?"

"Yeah, I guess so."

Bryant nodded, moved to the door, and left.

"Where's she going?" Krause asked.

"To find you a ride," Meeker explained. "Why don't you sit on the box and wait."

He didn't have to wait long. Bryant was as efficient as ever. When she returned, the assigned patrolman was by her side.

"Dale, this is the man who seems to have gotten lost from Great Lakes. Do you think you could help him get back there?"

"Sure. What's your name?"

"Ben Krause."

"I'm Dale Crawford. You look like you could use a bite to eat. I've got a car outside—we'll get you a meal as we wait for the MPs to take you home."

Krause nodded and walked to the officer. Just before he stepped outside, he looked back and admitted, "I'm still scared."

Meeker laughed. "The way you drove me into those shelves, I have no doubt you can take care of yourself."

"Sorry, ma'am."

Meeker watched Crawford escort Krause out of the building before turning toward Bryant. "Is he who he says he is?"

"If you're asking if I think he was sent to spy on us by Redman, then my answer is no. He's a kid who doesn't want to die. There are millions of others just like him. Now, I really need to head back to the hotel and grab some sleep. Are you going to be all right here by yourself?"

"Sure. Having my nerves rattled will keep me awake." Meeker followed Bryant out the door and looked up the lonely streets that made up the warehouse district. "Is Redman going to take the bait?"

"Time will tell, but, Helen, I do know this. Whenever I walk out of my hotel room, I feel eyes on me. I can't see anyone, but I sense I'm being observed. So, what happened tonight scared me as much as it did you. I think there's a battle coming, and we can't dodge it. And Redman has an advantage—he will choose when and where that battle is fought."

Meeker watched Bryant slide into the car and drive off. Closing the warehouse door, Meeker climbed the steps to the office, turned on the radio, collapsed into a chair, and waited. The question was, how long would she have to wait until she looked into the green eyes of a man who enjoyed delivering death?

CHAPTER 33

THURSDAY, OCTOBER 28, 1943
8:30 P.M.
LONDON, ENGLAND

"Why am I here?" Russell Strickland demanded.

Here was a small home on the east side of London. Since the day after the kidnapping, it had served as a hiding place for the soldier he now knew as Red Cloud.

"Look at this," Red Cloud demanded as he tossed a newspaper at the OSS operative. A huge circle had been drawn around one story.

Strickland glanced at page fourteen of the *Times* and shrugged. "Yeah, I've read it. Is this why you called me from my work? If that's the case, I'm not happy. I work far too much to be bothered by trivial matters."

"How did Meeker and Bryant find Horse?"

Strickland frowned and studied the two guards before leading Red Cloud into a bedroom, where he closed and locked the door. Once they were alone, he shook his finger in Red Cloud's face. "I'm angry, and I think I have a right to be. So, what I'm going to say is going to come off as really harsh. I work intelligence and have to keep secrets, so, you have no right to ask any questions or demand any answers. We're protecting you from the Germans as well as some folks back in the States who want to work you over and then throw you away. If you had leveled with us from the beginning, I could be using those men in the next room, those guys who are babysitting you, for something important. If you think about it, that story in the newspaper is your doing, not mine. Just look into the mirror if you're searching for someone to blame."

Red Cloud's expression combined both rage and concern. "You can't push me around."

"Actually," Strickland argued, "I can. Once you admitted you lied about who you were, you stepped over the line and are on the wrong side of the law. So, the OSS and the army own you. Your only way to avoid that is to come clean. And I'm guessing you're not willing to do that."

"The reason I haven't come clean is that I was protecting Horse. Now they've made him a target. His life's not worth two cents."

"Sit down," Strickland ordered. After Red Cloud found a chair, the OSS operative growled, "Horse is safer now than ever."

"But—"

"Shut up and listen."

"Helen has no idea where Horse is. She made a vow to Teresa Bryant she wouldn't look for him. This whole thing is a charade. The man you and Horse saw execute Jim O'Toole has resurfaced. He's now killed two people that we know of, possibly one more. On top of that, if not for Teresa's heroics, he would have punched Helen's ticket."

Red Cloud was confused, and it showed. Grabbing the newspaper, he waved it as he demanded, "Why did the story say they had Horse?"

"For starters, they never said Horse, they said they had a suspect who witnessed O'Toole's murder. The only people who know who that witness is are you and the murderer. So, Meeker's team is trying to force Redman's hand. They are luring him out into the open, so you don't have to worry anymore. Which means they are laying their lives on the line for you and someone they've never even met."

Red Cloud visibly relaxed as he apparently grasped the truth. Tossing the paper to one side, he folded his arms and sighed. It appeared his blood pressure was returning to normal.

Strickland, his eyes focused directly on the soldier, was not ready to so easily sweep this under the rug. "Redman can't be allowed to find your friend. Only you and Horse know what it is Hitler wants. So Meeker, Bryant, and their other team member, Napoleon Lancelot, have made themselves targets in order to capture or kill the man you and Horse are hiding from. If they're able to do that, then you're both free. If not, we will likely have to send flowers to their funerals."

"Who else is helping them?" Red Cloud asked. "Surely the FBI is involved."

"No, not even the Chicago police have been called in," Strickland explained. "They're doing this on their own."

"That's stupid."

"Yeah, it probably is. But they know Redman is too crafty to walk into any situation where there are heavy doses of Feds or cops. He'll only come out of hiding when he's assured Meeker and her team are the only ones involved."

Red Cloud suddenly went mute and studied the floor. "Who deserves to live?" he muttered.

"What?"

He looked and repeated, "Who deserves to live? That's the question I asked myself that night in France. I made myself a target so those who had far more to live for could escape. Helen Meeker is doing the same thing. She's decided whatever it is Horse knows is far more important than her own life."

"And the lives of her team," Strickland added. "And by the way, Nap and Teresa are like family to her. Ultimately, Helen is doing something that totally goes against who she is."

"What do you mean?"

"Helen has to know the answer to everything. She can't let anything go until the mystery is solved. Yet, if she takes out Redman, she has vowed not to pursue Horse or ask you to talk. She told me it was a promise she made to Teresa. You see, Teresa doesn't have to have all the mysteries explained. She feels some things are best not known. But Helen's nature demands she keeps digging until everything is answered."

Red Cloud walked to the far side of the room and back. When he was again face-to-face with Strickland, he announced, "You just described a lot of the difference between my people and yours. We don't have to know everything about everyone. We don't have to possess things to assure ourselves we have worth."

"Maybe that's true. Maybe we wouldn't be fighting this war if we were more like your people. We are driven by ambition, we do like to own things, we love to solve mysteries, and often we can't leave well enough alone. Maybe that causes conflict, mistrust, dishonesty, and war. Those are the way things are played in my world, and I live within those parameters. In my mind, for all our flaws, England and the United States are far better than Germany or Japan."

Red Cloud nodded and smiled, "I've admitted I'm fighting for the lesser of evils."

Strickland understood what Red Cloud was saying. It made sense. Yet, it was still not a good enough reason to drag him away from his work. But at this moment, he was suddenly glad he was here. It was time to teach this stubborn man a lesson.

"Listen, Horse is safe and so is his secret. It's Meeker, Bryant, and Lancelot you need to worry about. And I hope that does worry you. I pray you stew over it, and it costs you sleep. Because, if you think about it, you're the one who put them in this situation." Strickland's face showed disgust as he turned and headed to the room's door.

"Wait."

The OSS operative turned and angrily snapped, "What?"

"Can you get me back to the States? Can you send me to Chicago?"

"Why?"

"I want to help."

"Seriously?"

"Yeah. If Redman finds out I'm with them, he'll really be convinced Horse is there as well."

That made sense. In fact, Strickland wished he had thought of it.

"So," Red Cloud pleaded, "can you arrange it?"

Strickland nodded. "It might take a couple of days. I'll let you know. But if this works, if Redman is captured or killed, will that free you up to tell us what Hitler wants so badly?"

"No," Red Cloud firmly replied.

"Why?"

"Because I'm just as afraid of what others might do with it. Remember, I'm not fighting for the good guys, I'm in the service to help the lesser of the two evils."

Strickland shrugged, opened the door, and left, but the final words stayed with him. What was so powerful or valuable that even Uncle Sam or the Union Jack couldn't be trusted with it?

CHAPTER 34

Friday, October 29, 1943
9:15 p.m.
Urbana, Illinois

Within twenty-four hours, all four of the men Ruffin Redman telegrammed had replied. On phone calls, he shared that each would make over six figures for a job lasting just a few hours. He assured them the plan was solid but only if they worked as a team. What he failed to reveal was who they'd be taking out and why. He'd leave that for their face-to-face meeting.

Redman fully expected only half of those he'd telegrammed to show up at the abandoned farmhouse outside of Urbana. His reasoning was that coming halfway across the country was difficult and expensive. If they traveled by car, they'd have to possess enough ration coupons and the correct sticker. If not the highways, it would be either train or plane, and most of the spots on those means of transportation were taken up by the military. It was already fifteen minutes past the assigned time, and no one had arrived. If he couldn't get at least two men to join him, then Redman would call the whole thing off. Meeker and her team were simply too dangerous to proceed shorthanded.

As he waited on the porch, his collar turned up to fight off the chill in the air, Redman reassessed what he'd learned on his recent trip to Chicago. He'd be able to follow Napoleon Lancelot to the warehouse. He knew that only one cop regularly patrolled the area. He'd learned Meeker, Bryant, and Lancelot worked in eight-hour shifts. Best of all, there was no other group involved in the operation. Though this hit added kidnapping to the mix, the job appeared to be far easier than taking out a federal judge, which he had done all by himself. Still, to stack the odds in his favor, he needed help.

Car lights shining brightly down the gravel road yanked his mind from what he'd observed in Chicago to the hopes one of the guests was about to join him. When a gray Buick pulled into the drive, it brought both relief and a passenger. Now, Redman was halfway to the number he needed for the operation.

The guest slowly stepped out of the big car. Tom Sears, a bit grayer and heavier than when Redman had last seen him a decade before, was still a man fit for duty. Sears wore a dark suit, shirt, and tie. His fedora was cocked to the right side. If you didn't know his reputation, you would have sworn he was a successful banker.

"Redman," he announced as he strolled across the grass, "traveling right now is a real pain. This better be worth it."

"I think you'll be pleased."

"I need to be more than pleased, I need to be ecstatic."

Sears had never been the type to mince words. The passing of the years had not changed him.

"Tom" Redman explained, "there's booze on the table in the dining room. It's the good stuff. Why don't you go on in. I'll wait on the porch for the others."

"I want the job to be as good as the liquor."

"It is," Redman assured him.

After Sears climbed the steps and stood on the porch, the two men eyed each other. Neither spoke nor offered a hand before the guest made his way inside. One down! In only sixty seconds that number doubled.

Redman was shocked when Santo Sappelli stepped out of a three-year-old Cadillac. Sappelli was the one colleague he hadn't expected. The man hated people in general and despised competition. Even when he'd promised he'd come and listen to the offer, Redman didn't expect him to follow through. Maybe the big, ugly brute had mellowed.

"Nice blue suit," Redman announced as the big man approached the porch. "It looks like it glows in the dark."

His eyes no more than slits, Sappelli chewed on his cigar and frowned. It appeared as though he eaten something that was waging a war for ownership of his large, round stomach. "I'll listen," he barked, "it would be stupid to not consider taking a job worth a hundred grand, but this better be good. If I pass, I want something for my time and trouble."

Sappelli's gruff reply was expected. The man was a snake. If truth be known, his own mother probably regretted giving birth to him. But if he chose to come on board, he could be used and used well.

"I'm waiting to see if the others show up," Redman explained. "Why don't you head into the house and pour yourself a drink. Sears should be in the dining room."

Sappelli didn't respond, just pushed by and stomped into the old house. In a world full of rats, he had to be the biggest.

For the next five minutes, as Redman waited alone in the cool air, he pondered on how to best use Sears and

Sapelli. They were two very different men. Could he find a way for them to work together well enough to grab Horse while getting rid of Meeker's team? He was trying to come up with a strategy to keep the two men on the same page, when a third car drove up. The driver turned into the lane, parked beside Sears's Buick, and stepped out.

Nic Ellis might have been a hired gun, but when he wasn't murdering folks, he was a really nice guy. Some had suggested he even had a soul. In his spare time, he was a pastor.

"Well, here comes the preacher," Redman called out when Ellis stepped out into the night air.

"Good to see you, brother," Ellis announced with a smile. "What's it been, a decade?"

"Twelve years. We ran into each other in Los Angeles. Luciano was throwing a cookout."

"Yeah, and I was heading up a revival. Have you been saying your prayers?"

"I figure you've been saying enough for both of us. You know, I've always wanted to ask you something."

After the two shook hands, Ellis grinned, "Whatever you want."

"Does it ever bother you that you kill people for a price? I mean, with your quoting Scripture all the time, how do you deal with what pays the bills?"

Ellis laughed. "The ones I kill are a blight on humanity. They're moral scum. So, even when I'm putting my hands around their throats, I'm doing the Lord's work."

Redman smiled. "I've never thought of it that way. Anyway, there's booze inside. Sears and Sappelli should be reliving old times. Why don't you join them? I need to wait and see if Hooten shows up."

"You forgot," Ellis scolded, "I don't drink. That's not a good look for a man of the cloth."

"What Bible do you use when you preach?" Redman asked.

"I choose my passages carefully. I try to steer clear of my own sins. Much more fun pointing out the sins of others."

"I'm sure it is."

After Ellis entered the house, Redman turned his attention back to the gravel road. Would J.J. Hooten leave Florida? After all, the guy had lots of money and lived on the beach. He literally had it made. A few minutes later, when a Lincoln-Zephyr rolled into the lane and parked, the question was answered.

"Redman," Hooten grumbled as he got out. "It's never good to see you."

"Not even if it means a hundred grand?"

As the big man ambled across the yard, he shook his head. "Are the others here?"

"Are you surprised? With the money we're talking about, didn't you think they would all come?"

Hooten stopped on the porch, popped a piece of hard candy into his mouth, and made an admission. "I talked on the phone with Sears, Ellis, and Sappelli. We decided to, at least, come here and listen. If we didn't like what we heard, and this turned out to be a colossal waste of time, we figured we'd get some satisfaction out of killing you. It has been a while since I've seen someone die. So, let's go inside and hear your pitch. As your life is on the line, it better be good."

"If all four of you decide I sold you a bill of goods," Redman observed, "then who gets to take me out?"

"We figured we'd draw lots. No matter what happens, Ellis will say a prayer."

That thought was sobering. Redman hadn't considered they would punch his ticket if the deal didn't smell right.

It was now vital he make a really good pitch. If that meant adding more money, he was willing to do so.

Redman followed Hooten through the living room to the dining area. After each of the four visitors were seated at the round maple table, the host poured a glass of whiskey and eased into a chair.

"Gentlemen," Redman began, "first of all I want to thank you for—"

"Can it," Sappelli spat. "Lay out the job and why there's so much money in it."

"And why you want all of us involved?" Ellis added. "We always work alone."

"I need all of you," Redman explained, "because the target is too much for one man to handle."

"Who's the target?" Sears demanded.

"Give me a second," Remand suggested. "First of all, thank you for wearing gloves. I don't want to leave any signs we were here."

"The target!" Sappelli shouted.

"In reality, there are three targets. I think you will recognize their names." He paused before saying, in a very deliberate tone, "Helen Meeker, Teresa Bryant, and Napoleon Lancelot."

It took thirty seconds before any of the guests found their voice. Sears was the first to state the obvious. "You do know they work with FDR?"

"Who doesn't know that? They've been featured in every newspaper and magazine in the country."

"Who's paying for this job?" Ellis asked. "Who's stupid enough to want to bury that trio? This isn't playing with fire—this is juggling nitro."

"I'm paying," Redman assured his guests. "I have two hundred grand with me right now."

"Where did you get that kind of cash?" Sappelli asked.

"It's part of my retirement account. I'm cashing it right now in order to invest in something much bigger."

"I don't get it," Sears snapped. "Why do you want them dead? What's Roosevelt ever done to you?"

"Bryant and Meeker have enough on me to put me away for the rest of my life. If I eliminate them, I silence the only two witnesses to any of my handiwork."

"This is too dangerous," Sears protested. "Even if we succeed, the hounds of hell would be after us until the day we die."

"There's more," Redman assured his guests. "While I want Meeker, Bryant, and Lancelot dead, I need to take the man they are protecting alive."

"Why?" Ellis asked.

"He's an Indian who witnessed me take out O'Toole."

"Then why don't you want him dead too?" Ellis demanded.

"Because this Indian knows something that's so valuable Hitler offered Jim O'Toole a ton of money just to obtain it. That was back in 1936, so I'm guessing it's worth even more now."

"How much was the price back then?" Hooten asked.

"Five million."

"What is it?" a suddenly intrigued Sears demanded. "What has that kind of value?"

"I'm not sure," Redman admitted. "But Big Jim had to have it. When he made the mistake of telling me the name of the person who possessed the information, I decided to cut O'Toole out of the deal."

"I don't feel right about doing any jobs for the Nazis," Hooten offered. "You have to draw the line somewhere."

"You don't have to draw this line," Redman assured him. "I mean if it's worth five million to Hitler, then Uncle Sam would pay that much or more."

Redman tried to read the room. Sears seemed intrigued, Hooten curious, and Ellis unconvinced. Meanwhile, it was clear Sappelli wanted no part of it.

"Okay," Ellis suggested, "if you can convince me we'd actually be helping the war effort, I might jump on board. Meeker has been responsible for taking out some of those who have paid me in the past. I could find a justification for killing her. After all, as the Good Book says, an eye for an eye."

Redman smiled. "What if I allowed you to okay the deal? When the Indian spills where this thing is, we trade it to Uncle Sam for a lot of money and full pardons for anything we have done in the past. In other words, we walk away rich and with clear names. We can live like kings and never have to worry about our past sins catching up with us."

"Glory be," Ellis quipped.

"You think this is that big?" Sears asked. "I mean, is it so huge they'd even forgive us for knocking off FDR's team?"

"To keep it out of Hitler's hands," Redman submitted, "I think so. What's the outcome of the war compared to three little lives? Here's what I'll do—each of you can have fifteen percent. I should get the rest because I've been chasing it for seven years. I'm sure your cut would be over a million."

"What are the risks?" Sears asked.

"First, Meeker, Bryant, and Lancelot are dangerous. We each know that. But they can't all protect the Indian, whose name is Horse, all the time. They work in shifts. One is guarding him for eight hours, then the next, and finally the next. There is one additional patrolman watching the warehouse district where the Indian is being kept. And that's it."

"If they're not together," Ellis asked, "how do we take out all three?"

"If we get the chance, we take out all of them," Redman explained, "but I'll settle for Meeker and Bryant. We can get them as one relieves the other. I don't mind giving the Negro a free pass. He was not a witness to anything I've done."

"And how do you know the setup?" Sappelli demanded.

"I spent a couple of days watching from a safe distance. The formula works this way. Bryant watches Horse in the evening until midnight. Meeker arrives to take over then and guards Horse until eight. Midnight is when we make the move."

The excitement was building. Most of the men were obviously intrigued by thoughts of being rich and getting pardons.

"Why's the FBI not involved?" Sears asked.

"My guess is," Redman theorized, "the FBI didn't want to use that much firepower to protect a witness to a single murder from seven years ago. After all, they're stretched thin right now. My sources tell me Hoover has no use for Meeker or Bryant, and it's well known he has no respect for Black people."

"I'd have to see the set up first," Sears announced. "If it's as clean as you have described, then I'll join you. But I want fifty grand before the job—you have to guarantee that piece of the action when we make the sale. Rather than fifteen percent, I think we need twenty."

"You'll get fifty thousand tonight," Redman assured him, "and I can live with upping your shares to twenty percent."

"Count me in too," Hooten agreed, "but I'm like Tom, I have to see it first."

"I'll make it a trio," Ellis agreed. "I want the same rules. If we can convince Uncle Sam to give us a few million, I can think of ways to enjoy my golden years. Let's just say this would be an answer to prayer."

Redman turned to Sappelli. "What about you?"

"I don't like it," he grumbled. "It sounds too good to be true."

Redman shrugged, pushed his chair back, got up, and walked over to the desk. Opening a drawer, he pulled out three boxes then circled the table putting one in front of Sears, Hooten, and Ellis.

"Gentlemen, you will find your fifty grand in unmarked bills, as well as instructions on when and where to meet in Chicago. Be at that address no later than six o'clock on Halloween. When our team is assembled, we'll do some trick-or-treating. By the way, as the city will be dressing up for the holiday, I've decided that we will wear costumes. It will keep us from standing out. I'll have the costumes ready for each of you. Any more questions?"

The trio shook their heads.

"Good. I'll see you in two days." As the three got up and left the house, Redman moved back to the head of the table and eased into a chair. Once the cars had pulled out of the drive and were well down the gravel road, he switched his focus to the lone, remaining guest. "Now, Santo, as you don't want any part of this, I can't give you fifty grand. But I'll give you ten just for showing up. I'd like one more shot at convincing you."

"It's not going to work," Sappelli groused, "The risk is too great, and I have all the money I need."

"Fine. That's your choice."

Redman reached his hand slowly inside his suit coat and retrieved an envelope. After tossing it on the table and announced, "You can count it if you want."

Sappelli took the envelope, looked inside, and nodded. "I'll trust you."

"Good, let's have a drink."

Redman moved to the side table and poured two shots of whiskey. He returned and handed one to his guest.

"To you, Santo!" Redman announced while lifting the glass, "You're a man who isn't afraid to stand alone."

"Not so fast. I'll drink with you, but let's switch glasses."

"Fine," Redman laughed, "but I'm kind of hurt you don't trust me."

Once they had exchanged glasses, Redman smiled and downed the liquor. Sappelli held his glass for another minute before following suit.

"Your career has been remarkable," Redman announced after the men set their glasses on the table. "Santo, the rest of us have a style, and yet you employ all styles. It's often messy but effective. I've always admired your diversity."

"A killing is a killing, there is no reason to sign your work. I'm not DaVinci. What I do is hardly the Mona Lisa."

"I guess you're right."

"I need to go," Sappelli declared, "but ten grand's not enough to pay for my time. I want the other forty."

Redman pointed to the desk. "Drop the ten I gave you on the table and take the box you'll find in the desk. I can part with it if it will make you happy."

Sappelli pushed off his chair and made three steps toward the desk before he wobbled and fell. As reality set in, he whispered, "No."

"Yes," Redman laughed. "I knew you'd want my drink. And in case you're wondering why you must die, we can't have any witnesses to this meeting. I decided when this thing was set up those who opted out would exit life as well."

As Sappelli's eyes closed, Redman retrieved some rope, dragged the big man across the room, and tied him to a chair. After checking his watch, Redman walked into the kitchen, scrambled two eggs, and fried three strips of bacon. He'd just finished his meal when he heard his guest stir. Picking up a gun reserved for this moment, he returned to the dining room.

"Goodbye, Santo," Redman announced. "You should be grateful; I have no need to beat you up."

Stepping behind his next victim, Redman pulled the trigger. The smoke hadn't even cleared the room when he placed the Smith & Wesson on the floor.

After retrieving the final box and getting the ten grand off the table, Redman strolled out of the house, got into his car, and drove down the lane. Tomorrow, he would phone in an anonymous tip about where to find Sappelli's body. How he was looking forward to reading about the hitman's death in the newspaper. It would serve as another example of the FBI knowing who did a job but having no evidence to arrest him. Besides, who was going to mourn Santo Sappelli's unfortunate passing?

CHAPTER 35

Monday, October 31, 1943
11:05 P.M.
Fort Sheridan, Illinois

Because of the importance of Red Cloud's heroic service, as well as the urging of the President, the Army Air Corps got him on a flight across the Atlantic with a stop in Canada, then a change of planes to the Windy City. Sensing that the soldier would feel most comfortable around Teresa Bryant, Helen Meeker had taken the afternoon shift at the warehouse. Initially, Bryant protested, using the excuse the late flight would cause Meeker to be stuck at the warehouse longer than normal, but it did no good. Meeker essentially demanded Bryant accept the task of picking up Red Cloud from Fort Sheridan.

Bryant still didn't feel comfortable using Horse as bait. She figured Red Cloud surely resented it too. The cold shoulder he gave her at Fort Sheridan assured her she was correct. Except for a handshake and the necessary greetings, neither Red Cloud nor Bryant spoke until they were well off the base. And she was the one who broke the awkward silence.

"We were surprised you wanted to come visit," Bryant announced, her tone as cold as her words. "You'd made it clear you didn't want anything to do with Helen or me in this life or the next. You also made it known you didn't want to see us continuing to dig into this case."

He nodded. "That's before I realized what you were doing and how you were doing it. This was all about protecting Horse. Now I'm convinced you're a woman of your word. That motivated me to want to help. I haven't said anything because I don't know what to say. I think I owe you an apology."

As the door was now open, and real feelings were being exposed, Bryant dug deeper. "Was I going to lie to you? We may not share a tribe, but we share a heritage. You should have known you could trust me when we met. I was never going to betray you. If this had no bearing on national security, we would have walked away."

"You work for the government," Red Cloud argued. "If you remember, the United States has never been very good at living up to its promises when it comes to Indians. So, because of who signs your paychecks, how was I to know if you were one of them or one of us?"

"Next time, don't doubt me. I will not compromise my heritage. And guess what, with what I'm doing, I don't have to. Helen allows me to be exactly who I am. She doesn't try to make me White."

"Okay, I get that ... now."

"Good, do you need anything to eat?"

"No, they fed me at the base. But there's something else I need."

After passing a produce truck, Bryant asked, "What's that?"

"What can you tell me about what's going on?"

Bryant made a right turn, pulled the Packard into traffic, and glanced at her passenger. For a man who'd likely had very little sleep, he looked pretty good. His eyes were clear, and his posture defined a person ready for action. But before spilling everything she knew, she decided to find out what he'd already been told.

"What did Strickland tell you?"

"He told me about the plan to lure Redman to the warehouse. That's about it."

"That's all there is," Bryant assured him. "So far, Redman hasn't bitten. For all we know, he might have escaped the country. That's what the FBI thinks happened."

"Do you think he's still around?"

"I can feel him," Bryant admitted. "I get the sense he's just waiting for his moment."

He glanced down at the seat and picked up a copy of the *Tribune*. "What's in the news?"

Bryant shrugged, "I bought the paper this morning but haven't had time to read it. I'll switch on the dome light and you tell me."

The next five miles were spent in silence as he scanned the headlines. If there was anything worth knowing, he hadn't shared it. He continued to remain mute until he turned to page three.

"Your gut was right," Red Cloud calmly announced.

"What do you mean?"

"There's a story here about a man from the West Coast with underworld ties who was murdered in Urbana, Illinois. They found his body yesterday."

"Why is that so important?"

"When he took me to catch my flight, Strickland told me about Redman and how he operated. The victim in this story was tied to a chair and shot through the back of the head."

Bryant quickly did the math. That was about one hundred and twenty miles from Chicago. So, that meant Redman was in the area. This was no longer a leisurely drive to a hiding place. This story had given it purpose.

"Red Cloud, I was going to take you to the Lincoln Hotel to let you get some sleep, but we'll have to put that off. Right now, we must get to the warehouse. I've got to tell Helen this news. Hold on tight, I'm about to break some speed records."

It took twenty minutes of cutting in and out of traffic, gunning the engine and laying off the brakes to make it to the warehouse as quickly as possible. During that time, Bryant said nothing. Even before she switched off the ignition, she retrieved her gun.

"Where's the patrolman?" she whispered.

"What?" Red Cloud asked.

"Stay behind me, and if I give you an order, follow it without question."

Bryant got out, moved quickly to the door, and tested the lock. It was open. Stepping inside, she flipped the lights on. The policeman was between two rows of shelves. The large pool of blood assured her there was no reason to check for a pulse. Glancing toward the office revealed just what she feared. Everything appeared empty.

With her gun ready, she took the stairs two a time. Grabbing a deep breath, she swung the door open. The room was void of life. Meeker was not there, but there had been a struggle. A chair was overturned, a table was on its side, and magazines were scattered all across the floor. Thankfully, there didn't seem to be any blood.

"Where's Miss Meeker?" Red Cloud asked.

"Obviously not here."

"Is she dead? Did they kill her?"

"No," Bryant answered while spying a hypodermic syringe and needle that had been tossed onto the floor. "But it looks like she's been drugged."

Red Cloud seemed shocked. "So, Redman didn't kill her? Does that make sense?"

"Yeah, Horse wasn't here. He wants Horse. He must believe Helen knows where Horse is, so he took her someplace to beat it out of her. He won't kill her until he finds out this whole thing has been a scam."

"How long will that take?"

"Not long."

Bryant picked up the phone and dialed the main office. Lancelot picked up on the second ring.

"Hello."

"Redman's got Helen."

"What?"

"She's gone. Our guard is dead, and we have to figure where Redman's taken Meeker."

"There are no hints at the warehouse?" Lancelot asked.

"Not that I can see. When was the last time you heard from the guys watching the family home?"

"An hour ago. No one has been there."

"Are there any other places he would consider safe?"

"I've had people watching the old butcher shop. He hasn't been there."

"Think, Nap. We likely don't have much time."

"Let me call his sister. Stay there until you hear back from me."

"Sure, but hurry."

Bryant put the phone down and scanned the room.

"Where do you think she is?" Red Cloud asked.

"Be quiet and don't move."

She didn't have time to talk or speculate. All she had at this moment were her eyes and a lifetime of experience of assessing her enemies. It was time to shut everyone and everything out and observe. There had to be answers right in this room ... if she could just see them. One step at a time, she covered the length of the room, her eyes constantly shifting, her brain recording every image. As she stood against the back wall, she studied the office from this new point of view. Except for what had been overturned and scattered in the struggle, things looked just as they did when she'd left. The last thing she'd seen was Meeker turning on the radio and getting a Coke out of the icebox. That was how she always started each of her shifts. The routine never changed. An empty Coke bottle was on the table, but the radio was off.

Bryant came back into the present and slowly strolled toward the door. Then, out of the corner of her eye, she saw it. There was a sack in the waste basket. That shouldn't have been there. The last thing Bryant had done before leaving was take out the trash. And Meeker hadn't had anything with her when she'd come in to take her shift. Why was there something in that basket?

The phone's ring momentarily pulled her attention away from the unanswered question. She wasted no time and answered during the first ring. "Bryant."

"Teresa, Redman's sister wasn't aware of anywhere else he would go. She said her brother would sometimes buy and sell rental houses, but she didn't know where any of them were. She pointed out he'd been gone a long time, so she doubted he owned anything but the store and the family home. I'm going to drive over and see if my men missed anything at either one of those places."

"Hang on," Bryant suggested.

She set the phone on the table and hurried to the waste basket. The paper sack was far too large for a food delivery, so it couldn't be something Meeker ordered and had delivered. She picked up the sack and frowned—empty. Shaking her head, she opened it anyway. Not everything was gone. Inside the bag was a handwritten receipt. She retrieved the paper and walked over to the lamp.

"Do you have something?" Red Cloud asked.

After scanning for any clues, she rushed back to the phone.

"Nap, I have a receipt for four clown costumes. They were rented by a Mr. Steven Black at 11345 Garland. What do you know about the area?"

"It's a residential district. The houses are older and they're cheap. Do you think that's where they took Helen?"

"Yeah, and this tells us something else too. Redman's not working alone. He's assembled a team. Let's get there as fast as we can, but we don't go in until we're together."

"Are you sure about this?"

"It's our only clue, we have to go with it."

"Already on my way."

"Come on," Bryant barked as she set hung up the phone.

"Why clown costumes?" Red Cloud asked as he hurried after her.

"Redman has always used disguises. This one is perfect for this occasion. They likely didn't put them on until they got here. When they got dressed up, they left in them, and someone tossed the bag into the trash without thinking ... or ..."

"Or what?" Red Cloud asked.

"Is this the bait? Redman may have turned the tables on us."

"If so, we'll be walking into a trap?"

Redman knew she and Lancelot were good. He was surely aware they saw clues in places others didn't. If

Helen wouldn't crack, if he could capture the rest of the team, he'd have a better chance at getting Horse's location. Which meant living the lie and not actually knowing where Horse was would sign all their death warrants. But trap or not, she had to go, she had no other choice.

"Red Cloud, I can smell out traps. We'll do our best to save Helen. We will do whatever that takes, but we won't go in blind. I'll figure something out on the drive over. If this is a trap, we'll find a way to spring it and not get caught."

CHAPTER 36

TUESDAY, NOVEMBER 1, 1943
12:30 A.M.
CHICAGO, ILLINOIS

The house at 11345 Garland was a brick, two-bedroom built in the early 1900s. The neighborhood had once been considered middleclass, but by 1943, it had become a street on the outs. It was no longer defined by who lived here but by who didn't. Half the homes along Garland were vacant, and those that were occupied would never be featured in a real estate ad.

Teresa Bryant, who'd parked in front of 11241 and walked the last block, studied 11345 Garland with an intensity usually reserved for a battlefield. Crouching on a dilapidated porch belonging to a vacant house across the street, her dark eyes searched every window and listened for any sound. The only obvious activity in 11345 was a radio playing swing music.

"It doesn't look like anyone's home," Red Cloud whispered.

The man's quick assessment didn't faze Bryant. Long ago, she figured out appearances were almost always deceiving. So, as she waited for Lancelot, she searched for anything that looked out of place.

"What do we do?" Red Cloud asked. "I mean there's no one here."

"How do you know when a possum is dead?" Bryant asked.

"What?"

Bryant, her eyes not diverting from the target, whispered, "You poke it with a stick."

The sound of footsteps hurrying down the brick walk caused Bryant to turn her gaze from the house to the street. Napoleon Lancelot had arrived. Like her, he'd parked well down the block in order to not call attention to his arrival.

"What have you seen?" he asked.

"Look at the coal chute on the side of the house," she directed. "There's a cellar. At first, you don't notice it because the basement windows have been blacked out. The fact there are two cars in the driveway points out someone is here. Despite seeing nothing, I think we're in the right place."

"So, Helen is here?" Lancelot asked.

"I think so," Bryant answered, "but we could be walking into a trap. Redman might have intentionally left the clue to lure us here."

"So, what's our move?"

She looked at Nap and offered a stern but reassuring smile. "Stay here with Red Cloud, I'll do a bit of scouting. When I get things sized up, I'll come back, and we'll work out a plan."

Bryant walked casually out of the shadows and down the street. She appeared to be someone on a late-night walk, but there was nothing casual about this stroll. Out of the corner of her eye, she studied 11345 from this new point of view memorizing every detail. When she was out of view of the house, she turned, and while staying in the shadows, returned. Now, it was time to get close. With gun drawn and ready, she stopped by the two cars. The Ford's radiator was cold, it hadn't been used in a while. The Lincoln's hood was still warm. Using her small flashlight, she peered inside. On the seats were several discarded clown masks and wigs.

Satisfied she was in the right place, she crept to up to the home and looked inside. As she gathered from her early inspection, there were no lights on, and except for the loud radio, it appeared no one was home. As she peered in window after window, 11345 looked just like another rundown rental—the furniture was worn, the wallpaper torn, and the rooms void of artwork or personal items. And then, she hit the jackpot. In the kitchen were clown costumes. While they left the masks in the car, they didn't pull off the costumes until after they'd arrived.

Coupled with what she'd seen in the Lincoln, she was now sure she was in the right place. But was it a trap? As her plan of attack would depend upon an answer to that question, she continued her trek around the house, testing each window and door and finding them all locked. Falling to her knees, she examined one of the basement windows. It hadn't been painted, there was something thick covering it from the inside. She crawled to the next one. It was the same way. It appeared Redman had soundproofed the basement. Bryant guessed his original plan was to bring Horse back here and beat a confession out of him. Now it was Helen Meeker who was likely feeling the hitman's rage. The radio was being used to cover any noise coming from the basement.

Bryant felt confident the bag had been left at the warehouse by mistake. It had not been planted to set up a trap. With that assurance, she hurried around the house and back to the men.

"Okay, if she's here, she's in the basement. The downstairs has been soundproofed. No one around this place could hear anything coming from that part of the house, but the radio's music gives them an added layer of cover. The good news is this is not a trap. The bad news is there are no outside entrances to the basement, so we'll have to go in the house from upstairs."

"That means they'll hear us," Lancelot observed.

"They'll hear you," Bryant corrected. "I actually want you to be noisy. I want to make sure Redman and his team are fully aware when you stumble in."

"What?" Lancelot demanded. "I'm a target?"

"No, a distraction. Red Cloud and I can move without being heard. We will be in position to cover you. Nap, did you bring firepower?"

"I have some extra forty-fives."

"Give one to Red Cloud, keep two handy for yourself."

Lancelot pulled a revolver from his pocket and gave it to Red Cloud. After both men checked their weapons, Bryant outlined the plan.

"I'll pick the backdoor lock—that will be no problem—then Red Cloud and I will enter that way. Nap, you have to give us time to find the basement door. When we do, we'll wait behind it. You'll walk in, making even more noise than usual." She turned to Red Cloud. "I figure Redman will send at least one or maybe two men up from the basement to investigate. We don't want any gunplay. We'll club those guys as they come out of the basement and catch their bodies before they fall to the floor. Then, we'll quietly drag them to one side." She turned back to Napoleon. "If they get by us, or if there are more than two, you shoot until they all fall. Are there any questions?"

The men shook their heads.

"Nap, you're going to have to break that front door in. Don't you dare crawl forward and unlock it. The house is too old, and the floors might creak. Give us three minutes to find the basement door, then you break in the front. I mean, slam it with your shoulder. Make enough racket to wake the dead."

"I can do that."

"Okay, let's move."

Bryant and Red Cloud stayed in the shadows until they got to the backside of 11345. Once they were at the rear door, it took Bryant twenty seconds to pick the lock and ease the old entry open. She was shocked it didn't squeak. Once inside, she used her flashlight to study the kitchen. There was a hall leading forward, and the first door on the right was closed. She crept to that point and reassessed the situation. Twenty-five feet ahead was the living room where the radio was blaring, to the left were two bedrooms—both of those doors were open. Ten feet forward and to the right was the bath. That meant the one closed door led to the basement.

Taking a deep breath, she twisted the knob. It was unlocked. She eased it open a quarter of an inch to discover stairs illuminated by a light in the basement. As she stood there, she heard a man's voice.

"Where is Horse?" he screamed.

Bryant recognized the speaker. She'd heard him in the cabin outside of Alamogordo. She also knew the next sound. It was fist driving into a person's face.

"Where's Horse?" Redman screamed again.

"I told you," Helen Meeker spat, "you'll need to go to Texas to get a horse. I've never even owned one. Though, now that I think of it, there might be a few at the stockyards. Isn't there a glue factory in Chicago? Maybe I can lead you to one."

Her voice was weak, but Meeker was alive. They'd gotten here in time.

"Why you little—" Redman yelled, the sound of a fist impacting flesh finishing the sentence.

"You're going to kill her," another man warned.

"Not until she talks," Redman barked. "She's tough, she'll live a lot longer. Besides, I'm enjoying this." He snarled, "Now, Meeker, you've played your game. You convinced me that you were hiding Horse in the warehouse. Now I know he's somewhere else. You'll die a lot easier if you just come clean and tell me where he is."

"But I'll still die," Meeker announced, "so do your worst."

Heavy footsteps on the front porch signaled Lancelot was moving into position. With Red Cloud beside her, Bryant closed the basement door and flattened against the wall. A few seconds later, Lancelot knocked the door off its hinges. As the entry smashed to the floor, the noise echoed all through the house.

The voices in the basement were now muffled, so Bryant couldn't hear what was being said, but the sound of two sets of feet rushing up the wooden steps were unmistakable. The man who tossed open the basement door was large and quick. The one who followed was tall and lean. Both held guns.

"Hello, boys," Lancelot called out.

As the pair turned toward the living room, Bryant and Red Cloud brought the butts of their handguns down onto the men's heads. The lean man immediately buckled. It took a second strike before the big guy collapsed into Bryant's arms. Both were quickly dragged into the kitchen.

Moving back to the open door, Bryant eased down four steps. Hidden by shadows, she studied the situation.

Redman was behind Meeker. She was bleeding from her mouth, one eye, and an ear. To the left was a man dressed more like a preacher than a hood. He even held a Bible in his hand.

"What's going on?" he asked Redman.

"Hooten, Sears," Redman called out, "report!"

"They're not answering."

"Shut up, Ellis."

"It's time you give it up," Bryant called out. "Your goons are licked, your one exit is covered, and I'm losing my patience."

"Teresa Bryant," Redman answered, obviously recognizing her voice. "I believe we were in the same position a couple of weeks ago."

"This time, I've got the upper hand," she argued as Red Cloud and Lancelot joined her on the stairs. "You can't see me, but I can see you."

"But once again," Redman argued, as he pulled Meeker out of Bryant's view, "I can easily murder your partner before you can get off a shot." He paused before shouting an order. "Ellis, pull that lever on the wall, it opens a door to a tunnel that'll get us out of here."

Bryant frowned. There was a second exit. That meant they could no longer wait things out. Yet, they also couldn't charge down the stairs as they would be easy targets. As she considered her options, she heard a door creak open. Time was ticking, they had to do something. If they didn't, Meeker would soon be gone or dead.

"Redman," Red Cloud called out.

"Who are you?"

"Remember when you killed O'Toole? There were two Indians who saw you. One was the man you knew as Horse, and the other was me. I've been hiding Horse from you ever since. I know where he is, and, better yet, I know what he knows. If you have me, you don't need Horse."

"You can take me to what O'Toole wanted?" Redman yelled.

"Yeah. Now, I'm coming down the steps unarmed. As I know what you want to know, you can't afford to kill me."

Bryant turned and glared at Red Cloud. "You can't do this."

He shrugged and whispered, "It's the only way to save Helen. I trust you'll able to track me. I'll make a trail—you just need to be able to read the signs."

Setting the gun on the stairs, Red Cloud moved passed Bryant, and with hands in the air, he made his way down the steps to the basement's concrete floor.

"You recognize me?" Red Cloud asked. "I surely haven't changed that much in seven years."

"I know you. You were with Horse in town. I saw you a couple of times before the cabin."

"Here's the deal," Red Cloud explained, "it's me for Miss Meeker. I'm worth a lot more to you alive than she is dead. So cut her loose, and we can start the trade. Otherwise, there's going to be lot of blood shed today."

Bryant couldn't see the far side of the room, so she couldn't get a read on the situation. What concerned her was how long it took Redman to respond. This was his chance to get what he wanted, but would he take it? A few seconds later, she had her answer.

"Ellis, cut the woman loose."

Bryant could hear a knife sawing through rope. So far, Red Cloud's plan was working.

"You don't have to do this," Meeker announced, her voice weak and her words slurred.

"Actually," Red Cloud calmly replied, "I do."

Bryant watched as the soldier pointed toward where Meeker must have been sitting. "Are you Ellis?"

"As God is my witness, I am."

"Take Helen over to the steps."

"Do it," Redman barked.

A few moments later, Meeker, leaning against a man holding a Bible, appeared. She was so badly beaten she could barely walk.

"No funny stuff," Redman ordered. "I can still kill her. Now, boy, you come back over to the door with Ellis. And Bryant, if you try anything, your partner and the Indian die. You got that?"

"I've got it," Bryant assured him.

Red Cloud looked up the stairs, smiled, and announced, "Morning Song, we'll always have Frontier Days. I'll never forget the magic, and I hope you won't either."

As Ellis and Red Cloud stepped out of view, Bryant leaned forward and took a quick inventory of the room. Redman was already hidden in the secret tunnel. The only thing she could see was his hand holding a gun.

"Get into the tunnel," Redman snapped. When Red Cloud was out of sight, Redman shifted his weapon and fired. A shocked Ellis, clutched his chest and fell backward. A second later, the door to the escape route closed.

Bryant took the steps two at a time and rushed by Meeker to where the wall had just closed. She couldn't get it open. It appeared Redman had locked the door from the other side. Behind her, Lancelot was picking up Meeker and climbing the stairs.

Dropping to her knee, Bryant grabbed Ellis's face and looked him in the eye. "Where does that tunnel lead?"

"Straight to Hell." Blood was pouring from Ellis's chest and puddling on the floor. He didn't have much time and likely knew it. A strange smile crossed his face as he whispered, "Vengeance is mine says the Lord." Then his eyes went blank.

Without being able to open the tunnel door, there was no use staying in the basement. Bryant took a final look around and charged up the stairs. She found Lancelot in the living room where he'd placed Meeker on the couch.

"She needs a hospital," Bryant suggested. "You get her there as fast as you can."

"What about Redman?" Meeker whispered.

"For the moment, he's gone. But Red Cloud promised he'll leave us breadcrumbs."

"What does that mean?" Lancelot asked.

"We'll know when we see them." She looked around the room before saying, "Why don't you go get the car."

A few minutes later, after Bryant had helped Lancelot get Meeker to the car, and they were safely on the way to the hospital, she angrily returned to the house. She'd underestimated Redman. She should have known he'd have an escape route. Worse yet, he now had a man who could lead him to what Hitler wanted. Did this blunder just shift the tide of the war? As she pondered that question, she pulled out her gun and walked into the kitchen. The two men Redman had called Sears and Hooten weren't there. They must have come to and escaped, but where did they go?

Bryant hurried to the front porch and looked toward the driveway. The Ford and the Lincoln were still there. So, the tunnel had to lead to another home or maybe a garage. They must have had vehicles there too. Still, even if she found where the tunnel exited, she knew the trio, with Red Cloud as their captive, were gone by now. While she didn't know the route they would take, she knew where the trail ended.

CHAPTER 37

Monday, November 1, 1943
10:33 a.m.
Chicago, Illinois

A nurse, clad in her starched white uniform and her flossie—a hat she'd earned upon graduation from school—walked over to where Teresa Bryant was sitting in the waiting room. "I'm Jean, I believe you're with Miss Helen Meeker."

"We work together, and we're friends." A concerned Bryant then added, "And I spend far too much time in hospitals waiting to get reports on her condition. So, how is she?"

"She's a very headstrong woman," the nurse announced. "She's not an easy patient to deal with."

"There are times she's not an easy person to work with, either," Bryant replied. "That's one of the things that makes her amazing. What can you tell me about her condition?"

"Well, she has bruises from her chin to her forehead, two black eyes, three loose teeth, the inside of her mouth was cut so badly it took stitches, a number of her ribs are cracked, her right ear drum burst, and there are a few other minor injuries as well. She should be begging for something to stop the pain, but instead she wants her clothes and directions to the front door."

Bryant nodded. That was the woman she knew better than anyone on the planet. When there was work to done, nothing else mattered.

"May I see her?"

"That might make it easier on all of us," the nurse suggested. "That's what she's been demanding for the last half hour. She's in room 421."

As she pushed off the chair, Bryant said "thank you" and hurried down the hall.

"Make her behave," Jean called out just before Bryant walked into the sterile, white room.

"It's about time they sent you in here," Meeker grumbled. Her bed was cranked high enough to allow her to sit up. "Have I ever told you how much I hate hospital gowns. I mean, why do they bother putting you in anything? And this place is no excuse for a hospital. They don't care about their patients. They haven't brought me a newspaper, won't give me a Coke, and let's not even talk about what they served for breakfast."

"I'll inform the staff you aren't happy. I'm sure that will make a difference."

"Is Nap with you?" Meeker asked.

"No, he's been trying to figure out where Redman went. Here's what we do know. They were likely thirty miles away before we discovered the tunnel led to another vacant house. There must have been a car waiting there. We don't know what kind. So, we have very little to go on. I can tell you this interesting fact, the tunnel was constructed during prohibition to hide illegal booze. It also served as an escape route on raids."

"I don't care about history—what about now?"

"Nap did some research. All three men at the house were hitmen—Tom Sears, J.J. Hooten, and Nic Ellis. You might not remember, but Ellis died in the basement. We figure they were brought in because Redman didn't want the risk of taking us on by himself. The guy that was executed in Urbana, the one that alerted me Redman was close, was a mob enforcer named Santo Sappelli. By the looks of it, Redman staged the Urbana farmhouse meeting to organize how he could get Horse and kill us. I figure Santo opted out and was murdered. I still can't understand the logic in taking out the guy in the basement. Hooten, Ellis, and Sears are all known hitmen."

"What happened to Hooten and Sears?" Meeker asked.

"Initially, Red Cloud and I knocked them out. They woke up when Red Cloud was swapping places with you. My guess? As they didn't escape in the cars parked at the house, they must have known where Redman was heading and met him there. If I'm right about them all being together again, then the three have a good chance of keeping Red Cloud in check."

"We need to get moving," Meeker announced. She winced and moaned as she tried to get out of bed.

"Just say put," Bryant ordered, "and let Nap and me handle what needs to be done."

"But we have to figure out where Red Cloud is taking Redman and his gang. We can't let him—"

"They aren't moving fast," Bryant explained as she gently pushed Meeker back down on the mattress. "Because of all the wanted posters and rewards, Redman can't afford to take a train or plane. He'll have to drive. And, as we found a suitcase filled with his disguises and his makeup kit, he doesn't have any masks to hide behind right now. I'm also sure Red Cloud will lead them on a wild goose chase, and it'll take several days, if not a week, for them to get to where they need to be."

"But where is that?" Meeker asked. "It could be a million different places. We don't even know what we're looking for."

"While you heal, I'm heading back to Alamogordo."

"That's where everything went down in 1936, so you figure that's our best place to start?"

"No, I know that's the area where it will end," Bryant corrected her associate.

"How do you know that?"

"Red Cloud mimicked a line from *Casablanca*. He told me we'd always have Frontier Days. Without Redman picking up on it, Red Cloud told me exactly where he was going. We just need to beat Redman and his gang to Alamogordo. We can fly. They'll be traveling by car and avoiding anywhere they could be spotted, so for them it's going to be a long, slow trip. Nap and I are leaving this afternoon and will get there in plenty of time."

"I'm going too," Meeker snapped.

"You're in no shape to travel."

"Try to stop me. Redman has now worked me over twice. When he goes down, I deserve to be there. Now get Miss Florence Nightmare in here."

"Her name is Jean."

"Fine, get Jean in here and make her give me my clothes. And before we leave town, I want a real meal."

CHAPTER 38

Monday, November 1, 1943
5:40 p.m.
In the Air over Missouri.

Thirty-three passengers normally rode in this plane, but today, it was only three. A few strings had been pulled, and the DC-3, which was temporarily out of service for routine maintenance, was given to Helen Meeker's team for the trip. It was fueled up and waiting when Meeker arrived at O'Hare. Teresa Bryant and Napoleon Lancelot were already aboard and visiting with the crew as Meeker limped up the stairs to the cabin and fell into a seat. For the first two hours of the flight, she slept so soundly, she didn't even remember taking off.

Now, as the DC-3 pushed through the air, Meeker, large dark glasses covering her eyes, was finally awake and looking toward the setting sun. Across the aisle, Bryant seemed lost in thought. She knew something, but she obviously wasn't ready to volunteer the information. Not knowing what was on Bryant's mind always bothered Meeker, and never more than today.

"I figured you'd want a Coke," Lancelot announced as he walked from the front of the plane. "Do you need an aspirin?"

"No," Meeker offered, "I don't want to block the pain. I want to still be feeling it when I'm face-to-face with Redman."

Lancelot smiled grimly. "I get that, but I thought you'd want to know we'll be landing in Oklahoma in about an hour."

"Thanks." After taking a long swig of the soft drink, their destination soaked in. Before Lancelot could turn and head to his seat, Meeker called out, "I thought we were headed to Alamogordo."

"We'll end up there," Lancelot assured Meeker, "but Teresa has something we need to pick up in Oklahoma. She wouldn't tell me what."

Meeker nodded. "Thanks for the Coke."

"Sure. Why don't you get some more sleep."

As Lancelot walked back to his seat in the front row, Meeker turned her attention to Bryant. What was so important she was willing to give up some very precious time? After draining what was left in the hobble skirt bottle, Meeker unleashed a world of pain by standing and moving toward Bryant.

"You need something?" Bryant asked.

"Yeah, why are we stopping in Oklahoma?"

"Sit down before you collapse."

Meeker eased into the seat beside Bryant and declared, "We need to get to Alamogordo. We have to beat them there."

"They aren't even out of Missouri," Bryant explained.

"How do you know that?"

"A piece of paper was dropped at a gas station in Charleston. My name and the Lincoln Hotel were written at the top. The Seminole word for hello was scribbled below. I talked on the phone to the guy who found the note.

Needless to say, they haven't made it very far, which proves Redman is being very careful. So, even after this stop and spending about twelve hours in Oklahoma, we'll arrive in New Mexico days before the action starts. Which is good, because you need some time to heal."

"Lancelot said you were picking something up."

"I'm going to try to get something we need from a Seminole elder. If he can help me, we have a much better chance of not only stopping Redman but of saving Red Cloud's life."

"What are you getting?"

"Just be patient. You can watch what I'm doing, see things unfold, and if my hunch is right, you can help me plan the next step. At the very least, you'll get to visit an Indian reservation and learn what White men have done to the people who were once stewards of this land."

"Another life lesson?" Meeker asked. "Do we really have time for that?"

"Helen, you can't grasp something until you have witnessed it in such a way that the memories not only settle into your brain but bore into your bones. For a long time, you've questioned who I was and have tried to get me to open up about my life. I've shared bits and pieces but only as much as I thought you could handle. My tribe is not on the land we are about to visit, but in many ways, all this country's native people are my people. We share a bond not because of being here long before your people but because of what your ancestors did to us." Bryant paused and licked her lips before adding, "And are still doing to us."

"I—"

"Wait before you speak," Bryant warned. "We are told time and time again to get over it. Maybe that works for people like you, those with White skin whose ancestors came from Europe, but the fact is you can only move on and get over it when you are no longer oppressed. When you visit the Seminole reservation, you might begin to understand the barriers my people face each day. For generations, we've been told to give up being who we are and become White. Many have tried. But even those with college degrees, who dress in the latest fashion styles, who speak English as well as I do, are still viewed as being anything but equal."

Meeker suddenly felt very uncomfortable. She suppressed an urge to apologize, though she felt it was needed. Deep down, she realized doing so would also be inadequate.

Bryant pointed toward the front of the plane, pulling Meeker from a place she didn't want to be. When her friend spoke, it didn't bring escape or relief, it made her more uncomfortable.

"Look at Nap. How many times has he saved us? How much valuable service has he given to this country? How many times has he offered his life for the Stars and Stripes? And he lives in a country where he's never quite seen as equal. He's not judged on his character but by his skin color. And when someone does offer compliments, they usually couch it, by saying he's a great guy for a Negro or he's smart for a Black person. Nap's one of the most amazing, intelligent, talented, and dynamic people I've ever met, and yet in our country even that's not enough for him to break out of the chains that have bound him his whole life.

"Don't get me wrong." Bryant continued, "Nap and I appreciate that you treat us as equals. We don't take for granted that you respect us and have given us a chance. But you must realize you can't understand us until you have been to someplace where you can see and feel the results of the laws and attitudes that hold us back."

"Teresa, I'm sorry."

Bryant nodded. "I've said what I've said because I'm taking you to visit a proud people who have been robbed of all they hold dear. Observe them, listen to them, and then leave them vowing to do more." As darkness consumed the night sky, Bryant glanced out the window and finished her lesson. "You didn't understand why Red Cloud would refuse the Medal of Honor. Let me explain the real reason. He brought value to a boy who was beaten and abused when no one else would. And he vowed to protect him, which meant denying his own dreams and the honors that came with his service in order to save that boy. This is so much bigger than one man."

Bryant turned her face back toward Meeker. "The Jesus Christ you worship—the one whose words mean so much to you. You must realize he brought value to those others deemed had no value. I have no idea if Red Cloud is a Christian, but I do know this—he's echoing the life of Jesus far more than most who go to church each week."

Meeker understood the emotions driving Bryant's lecture. After all, it was that same Red Cloud who'd also traded his life for hers. Before that he'd offered his own life to save two French women he didn't know. If her team did manage to save Red Cloud, and he accepted the Medal of Honor, he would still have no more rights or opportunities than he did before the war. Sadly, neither would her friend Napoleon Lancelot. That was very sobering.

CHAPTER 39

Wednesday, November 3, 1943
8:15 a.m.
Seminole Reservation, Oklahoma

"Someone does not like you," Grey Wolf announced as Teresa Bryant introduced Helen Meeker to the tribal elder.

The old man's dark eyes were kind, his voice strong, his body lean and muscular. He was dressed in a handmade coat featuring symbols that likely had meaning for his tribe. His collar was turned up to block the cold. His long, gray hair blew in the northernly wind. He was a man who carried himself with more dignity and strength than anyone she'd ever met. And his observation also proved he was man who understand the power of humor.

"There are a lot of people who don't like Helen," Bryant explained. "She has been known to step on toes."

"In this case, I'm guessing she must have stepped on far more than toes."

Bryant smiled. "In this case, you are correct."

"Sometimes a woman must stand against the world," Grey Wolf offered. "And when she does, the world takes note. Welcome to our home, Helen Meeker."

He said home with little conviction. After all, this was not a tribal land, this place was a long way from Florida.

This was just property the United States government viewed as worthless.

"I am honored to be with you," Meeker said. "And I am more than honored to claim Morning Song as my friend. She has saved my life more times than I can count."

"I had to leave another friend at the airport," Bryant explained. "Napoleon Lancelot is someone you would like. He has character, courage, and heart."

"Bring him next time," Grey Wolf suggested. "We can sit by the fire and share stories. But I don't believe you came here just so your friend could meet me. Perhaps it's best if you tell me what you need, then I will decide if your need has value to my people."

As they stood on the ridge outside Grey Wolf's small cabin, Meeker observed a handful of children playing with a dog. The kids were clean but dressed in old and tattered clothing. She turned her attention to a group of women washing clothes in large pans. Their poverty was just as obvious. Worst of all, they were confined and doomed to poverty by government decree. Yes, they weren't in a prison or a zoo, but they were still unable to move freely. Their children had no chance at living the American dream. If fact, they likely had no opportunity to realize any dreams. As Bryant explained on the airplane, everyone seeks to be validated and respected. Yet that was being denied the very people who once tended to all the land that was now called the United States. The sound of Bryant's voice jerked Meeker from an uncomfortable realization to the moment at hand.

"Can we speak to you in private?" Bryant asked Grey Wolf.

The elder looked at Meeker and in a kind, caring voice asked, "Do you feel like walking?"

"I think it might be good for me," she agreed.

"Then let us go down by the creek. The trees will protect us, and the winds will not cut through us like they do here on the ridge."

Grey Wolf patted a small girl on the head, smiled, then began a trek down a dusty path. Bryant fell in line behind him. Taking a deep breath, Meeker brought up the rear. The next half mile was pure torture. With each step, her ribs reminded her she still should've been confined to a hospital bed. When they finally stopped and sat down on a huge, fallen tree trunk, Meeker offered a prayer of thanks. She doubted if she could have made it another hundred yards.

"What was the force behind your long journey?" Grey Wolf asked.

Bryant stared into the man's wrinkled face and announced, "When Red Cloud was sent to the Indian school, he witnessed something horrible."

"He lived through many horrible things," Grey Wolf corrected her.

Sensing her words would mean nothing, Meeker leaned back and observed a conversation she likely had no right to hear. The pained expression now etched into faces hinted at a horror she couldn't imagine.

"They had their lives stripped from them." Grey Wolf continued, "The schools taught them to hate who they were but gave them no path to become anything else. Many returned from those schools blaming us for the color of their skin and refusing to speak our language or share in our traditions. So, he saw a lot that was horrible. I'm sure you did as well."

Bryant nodded. "But there was one thing we need to revisit. Red Cloud saw a boy so badly beaten the child was left with mental issues. He couldn't talk or perhaps even think like a normal person. Red Cloud protected the boy from that day forward."

"If you say so."

"I don't think the boy was a Seminole," Bryant stated.

"You know as well as I do, the schools put people from all tribes in one place. They were trying to wipe away our heritage and all our histories. So, the boy could have been from another tribe." Grey Wolf agreed.

"I'm looking into your eyes," Bryant announced, "and I think you know more than you say."

"What is it you need?" For the first time, Gray Wolf appeared impatient.

"I think the boy Red Cloud took care of was Apache. I believe when Red Cloud came home to this place, he brought that boy with him to live with the Seminole."

"Apache, Sioux, or any brother or sister in any tribe can join us and become one with us. We would take you if you wanted to live here." He pointed to Meeker. "We would take her as well."

"I believe when Red Cloud left the reservation, this boy did too," Bryant continued. "In time, he went back to be with his people in New Mexico. Let me tell you something else you need to hear. This boy has or knows something that is so valuable Hitler wants it. On top of that, this boy and Red Cloud witnessed a murder motivated by this knowledge. Even today, people are being killed because of what the boy has or knows. Helen was beaten because of what the boy knows. A policeman in Chicago and a newspaper publisher in New Mexico were murdered because of what this boy knows."

"It is a good story," Grey Wolf admitted. "It sounds like something a White man would put into a book."

Bryant grimly nodded. "After witnessing that murder in 1936, Red Cloud needed to protect the boy who is now a young man. He brought him to you, then Red Cloud changed his name and entered the military. You have been hiding the boy, who is now a man, here ever since that time."

Meeker studied Grey Wolf's face. His expression didn't change, his body didn't tense, his emotions remained stoic. It appeared Bryant wasn't getting to him.

"As I told you on my other visit," Bryant continued, "Red Cloud took the name Redman and is a true hero. He has been nominated for the Medal of Honor but won't take it. And he admitted his reason for the change of his name and his refusal to be honored was because he needed to protect both the man called Horse and the secret Horse has held since childhood. I believe Horse has kept that secret because Red Cloud has told him how valuable it is. I think Red Cloud feels it has far too much importance to share with either Hitler or Roosevelt."

"It sounds like you have your answers," Grey Wolf suggested. "Besides, I told you to leave this alone. It is up to Red Cloud to speak."

"In most cases, I would agree, but Red Cloud has been taken hostage by one of the most evil men I have ever encountered. That man will do anything to obtain the secret. He will then sell it to Hitler. I think the only way I can keep that from happening and save Red Cloud, as well as the man known as Horse, is to know what the secret is and where to find it." She paused, took a deep breath, and said, "So, I need for you to let me speak to Horse."

"His name is no longer Horse. We call him Silent Wind."

"What does he know?"

"I've never asked him, and he wouldn't tell me if I did. He made a promise to Red Cloud to never speak of this."

"May I talk to him?" Bryant asked. "Maybe he will listen to me."

"He has been behind that oak tree the entire time we've been here," Grey Wolf explained. "He has heard everything you've said." The old man stood, looked over his left shoulder, and called out, "Come join us."

The man who stepped from behind the large oak was thin, his face drawn, and his dark eyes filled with pain. He was about five-eight, and his long, black hair was parted in the middle and hung in braids on both sides. He wore jeans, a flannel shirt, and a buckskin jacket. He had scars on his face that must have dated back to his days in the Indian school. When he spoke, he stammered.

"I ... I ... I don't speak ... good," he began. "But I understand."

Bryant nodded. "You have heard what I need, and you know why I need it."

"But Red Cloud told me ... a ... a ... not to tell."

Bryant glanced toward Meeker. Her look suggested a woman trapped into doing something she didn't want to do. Yet, she also had no choice.

"What do you want me to call you?" Bryant asked.

"Horse."

"Okay, Horse, can you tell me the secret place Red Cloud would go? I need to be there to save him from evil men. Can you tell me how to get there?"

"No." There was pain in the man's eyes as he spoke, "but ... but ... to save Red Cloud I can show you. But ... I ... I ... can't ... tell you what is there."

Bryant looked at Meeker, who nodded. The knowing where was far more important at this point than knowing what.

"You will come with us," Bryant suggested. "And if we save Red Cloud, he will bring you back to your home."

The young man nodded.

"You have what you want," Grey Wolf announced, "I hope you use that knowledge with wisdom. I will help our brother gather his belongings and meet you at your car."

Grey Wolf and Horse walked together up the hill. As Meeker watched, a sense of sadness washed over her. After standing and placing her hand on Bryant's shoulder, she whispered, "I'm sorry you had to do that."

"We sometimes do what we don't want to do in order to save others. I knew Horse would understand that."

"Did you also know he was listening as you spoke to Grey Wolf?"

"Yes, but I'm guessing you didn't."

"No."

"Well, in your defense, your eyes are almost swollen shut. Can you make it up that hill?"

"As long as we don't go too fast."

CHAPTER 40

WEDNESDAY, NOVEMBER 3, 1943
7:19 P.M.
JOPLIN, MISSOURI

Just because he had a man who could lead him to his quest, he wasn't lured into being reckless. As he had for seven long years, Ruffin Redman remained patient. Knowing there was a reward out for him and understanding his face was in every post office in the country, the route he planned to New Mexico was one that stayed off the main roads. They traveled at night with Sears, Hooten, and himself taking turns driving in four-hour shifts. When stops were made, the two who were off the radar made the purchases. Redman ate his meals in the truck and never put himself in the public eye. When Hooten and Sears wanted to hurry, Redman waved them off, reminding them time was on their side.

To ensure his hostage would not be seen, two days before the raid on Meeker's warehouse, Redman had purchased a 1937 Dodge truck. The company that originally owned it ordered just a chassis and a cab, and had a custom body installed by a coach builder. The entire rear of the ton-and-a-half rig was closed to make all-weather deliveries of dry goods. Though it had been bought to hide Horse, it worked just as well for Red Cloud. Except for brief walks to go to the bathroom, the prisoner was kept in the back chained to the wall and always guarded. If they were traveling in urban areas, he was also gagged.

When not driving or sleeping, Redman would sit in the back and visit with Red Cloud. At this point, there was no reason to pump him about the specifics of what was waiting down the road. Red Cloud had assured Redman the trail ended outside of Alamogordo. So, the visits turned to politics, sports, religion, and even fishing. Surprisingly, the conversations never grew heated or combative.

As the truck left Joplin with Sears driving, Redman once again sat opposite Red Cloud. In the darkness, he listened to the Seminole breathe, trying to gauge if he was awake or asleep. Somehow the prisoner read his mind.

"I'm awake," Red Cloud volunteered.

"That's good, because it's time to cut to the chase. Over the past couple of days, we've wasted the hours talking about a lot of different subjects. Now, it's time we come to some agreement on a few important issues. First—and you need to know this—if you don't lead me to what I want, you will die. I'll make it a very painful death."

"I figured no less, but that doesn't scare me. I've been beaten before, and we all die."

"You also need to know there's another price to pay if you fail to do as you promised." Redman continued, "Just because we didn't find Horse doesn't mean Meeker and Bryant haven't. I know Bryant went to the Seminole Reservation on September 25. If you're wondering how I learned this bit of information, once the story was published on me taking out O'Toole, I started to get to know the people who tagged me as the killer. That included seeing where they had recently been."

"So, you know I was raised on the reservation, and you know Meeker and Bryant know me. But you have no idea what that visit means. Maybe she was visiting a relative."

Redman chuckled before explaining, "In my mind, it means they found Horse there. Then when things got hot, they moved him to Chicago. He wasn't at the warehouse because that was a trap meant for me, but I'm sure he was in town. When things calm down, they'll send him home. I can assure you of this, if you don't come through, I'll find Horse and will torture him until he gives me what I want. Then, I'll give him the same kind of death I've promised you. And it won't end there. I'll track down Meeker and Bryant and kill them too. If you fail to level with me, three people you seem to care about will die. I just want you to think about that."

"I kind of figured that was the way you planned things when I traded myself for Helen," Red Cloud admitted. "So, I was always going to give you what you wanted. But, when I do that, what happens to me?"

"I haven't decided yet. But, if I don't let you go, I promise your death will be quick."

"I have a warning for you."

"I don't think you're in any place to warn me about anything."

"Once you get want you want, it will haunt you for the rest of your life," Red Cloud quietly declared. "These spirits won't leave you alone. They will follow you everywhere. They will invade your daydreams and own your nightmares. When you die, you will die screaming."

"If the Indian mumbo jumbo is supposed to frighten me, it doesn't." Redman sighed. " I don't believe in your God or any other god. The only life I think is precious or has value is my own. So, I'll take that chance of being haunted." He laughed and added, "I've killed more than forty people, and none of those deaths have ever cost me a moment's sleep."

Redman leaned against the truck and smiled. He had Red Cloud where he needed him. The Indian had a flaw that could be easily exploited—character—the undoing of all good men. How he wished there were more people with empathy and principles. It would make his life so much easier.

CHAPTER 41

Thursday, November 4, 1943
2:05 a.m.
Alamogordo, New Mexico

It seemed natural for Horse to bond with Teresa Bryant. They shared not only a heritage but the connection of having been in the Indian schools. So, during most of the flight from Oklahoma, Bryant devoted her time learning to read the young man's eyes, body language, and facial expressions. In time, his difficulties putting his thoughts into words were eased. She could ask a question, and his face would reveal the answer. Then they crossed into an even better way of communicating—a method different tribes with different languages had used for centuries—sign language. By the time their plane landed in New Mexico, she had a firm grasp on the amazing brain hidden because of the damage done by abuse.

After checking into the hotel and settling Horse into a room with Napoleon Lancelot, Bryant walked down to meet with Helen Meeker. Combined with the toll from the beating, the trip had been hard on her friend and coworker. Meeker looked more dead than alive.

"You feel like talking?" Bryant asked.

"The way my head is hurting, I feel more like listening." Meeker admitted. "Do you know any bedtime stories?"

"Not that you'd enjoy, but I do have a few things to tell you."

"Go for it," Meeker announced as she lay down on the bed.

"Red Cloud has been protecting Horse for years, but we were wrong—it's Horse who decided to keep what he knew secret. The only people he ever told were a teacher, who literally beat it out of him, and Red Cloud. No one else knows, and he won't tell me."

"So," Meeker posed, "he'll take us to the place, but not show us what we need to see?"

"Maybe we don't need to see it, perhaps we just need to keep it out of Hitler's hands."

"Speaking of that," Meeker observed. "If Horse only told two people, how did Hitler find out?"

"The teacher who beat him was originally from Germany. After he left the Indian school, he went back to his home in Berlin. His name is Peter Berghaulter. That should mean something to you."

"Sure, he's an advisor to Hitler. He's ruthless and will do anything to anyone to get information. He's responsible for torturing hundreds who were suspected of working in the resistance." She sat up suddenly and snapped her fingers. The immediate pain brought from her quick movement caused her to moan. When she caught her breath, she added, "And, it makes sense he'd have ordered the raid to kidnap Red Cloud and the French women. He would've known about the friendship between Red Cloud and Horse from his days as a teacher."

Bryant nodded. "Yes, we now have the route to Hitler knowing what Horse knows. I think the connection to

O'Toole and Berghaulter is something we could likely find too. In fact, the FBI or OSS might already know it. When we discover that, it ties up all the threads."

"How did Horse fall in with Taylor Owen and get the job working at the bank?"

"He's an Apache. He was born in this area and grew up exploring the mountains and desert. As we already learned, when he left school, Red Cloud took Horse to the Seminole Reservation. Only when Red Cloud left Oklahoma to seek a better life did Horse come back to New Mexico. O'Toole knew about Horse, which means he had to have been given the information from Berghaulter. When Horse was spotted here, Big Jim ordered Owen to get close to him and obtain the information. When Horse wouldn't talk, O'Toole likely brought in Redman to beat it out of the young man. But things got derailed when Red Cloud showed up in Alamogordo."

"And why did he come to town?" a perplexed Meeker asked.

"That was sheer luck. Red Cloud went home to Oklahoma, discovered where Horse had gone, and simply came to check on him. That's when Horse took Red Cloud to the very place everyone was looking for. They were coming back from there, and had just found the bags of money in another cave, when they witnessed what happened at the cabin."

Meeker leaned forward. "Why did they take that route?"

"Because when he was a child, Horse knew Grant Winters and liked him. He was also privy to where Winters kept all the stuff he'd taken from the tombs. It seemed the professor would borrow the items, study, and catalog them. Then he and Horse would return them. Winters respected the ancients in ways most Whites don't. In a way, Winters was a mentor to Horse."

Bryant handed Meeker a piece of paper. While Meeker was studying it, Bryant explained what it meant.

"This is the map you found that Winters drew. Horse recognized it. He assured me this is where we are going."

"But there are three different places," Meeker pointed out.

"And all three locations contain parts of what Hitler wants," Bryant explained.

"So, that means we don't really know where to go." Meeker frowned. "I think we have to bring in some help. The FBI can surround the places and—"

"We can't do that. First, Redman would spot them and never approach. So, we wouldn't get Red Cloud back or capture the men. More importantly, until we find out what Horse and Red Cloud won't tell us, we probably don't need anyone else to know about it. This might be a secret even Roosevelt will want us to keep. So, this is something we have to do all on our own."

"Then how do we cover all three places?"

"We don't have to."

"What?"

"Red Cloud has only been to one of the three. So, he will only know this one." Bryant tapped the middle dot on the map. "This is where you and I will be waiting."

"What about Nap and Horse?"

"Horse will lead us there and show us how to get in. Then, I want Nap to bring Horse back to town. I don't want him near Redman."

"We'll be outnumbered," Meeker pointed out.

"Sure, but we'll have surprise on our side. We can be in sniper positions. You and I have been outnumbered before, and we have always come out on top."

"Are you sure about this?"

"It's not ideal, but it's the best choice. That is, if your injuries are healed enough to handle it."

"No matter how I look, I'm fine. Is there anything else I need to know?"

"Maybe not about the mission," Bryant offered. "However, there is something I want you to know. Horse is remarkable. He's smart, so while the beating created an inability for him to translate what he thinks into words, his brain still works. He is well read, a student of nature and man, he can write detailed descriptions on paper. He is an amazing young man whose life took a tragic turn because he trusted a White teacher and shared a secret."

Meeker sadly shook her head.

"Helen, whatever he has protected all these years means more to him than his life. He senses that if it's discovered, the world will misuse it."

"I wish he would just tell us. It would make things so much easier."

"He won't. And perhaps, when we are face-to-face with it, we won't feel comfortable sharing it, either."

"That's sobering," Meeker admitted as she lay her head back on the pillow. "Let's get some sleep. We have to get things set up tomorrow and begin the wait. Wonder how long before they'll get here?"

"My guess, the day after tomorrow. And once they get here, they will move quickly. Good night. Sleep well."

Meeker was showing a great deal of confidence in Bryant. If this blew up—if they didn't get Redman and he got a hold of the secret—Meeker would have to take the fall because she was the team leader. For whatever it was Horse and Red Cloud were protecting, along with justifying Meeker's faith in her, Bryant's plan had to work.

CHAPTER 42

Friday November 5, 1943
8:45 a.m.
Outside Alamogordo, New Mexico

Horse had been true to his word. He guided them to the cave and helped them get in. During the fifteen minutes Teresa Bryant, Helen Meeker, and Napoleon Lancelot roamed the chamber, using flashlights for illumination, the guide remained quiet. Even when it came time for him and Lancelot to leave, he was mute. Once the entrance had been closed from the outside, Meeker, her eyes not as swollen but still little more than slits, shined her light in all directions.

"We're locked in," Meeker cracked as she studied the bones of what appeared to be a woman. "There is no way out."

Bryant shrugged, "They'll come back with fresh food and water every day until something happens; so it's not as bad as it sounds."

"As long as nothing happens to Nap and Horse."

"There's a letter I gave the sheriff. He promised not to open it unless he didn't hear from Nap for forty-eight hours. It gives directions on how to get here. In the meantime, Nap is checking in with Kolb each day. So, I have a backup plan too. This place isn't going to become our grave."

Meeker nodded and slowly moved her light from one part of the room to another. "What do you have in mind?"

"The back of the cave is fifteen feet higher than the entrance. There are stacks of artifacts to hide behind. I think we grab our bags and supplies and go up there. Then, we make ourselves comfortable and wait."

With Bryant leading the way, the women waded through thousands of objects that had once meant a great deal to the natives who left them with the bodies of their loved ones. There were clothes, blankets, weapons, toys, pottery, and leather scrolls. There was no silver or gold, and the jewelry appeared to be only beads. As the cave was massive and—except for the area around the entrance—almost full of relics, it would take a team of archeologists years to catalog.

When Bryant had climbed to the highest point in the cavern and dropped her gear on the floor, Meeker made a confession. "I don't get it. I don't see anything of value here. Why would Horse and Red Cloud be willing to die for what's in this cave?"

Bryant spread a blanket on the ground, laid her gun where it would be easy to retrieve, and put her backpack against the wall. After sitting down, she turned off her flashlight.

"Should I do that too?" Meeker asked.

"You might as well. I doubt if we'll have any visitors for a day or more. Get comfortable and turn off the light to save the batteries."

Once Meeker created her nest, she switched off the flashlight and posed a question Bryant was going to answer if she wanted to or not. "What's the plan?"

"When they roll back the stone, we'll be able to see a part of floor area from up here. If we catch them as they walk in, they will have no cover. As we are hidden, we have the advantage."

That made sense. In fact, the odds seemed to be in their favor. Though outnumbered, they had surprise and position on their side. As the light was in front of them rather than behind them, they would be very hard to spot.

"You didn't answer my first question," Meeker announced as she leaned against the cool stone wall. "Why would this place be worth millions?"

"It's a sacred place," Bryant explained, her voice echoing against walls and ceiling. "There are many who believe great power is to be found in scared places."

"It might be dark, and my face might be swollen, but I can still see when you're stalling. Are you as confused as I am about what Horse found that is so important?"

Bryant didn't immediately answer. So, in the darkest place she'd ever been, Meeker waited. A minute became two, and two became five, and then, it became ten minutes of silence. Was Bryant thinking or was she as confused by what was here as Meeker?

"Helen," Bryant finally explained, "we can't see an atom, yet we have been assured that by somehow splitting something we can't see we can produce a tremendous amount of power. There are ancient buildings across the globe that we can only guess at what their original purpose was. Archeologists and historians can guess, but they don't know. What we're looking for in this cave might be easy to see if someone pointed it out to us. But like you, I don't see it."

"How did Horse know what it was?" Meeker demanded.

"The Bible speaks of people who could find meaning in things the rest of us miss. Maybe Horse is one of those."

"You think so?"

"Or maybe Grant Winters found it—after all he was a scholar—and shared it with Horse. I'll be honest with you. I'm glad I can't see whatever it is. That means I can't share what might be so dangerous."

Bryant was still set on keeping the secrets of this place secret. Meeker knew her friend felt that way out of mistrust for what White men might do with great wealth or knowledge, but her curiosity couldn't be quieted so easily. Something, perhaps within touching distance, was in this cave, and she wanted to know what it was.

"Why don't you get some rest," Bryant suggested. "I need you ready for action when Redman and his crew arrive. The more sleep you have, the more you'll heal."

Meeker put her head against the wall and relaxed. The long hike had worn her out. Maybe it was time to forget about secrets and head off to dreamland.

CHAPTER 43

Saturday November 6, 1943
11:15 a.m.
Outside Alamogordo, New Mexico

Red Cloud knew his life would soon be over. As he sat in the back of the truck, chained to the wall, he considered his options. In truth, barring a miracle, there were none. He would lead Ruffin Redman, Tom Sears, and J.J. Hooten to the place that had been hidden for centuries, and then they would kill him. Strangely, he didn't fear death—his only regret was having to give up a secret in order to save the lives of people he cared about.

As he reviewed his time on earth, he remembered once again his traumatic youth. One of the few saving graces of the Indian school had been a kindly old pastor, Steven Stiller, who often visited with the students. He shared Bible stories and taught the kids songs. After Horse had been beaten, the preacher took a special interest in the boy. He treated him just as he would treat everyone else ... with respect and love. It was Stiller who ingrained into children the need to keep secret anything greedy men could use to gain wealth or power. He and Horse had embraced that lesson, but now Red Cloud was going to toss it out the window.

"We're approaching the cabin," Redman announced as he moved from the cab to the back of the truck. "Where do we go from here?"

"It's about a three-mile walk," Red Cloud explained. "We won't be able to take the truck. We'll have to make the final trek on foot."

"You know what happens if you're lying."

"Yeah, the same thing that happens if I'm telling the truth. But I value the lives of others far more than I do my own, so you're going where you want to go. You can have faith in that."

After Hooten parked the truck, he, Sears, and Redman got out but left the prisoner chained inside. He waited in the darkness for at least ten minutes before the back door opened and Redman climbed in. Once he released Red Cloud from the chains, the hitman pushed him out of the truck onto the ground. It took several seconds for Red Cloud's eyes to grow accustomed to the bright sunlight.

"Which way?" Redman barked.

"Follow me," Red Cloud announced as he started down a trail that began behind the shack.

Each step Red Cloud took was filled with agony. It wasn't physically painful, but was the weight of trading something he knew he shouldn't trade. Long ago, his father told him he was to never compromise his principles, and yet now he was. Would his father understand the reason why?

Silently, knowing he was on a death march, Red Cloud led the men over two ridges, across valleys, and into the mountains. The trio looked so out of place in their suits and white shirts. Their shoes weren't equipped for the hike, either. But their lust for riches was so great, they kept stumbling along. It was over an hour before any of them spoke.

"How much further?" a winded Redman demanded.

"It's ahead and around a bend," Red Cloud assured him.

"You better not be lying."

Red Cloud stopped and turned to face his captors. "You're close to what you want, but remember, I'm the only one who can get you there."

"Horse can," Redman argued.

"But you'd have to find him." Red Cloud studied his executioners' angry faces and smiled. "Each of you has spent your life killing. You're numb to it. When you murder someone, you feel nothing. To a man like me, that means you don't have souls, and I feel sorry for you. You can't know joy if you don't feel the presence of something bigger than you. What are you going to do with the millions of dollars that might soon be coming your way? How is it going to make you happy when the ghosts of those you killed are tormenting your dreams?"

The confused trio, visibly tired and not wanting to be lectured to by a man they deemed as not worthy of respect, said nothing. But if looks could kill, Red Cloud would've been dead.

A cold wind came off the mountain as clouds began to form. Rain was coming, Red Cloud could smell it. If it came in buckets, the truck would get stuck long before it made it back to the highway. The thought made him laugh.

"What's so funny?" Redman growled.

"There's so little we can control," Red Cloud announced before turning and leading the trio to a spot alongside a large, rock face. He paused and announced, "We are here."

"Where?" Redman demanded.

"Follow me." Red Cloud stepped between two huge boulders barely a shoulder width wide. Forty feet later, he led the trio between two rock walls for a hundred yards until the rock came together. As the walls on both sides were sheer, it seemed he'd brought the hitmen to a dead end. He hadn't. This was the destination. After taking a deep breath, Red Cloud said, "It's right here."

"What is it?" Redman asked as he searched the cliffs.

"Have your men roll this boulder away," Red Cloud explained. "It won't be that hard. It was engineered to move."

Redman signaled Hooten and Sears to put their shoulders to work. As promised, the huge stone readily shifted to one side revealing an opening into a cave.

"What you want will be found in there," Red Cloud promised. "Now you know why I told you to bring the flashlights."

"Hooten," Redman barked, "you go in first."

The ice pick assassin switched on his lamp and entered the five-foot-high opening. "It's clear," he yelled from inside, his words echoing off the cave's walls.

"You're next," Redman announced as he pointed to Red Cloud.

"Sure."

Once back into the cave he'd visited seven years before, Red Cloud studied what Hooten's light revealed. It was a reverent moment, a time to be awed and overcome with a sense of history. Yet, it still pained him these graves were being desecrated.

Redman and Sears followed. Now there were three beams of light searching the cave.

"There's nothing here but bones, Indian junk, and outdated weapons," Redman announced in disgust. After picking up and breaking two arrows, and throwing them to the ground, he growled, "What kind of a con job is this?"

"This is what Hitler was looking for," Red Cloud assured the visitors.

"You can buy stuff like this at roadside stands in reservations," Sears declared. "Redman, what have you gotten us into?"

"You look, but you don't see," Red Cloud explained.

"Are you trying to quote the Bible?" Hooten asked.

"I might have done just that, but let me assure you, you're surrounded by more wealth than you can imagine. It's everywhere."

The confused men shined their lights in every direction, but they saw nothing of value.

"Check the piles of junk," Redman ordered. "Maybe it's hidden there."

For ten minutes, Hooten and Sears searched through clothes, blankets, pottery, ancient weapons, and hides. They shined their lights on mummified remains and examined beads. Their faces told the story. They saw nothing that spelled out wealth or power.

"Okay, Indian," Redman screamed. "Now take us to the real place."

"You're standing in the real place." Red Cloud pointed to a spear leaning against the near wall. "Would you allow me to pick that up?"

"If you want to use it to kill me," Redman barked, "you'd never get close enough before I'd shoot you."

"I know that, but the spear will make my point. I hope you'll pardon the pun."

"Fine."

Red Cloud walked over, retrieved the five-foot-long weapon, and used it to scrape the wall. He smiled before ordering, "Shine your light there."

"My lord!" Hooten exclaimed.

"Yeah," Red Cloud announced, "you see it now. The walls, the floors, and ceiling are all gold. The deeper you go into this cave, the more gold there is. I have no doubt there is more gold in this cave than there is in Fort Knox. This is the gold the Spanish explorers had heard about but never found."

"Why didn't the Indians take it?"

Red Cloud leaned against the wall and shrugged. "To a people without money, to a people who didn't own property, this gold meant nothing. But there was a legend that in the next life, the paths the people walked were made of gold. So, this gold reflected the spirit's light. When these people died, they were laid to rest with the things they needed to go toward the light. So, burying them in a place that reflected the light was natural."

"Then why paint the walls, floors, and ceiling?" Redman asked.

"For centuries, they were not painted. But when the ancestors of these people learned of the White man's greed, when they were told of his need for ownership of anything of value, they hid the gold from him. Later, they hid the burial places. In time, even their ancestors forgot where these caves were located. Then a professor, who was consumed by grief, and a curious Apache boy rediscovered the burial places. You three are the only people, other than the boy, the man, and me to have seen this place in centuries."

"We're rich," Sears whispered. "Redman, you were right, we're rich! And we're not just rich, we are filthy rich."

"We can buy the world," Hooten declared.

Red Cloud laughed.

"What's so funny?" Redman demanded.

"To get the gold out of this cave will take a large-scale

mining operation. You'll also have to make a deal with the people who own this land. You'll have to find someone to sell it too."

"Hitler wants it," Redman observed.

"He's a little busy right now," Red Cloud pointed out. "And how would he get all this gold to a place where he could use it? As you all dream about your wealth, let me give you something else to consider. All of you are wanted. You kidnapped Helen Meeker, and the FBI finally has something they can pin on you. Now if this were cash, you might be able to buy your way to South America and live the good life. If it were a great and powerful weapon, you might trade to the United States for a reward and pardon. But because it's gold, it's worthless to you. All, you can do is talk about the gold you found but couldn't use." Red Cloud laughed. "You're surrounded by more wealth than any White man has ever seen, and it's worthless."

"Why didn't you get it seven years ago?" Redman asked. "You'd be the richest Indian in the world."

"These are sacred grounds to these people. I respected that then and respect it now. Besides, the spirits who live here will haunt anyone who disturbs this place."

"Redman," Sears screamed. "We were clean, the law couldn't pin anything on us until you got Hooten and me into this mess. You're the reason we can't cash in."

"You didn't have to join me," Redman insinuated. "Don't overreact. I have enough cash to get us to South America. We might not live like kings, but we will live well. So, let's not do anything stupid."

"Like we've already done?" Hooten grumbled.

"White men and their need to have power and wealth." Red Cloud chuckled. "It usually ends with them sniping at each other, and then, someone always ends up dead."

A seething Redman turned toward Red Cloud. "You're

going to die here with all your ancestors. I have no more use for you. So, just think how meaningless your life has been. That thought will bring me a lot of satisfaction when I'm enjoying the carnivals in Brazil."

Red Cloud didn't respond, but he also showed no fear. Instead, he remembered something the preacher at the Indian school had taught. There is no greater way to be like Jesus than to give your life for others. Red Cloud had almost done that in France, so he was already living on borrowed time. The way things had turned out, Horse would be safe. Redman would never find him. Everything had worked out.

"We need to get out of here," Hooten suggested.

"Let me take care of one final piece of business," Redman said. "Get me something to tie this guy up with."

Sears walked over to some of the artifacts until he found a blanket. He ripped several pieces and brought them back to Redman.

"Take him over to that pole thing and tie him to it." As Red Cloud was led to the ceremonial pole, Redman reached into his backpack and retrieved a Smith & Wesson. As he loaded it, he smiled.

CHAPTER 44

Saturday November 6, 1943
1:01 p.m.
Outside of Alamogordo, New Mexico

From the back of the cave, Teresa Bryant heard everything Red Cloud told the men. With Ruffin Redman setting a hit into motion, it was now time to step in and save the man who'd made such a noble effort to spare a friend from torture and death. She touched Helen Meeker's shoulder.

"It's now or never."

"I'll yell out a warning to drop their weapons," Meeker whispered.

"And when they don't," Bryant replied, "then we open fire."

Bryant crouched low and hid behind a large ceremonial drum as she waited for Meeker to alert the visitors they weren't alone. Spotlighted by Hooten's flashlight, a hundred feet ahead, Ruffin Redman, his face displaying a mixture of rage and disappointment, was slowly walking toward Red Cloud. Bryant steadied her arm. If Meeker didn't put out the alert soon, she would fire anyway.

"Place your weapons on the floor and raise your hands," Meeker yelled.

As all three of the men had flashlights, they were easy targets and surely knew it. What they didn't realize was there was also enough light coming through the cave's opening—if they didn't back into the deep dark shadows, the women had nicely silhouetted forms to use as targets. Initially, it appeared Sears and Hooten were going to comply. But when Redman extinguished his flashlight and fired a shot, the two followed his lead.

Relying on instincts, Bryant fired where Hooten had been standing. His screams and a thud assured her he was, at least, wounded. Meeker was concentrating on Redman. As there was no reaction, it appeared her three rounds had done no damage. In the meantime, Sears raced into the area where the artifacts were stored. For the moment, he was no longer in view.

"Teresa," Meeker whispered. "Can you weave through the maze to where we last saw Redman?"

"I can try, but there's so much stuff I'm bound to hit something."

"Do your best. And if anyone gets close to the opening, fire until they fall. No one is getting out of here with the knowledge of what this cave is made of."

Bryant, her eyes paving a path between bones, pottery, weapons, and drums, slowly made her way through the darkness. Between each of her steps, she stopped and felt around her, carefully moving anything that she might trip over. She'd only covered about twenty feet when Sears made a break. Meeker stopped him just in front of the door. From the way he fell, Bryant was sure the man had died before hitting the cave's cold floor.

"You're down two," Meeker called out. "Why don't you just give up?"

"And go to the chair?" Redman screamed. "I'd rather die here among the bones."

Based on his voice, Bryant tried to locate Redman. But the echoing created by the cave walls distorted everything. All she had to go on was a general idea of where he had been when he pulled away from the cave's entrance.

"Meeker," Redman yelled.

"Yeah."

"This is just like it was at the cabin. If you want Red Cloud alive, you have to let me go. It has to be his life for mine. I'm right behind him, my gun barrel is parting his hair, so what's it going to be?"

Undeterred by the threat, Bryant continued to feel her way through the maze. She'd made it another twenty feet when an impatient Redman barked, "Meeker, what's your call? Do I shoot him now?"

"We can talk," Meeker suggested, buying Bryant a bit more time.

The area where Redman was holding Red Cloud was bathed in complete darkness. The only way to see into it would require using a flashlight. The second Bryant turned her lamp on, Redman would shoot in her direction. She'd likely die before she could return fire.

"I'm walking him back to the entrance," Redman declared. "If you shoot, you'll hit Red Cloud. As he gave his life for you back in Chicago, I'm betting you don't want to do that."

"Shoot anyway," Red Cloud yelled. A second later, Bryant heard a gun's barrel coming down on a head—a sound she knew far too well. Red Cloud was likely out cold, and surely Redman was dragging him toward the cave's entrance. She had to get there first.

Yesterday, when they'd first entered, she'd mentally mapped the layout. To her left was an aisle that led between the stacks of bodies and the far wall where many of the artifacts had been stored. Ahead of that were the remains of what must have been a very important man. He'd been laid to rest on a raised platform. He was holding two spears, one in each hand. She'd admired those finely crafted weapons and how those who'd placed the body had fastened the five-foot-long end of the shafts into the floor in a fashion that pointed toward the cave's mouth. When she'd tried to pick one up, it hadn't budged. If she could get to that spot without alerting Redman, she might be able to circle behind him and flash her light just long enough to get off a shot. For her to accomplish that trek, Meeker needed to give her more time. As if on cue …

"Redman," Meeker called out. "Even if we let you out of this cave, the odds of you getting back to your vehicle are against you. We have people in the area. I'd fire off a shot as soon as I got out of the cave, and it would alert them. Half of them will come here, the other half will fan out and block all routes of escape."

"I'll take my chances," Redman vowed.

"Not a smart move."

Rather than reply, Redman fired off three shots in the direction he thought Meeker was hiding. As the noise was echoing in all directions, Bryant scurried down the aisle, past the old chief's body, and raced by the cave's entrance. As she did, Redman squeezed off three more rounds toward the raised area at the back of the cave. As the noise echoed, Bryant rolled into the darkness and waited on her stomach.

It was now time to consider the weapon Redman always used on his hits. The chamber held six rounds. If he didn't have a backup gun, he was out of ammunition. But, as he probably only brought the Smith & Wesson for Red Cloud's execution, surely he had another fully loaded firearm. Even if he didn't, he had enough time to reload. Therefore, she

TIME WALKER

still had to wait. As Redman needed Red Cloud to provide cover, she could be patient.

"Redman," Meeker cried out, "you missed me. You want to try again?"

"Woman, why didn't you shoot back?"

"I didn't want to risk hitting Red Cloud. But you knew that."

"I'm still holding the cards. Where's your Indian sidekick?"

"There are three caves like this one. She's waiting in another one for you," Meeker lied. The lie continued when she announced, "This battle is just me and you. Well, it is now. It appears Sears and Hooten are no longer any use to you."

Bryant could hear Redman dragging Red Cloud toward the entrance. It sounded as if he were no more than ten feet in front of her. While she couldn't take a chance on shooting, for fear of hitting Red Cloud, perhaps it was time to do some hand-to-hand combat.

Pulling herself to her feet, Bryant took a deep breath, slipped her weapon into her belt, lowered her shoulders, and rushed to where she sensed Redman was standing. Five steps later, they collided. The force of impact knocked Redman backward, causing him to lose his grip on Red Cloud, but somehow the hitman managed to stay on his feet. Pushing Bryant with his left hand, he pulled his right arm up for a shot. Before he could squeeze the trigger, she shoved his wrist upward. A bullet sailed past her ear and ricocheted off the wall. Three more wild shots followed. Then Meeker's flashlight put the battle in the spotlight.

Redman likely had two more rounds in his gun, so Bryant had to keep his arm pointed in any direction but at her. Spinning, she pulled around to his side while delivering a fist to a kidney. He yelled, but the punch didn't slow him down. As she tried to scoot behind him, he grabbed her neck with his left hand and pulled her close. Moving his arm around her throat, he pinned her, jerked his gun to where it was pointing at her head, and cursed. Then everything seemed to slow down.

Bryant grabbed his arm with both hands, but he was too strong. She couldn't get free from the chokehold. She tried kicking backward but failed to strike the target. Out of the corner of her eye, she observed Redman's finger tense on the trigger. Then, with no warning, his grip loosened, and his arm dropped from her neck.

Whirling, she saw Red Cloud, now free from his restraints, head bleeding and bruised, fighting to pull the revolver from Redman's hand. As they struggled, two more shots fired. One flew over Bryant's head, and the other went straight to the ceiling and bounced toward the mouth of the cave.

Red Cloud, weakened by the earlier blow to the head, was fading fast. After delivering a knee to the gut, Redman jerked away and tossed the Indian to the floor. He was about to deliver a second kick to the head when Bryant lowered her shoulder and aimed at the hitman's chest. Filled with rage, she struck with such great force it drove Redman backward. Like a running back pushing a linebacker, she lifted him in the air, and kept driving. She drove him for ten more feet and then his screams echoed off the walls, floor, and ceiling. A second later, his body went limp.

A panting Bryant pulled back, reached for her gun, and aimed. But, as the light from Meeker's flashlight bathed Redman in a white glow, she realized the battle was over. Bryant's charge drove one of the chief's spears all the way through the hitman's body. Two inches of the tip were extruding from his chest. Redman's eyes were open, his mouth still forming a silent scream, and his feet dangled three inches off the cave's floor, but there was no movement. Those spears, anchored in the cave's golden floor hundreds of years ago, had claimed a victim.

"Are you okay?" Meeker called out?

"Yeah, I'm fine," Bryant assured her associate as she moved to where Red Cloud was sitting up on the floor. "How about you?"

"I'm good. Thanks."

"Thank you," Bryant said. "Without your help, I'd have a hole in my head right now. It seems like you're in the business of saving everybody."

As Meeker worked her way back toward the entrance, Bryant grabbed her flashlight and checked on Sears and Hooten. It was time to notify their next of kin. Bryant grimly smiled, no one would be leaving the cave with any secrets. At least no one who would misuse them.

CHAPTER 45

Saturday, November 4, 1943
4:17 p.m.
Outside Alamogordo, New Mexico

It was a relieved Teresa Bryant, Helen Meeker, and Red Cloud who walked out into the afternoon sunshine. As they grimaced in pain, a thankful Bryant studied her two comrades. Meeker still looked horrible. Her face was swollen, bruised, and displaying a range of colors from green to purple to black. Red Cloud had a huge bump on his forehead and a scrape around his ear. His eyes revealed he'd slept very little in days, yet they were each far better off than the three in the cave.

"All of this because of man's lust for gold," Meeker muttered.

"Not every person succumbs to that lust," Red Cloud corrected her. "To some on this earth, owning things is not important."

"How much gold is in there?" Meeker wondered out loud. Before anyone could respond, she answered her own question. "Likely a lot more than is in Fort Knox."

"The other two caves have even more," Red Cloud volunteered. "At least that's what Horse told me. Now, are you going to tell Roosevelt about this?"

Bryant's eyes locked onto her associate. Meeker wore the expression of a person looking for an exit.

"Helen," Bryant explained, "these caves might be the largest gold strike ever, but this is a sacred place. Besides, we don't need more gold in Fort Knox. Think about all the new construction that would have to take place just to house it. We're too busy fighting a war for those kinds of projects."

"What do you think?" Meeker asked Red Cloud.

"For me, this isn't just about the gold, it's about something that has been forgotten and needs to stay that way. Sacred places have been destroyed all over this planet. Hitler raids them on a regular basis and steals what's inside. So, even though I care nothing about the gold, I don't want the White man to get it."

"Wouldn't all this wealth," Meeker asked, "help your people?"

"No, this land no longer belongs to Horse's tribe. This is federal land."

Meeker shrugged, "Okay, then we'll keep the secret. We'll hide everything." She laughed and added, "Besides, uncovering this much gold wouldn't be good for the world economy. A find like this would drive down the price of precious metals everywhere. Wall Street would hate us."

Red Cloud smiled. "Thank you. Now, what do we do with the three men who died in there?"

"I'd rather just leave them and seal the cave," Meeker admitted, "but that would be desecrating a sacred place."

"I don't think it would," Bryant offered. "They came into that cave looking to loot it. They paid a price. Redman was even killed by one of the dead chiefs. So, he died at the hands of a ghost. Maybe leaving the bodies of White men who were defeated by natives actually tells a story that

TIME WALKER

someone who finds this cave in a few hundred years from now needs to know."

"So, we pretend like it never happened?" Meeker asked.

"Did it?" Bryant laughed. "Who would believe a person who had been dead for five hundred years killed the most successful and ruthless hitman of our time? Besides, if we shared any of this news, people would be lured to this place. If you're serious about protecting it, we can't reveal anything that happened here. So, leave them in the cave."

Red Cloud nodded. "None of us need credit, there is enough of a reward in knowing the job is finished."

"We have a long walk," Meeker pointed out. "Let's roll that stone back in place and hide all signs we've been here. Then we can get moving."

"Could Red Cloud and I go in one more time?" Bryant asked. "If we are going to leave the bodies, there's a cleansing ceremony we need to perform. And as we can't have anyone outside our race witness it, you will need to wait here."

"Does it take very long?" Meeker asked.

"No, not long."

As a bruised and battered Meeker wearily strolled over to the cliff wall and sat on the ground, Bryant grabbed a flashlight and led the way back into the cave. Red Cloud quickly followed. Once they were thirty feet from the entrance, he made a confession.

"I don't know of any cleansing rituals."

"Neither do I," Bryant admitted, "but Helen doesn't realize that. Now, listen, we only have a couple of minutes, so give me some straight answers. You wouldn't die for gold—neither would Horse. It doesn't mean anything to you. And the spirits that were here left hundreds of years ago, so there's something more, isn't there?"

Red Cloud remained mute.

"Be honest with me," Bryant demanded. "You owe me that much for making sure this place will remain hidden."

"Will you be honest with me?" he asked.

"I have been," she declared.

"Morning Song, my people and your people have stories of time walkers. I'm sure you know what they are."

"I've heard the legends."

Red Cloud turned out his flashlight. "Let me refresh your memory. A time walker is someone the Great Spirit chooses because of honesty, compassion, wisdom, and willingness to serve others. They are given great responsibility along with more years to walk on this earth than others. They grow older, but they don't age."

"You believe the myth they are immortal?" Bryant asked.

"No, they bleed, they know pain, likely far greater than any normal person, and they do die. But they don't die of old age—they die giving their lives for others. In fact, they live always giving their lives to others. It's just not in our culture, the Old Testament is filled with stories of those who walked this earth far longer than others. There are stories of them in India, China, and other places."

"Why do you bring up this legend?"

"You want to know what is in the caves that's worth my dying for?" Red Cloud asked.

"Yes."

"I will tell you, but not until you admit you're a time walker."

"If you have heard the legend, then you know that a true time walker must never reveal who they are or the gift they've been given. If they do, they will immediately drop dead."

Red Cloud turned his flashlight back on and shined it into Bryant's face. "You can't answer with your lips, but you have answered my question in other ways."

"You sound like Grey Wolf," Bryant snapped. "Now, what's in here?"

"There was time, centuries ago, when the ancients had access to powers that have now been lost. Hidden in this place are a third of the explanations of how some were able to cloud the minds of others. Those who mastered this art could hide themselves in plain sight. People who knew them would not recognize them. To learn everything, you must combine the knowledge found in all the caves. Those who correctly used this power could ease fears and suffering. The Whites might have called them guardian angels. But like all good things, the powers could be abused. The knowledge that is hidden can be used to cause mass hysteria, hypnosis, or even death. It can cause good men to do horrible things. It can drive people insane. To use it wisely, you must have a pure heart. The few who had this power decided not to pass it on to others for fear of what would happen if people outside their tribe found out about it. Grant Winters and Horse discovered these lost secrets. That is what was beaten out of Horse, though he never gave up the location."

"So," Bryant suggested, "Hitler didn't want the gold, he wanted to have access to what the ancients knew. He needed those scrolls."

Bryant shined her light around the cave a final time, nodded, and walked out. After Red Cloud joined her, she announced, "Okay, Helen, let's move this stone and never speak of this place again."

CHAPTER 46

WEDNESDAY, NOVEMBER 17, 1943
9:00 A.M.
SEMINOLE RESERVATION, OKLAHOMA

The United States and the President wanted to award Red Cloud the Medal of Honor at the White House, but the man whose courage had earned him this distinction requested the ceremony be held on the place he had been born. He wanted his mentor, Grey Wolf, his friend Horse, and his tribe to be there when the medal was pinned to his chest.

The Vice President of the United States, Henry Wallace, traveled to Oklahoma to present the award. He, a senator, two members of the House, and three men who'd served with Red Cloud on the mission in France, were on hand to give remarks and interviews. Yet, it was Grey Wolf who perhaps defined this moment better than any of the other guests. When standing on the platform, he told the crowd, "Red Cloud has always been a man who put others before himself. The fact this honor has come to him is ironic, because, even as a child, he never sought the spotlight and never wanted credit for anything he did. He told his commanding officer, the very person who nominated him for this honor, that the others in his unit had much more to live for than he did. He was somehow protected and did not die. By living, he has given the natives in this nation a reminder of our value and our worth. Perhaps Red Cloud has also taught that lesson to many others who live in this country but have never seen us as equals. We can only hope."

As the several thousand applauded, Helen Meeker looked with pride at Teresa Bryant. Today she appeared much different than the exotic creature who normally wore stylish suits. She was dressed in a buckskin dress and moccasins and wore a beaded necklace. Her long hair was parted down the middle, fixed in braids, and she wore a beautiful, feathered headdress.

Stepping closer to Lancelot and Bryant, Meeker whispered, "I see things differently now. I want you to know that."

"We have a long way to go," Lancelot suggested.

Bryant nodded.

On the small stage, the vice president stood and motioned to where the honored guest was. As members of his military unit stood and applauded, Red Cloud rose and solemnly walked toward the platform. Four army officers, all White, stood and saluted the private. A hush fell over the crowd. The only thing that could be heard was the wind blowing through the trees.

Meeker lifted her eyes and observed an eagle circling the scene. The sight of the bird in flight sent a chill down her spine. When she shifted her gaze back to the stage, Red Cloud ascended the four steps and stood in front of Wallace. All eyes were on the men. The vice president fumbled with getting the medal's pin placed, but when it was properly attached to the uniform, he stepped back and saluted. Red

Cloud returned the gesture, turned, solemnly studied the crowd, and walked off to where Horse was standing. The two then strolled over to join Grey Wolf.

"It's over," Meeker observed. "With the man who earned this medal honored, our mission has been completed."

"It's not over yet," Bryant announced. With an urgency in her stride, she made her way through the throng toward Red Cloud. Meeker and Lancelot followed three steps behind.

"What's she doing?" Lancelot asked.

"I never know anymore," Meeker said with a laugh.

With Red Cloud surrounded by photographers and newsmen, there was no easy way for Bryant to get to him. Surprisingly, she didn't try. Instead, she took Horse by the arm and pulled him away from the crowd.

When they were out of earshot of everyone but Meeker and Lancelot, Bryant spoke, "I've found a school, a place where you will be respected, where you can complete the classes you need to go to college. They will teach you how to speak American sign language. Once you have learned that, you will be able to use your incredible brain to earn a degree, and if you choose, you can help our people. You will be an example for all of us to push beyond our limitations to do great things. I promise this school will be a safe place, everything will be taken care of, you will be able to come home between terms, and there will be no cost. I want this for you, but it's your choice."

Horse smiled, nodded, and said, "Thank you."

"You can contact me anytime you need something," Bryant assured him.

Bryant was not a hugger, she never had been, but she made an exception in this case. After that moment quickly passed, she rejoined her team.

"Time for us to go," Bryant announced. "I've made a decision. After the war, I'm going back to being called Morning Song."

"Why wait?" Meeker asked.

"Too much trouble to change all that information and fight a war. What do we do next?"

"We go back to Chicago. We've been given a few weeks off."

Lancelot laughed.

"What's so funny?" Meeker asked.

"That dog won't hunt. They always promise a few weeks off to regroup and rest, and then a day later we're on a plane, train, or in a car, headed to a new assignment."

Meeker nodded and looked at Bryant, who had walked over to Grey Wolf. They weren't speaking, but they were communicating. Judging by the look in the old man's eyes, Red Cloud was not the only person he was proud of on this day.

ABOUT THE AUTHOR

Citing his Arkansas heritage, Christy award winner **Ace Collins** defines himself as a storyteller. In that capacity, Collins has authored over a hundred books that have sold more than 2.5 million copies for twenty-five different publishers. His catalog includes novels, biographies, and children's works as well as books on history, culture, and faith. His two most recent books are *The Imprint*, released by Elk Lake Publishing in 2023, and perhaps one of his favorites, *The Story of Grady Bear, The Only Bear Who Ever Stayed Awake for Christmas*, also published by Elk Lake.

Beyond books, Collins has penned more than 2000 magazine features, appeared on every network's morning television show, as well as news and entertainment programming on CNN, MSNBC and CNBC, and does scores of radio interviews each year. His speaking engagements have taken him from churches and corporations to the America's Dog Museum in St. Louis and the National Archives in Washington DC. Collins has penned several production shows and regularly speaks to college classes on the art of writing. He has also been the featured speaker at the National Archives Distinguished Lecture Series, hosted a network television special, and has appeared on all the morning TV shows.

Ace's hobbies include sports, restoring classic cars, watching and reading about classic films, tinkering with Wurlitzer jukeboxes, and playing guitar. He lives in Arkadelphia, Arkansas, near Ouachita University, and has two grown sons and a daughter. Ace continues his late wife Kathy's calling by mentoring college students.

Ace is represented by Greg Johnson at the WordServe Literary Agency.

Other Elk Lake Books by Ace Collins:

- *Touchdown Tommy*
- *The Last Imprint*
- *The Story of Grady Bear: The Only Bear Who Stayed Awake for Christmas*

In the President's Service Series:

1. *A Date with Death**
2. *The Dark Pool**
3. *Blood Brother**
    Set of Books 1-3
4. *Fatal Addiction***
5. *The Devil's Eyes***
6. *The Dead Can Talk***
    **Set of Books 4-6*
7. *Bottled Madness*
8. *Shadows in the Moonlight*
9. *Evilution*
10. *Uneasy Alliance*
11. *The 13th Floor*
12. *The White Rose*
13. *The Red Suit Case*
14. *The Cat's Eye*
15. *Set for Danger*

16. The Trojan Horse
17. The Wolf Pack
18. Black or White
The Yellow Packard, 2nd Edition